AN ENCHANTED SPRING

MISTS OF FATE

BOOK

NANCY SCANLON

DIVERSIONBOOKS

Also by Nancy Scanlon

The Mists of Time series
The Winter Laird

Diversion Books
A Division of Diversion Publishing Corp.
443 Park Avenue South, Suite 1008
New York, New York 10016
www.DiversionBooks.com

For more information, email info@diversionbooks.com

First Diversion Books edition May 2016.
Print ISBN: 978-1-62681-727-2
eBook ISBN: 978-1-62681-726-5

For Sean, C., and E.

CHAPTER 1

Colin O'Rourke watched his cousin-in-law, many times removed, absently roll a pencil between his fingers. They were closer than brothers, and had been for the better part of eight years. Over that time, Colin had observed, helpless, as Aidan MacWilliam's countenance slowly changed from easygoing to aloof. But most worrisome was this latest visit.

Colin's voice was quiet. "It may be time to accept that your future lies here."

The pencil froze midroll, and Aidan's sharp green eyes pierced Colin's dark brown ones. "I will never accept that. I *will* get back, or I'll die trying."

Colin wisely held his tongue. Despite his refusal to accept that he'd been brought forward in time for good, Aidan had become immensely successful. He had more money than he knew what to do with and an extended family who understood clan loyalties.

But Colin knew that wasn't enough for a fifteenth-century Irish warrior. Aidan needed something to live for, something to spark his interest in life again. "Aidan, what's left to try? You've exhausted all possibilities."

Aidan angrily flicked the pencil onto the desk and stood. "I know there's a time gate somewhere. All manner of strange folk traipse through O'Malley's garden—they're coming from somewhere, without the aid of anyone. So there's something out there that will get me back." His tone turned surly. "I simply haven't found it yet."

Colin held back a frown and changed the subject. "Well, if you need a distraction, I could use your aid."

Aidan reluctantly sat back down. "Aye?"

It was becoming harder to simply sit by and watch someone he loved creep ever closer to a dark precipice that was neither acknowledged nor denied. Colin knew that if Aidan didn't find a way home soon, he might tumble headfirst into that abyss and never return.

"I'm expanding Celtic Connections into the UK and Ireland."

Aidan nodded. "The LA office doing well, then?"

Colin's elite matchmaking service had had such success in Boston, he had opened two other offices in Toronto and Los Angeles. Both were fully booked with an impressive clientele list.

"Sure is. But with so many offices, I need a new department for publicity and public relations. European expansion isn't something I'm ready to make public yet, and I need someone to handle the department setup."

Aidan shrugged. "Sorry, mate. I don't know anyone in that field."

"I realize that. What I need is for you to do some recon."

Aidan sat forward slightly though his face remained impassive. "Recon," he echoed.

"Yes." Colin watched him carefully. "The sword you brought with you, when you arrived in this time—it's on the auction block."

"What?"

Colin nodded. "One of our clients is facilitating the auction, which has loads of medieval artifacts up for grabs. Your sword is one of them." He flipped open a binder to a marked page, then handed it to Aidan. "Looks like the owner died suddenly, and he left all his relics to his son. Luckily for us, the son has zero interest in medieval history, but he seems awfully interested in the money it could fetch."

The curses that flew from Aidan's mouth were inventive, and Colin barked out a laugh. "The auction is in a few days, in New York City. Which is exactly where the person I'm looking to hire is located. This would kill two birds with one stone. You'd get your sword, and I'd get my PR person. So—you in?"

Aidan nodded curtly. "You know it. I've been tracking down that damn sword for years."

"Well, here's your chance to get it back," Colin replied. *And*, he added silently, *I'm talking about much more than the sword...*

* * *

To: Emmaline MacDermott

Emmaline Perkins stared in apprehension at the large envelope on her desk. The red CONFIDENTIAL stamp seemed to stare back at her, challenging her to break the seal. But that wasn't what held her back.

It was addressed to Emmaline MacDermott.

Even now, seven months later, Emma shuddered at what would've been her surname, had fate not intervened.

She took a closer look and noticed the seal was already broken. That explained why her bullying, brownnosing coworker had so gleefully dropped the envelope into her lap earlier. Heidi Swanson was only gleeful when someone was about to fall hard on her face.

Emma was on her way to the top at Price Publicity. Her A-list client roster grew weekly, and her boss had hinted that she was up for a promotion. Her hard work and dedication to being the best publicist possible wasn't going unnoticed by the movers and shakers of New York City. Her job was to calm down, smooth over, and cover up any situation before people found out there was something to find out.

Heidi *hated* her for it.

Her talents weren't limited to her professional life, either. She was quite successful in ensuring no one knew anything about her cheating ex-fiancé, or his threats against her.

She gave her head a small shake to dislodge the bubble of fear, and her sleek, dark blond ponytail swung gently against her neck. She reminded herself that she was sitting in her office, perfectly safe. Benjamin MacDermott was currently hanging out in a ten-by-ten cell on an aggravated assault conviction. The attack on

7

a bouncer in a nightclub was just one of many things she hadn't been aware he was capable of…and she knew not to underestimate him anymore. Despite the fact that he'd been behind bars for five months, a shiver of dread raced up her spine whenever she saw, heard, or even *thought* his name.

And now, she thought with a shiver, *here it is, staring me in the face.* She looked at the envelope again and blew out a slow, shaky breath.

To: Emmaline MacDermott.

Whoever sent this envelope to her was playing a sick joke, to be sure.

Emma peeked inside the folder, and she had to swallow the bile back. Her heart sank. She grabbed the envelope and headed for the nearest conference room, her phone to her ear, giving the appearance of leaving to take an important client call. She carefully closed the door and drew the blinds, then dumped the contents onto the polished wood table.

She drew a sharp breath.

Her ex-fiancé, dressed in some very inventive bondage gear, was tied to a bed. A red-haired woman, dressed in a similar getup, was midstrike with a whip and a ferocious look on her gorgeous features.

In a detached way, Emma thought the woman rather looked like something out of a movie. Perfectly placed, midmotion shot… Emma understood how the woman was such a huge star.

Emma would know, of course, since the woman in the pictures was her biggest and most demanding client, Jenny Kincaid. The same Jenny Kincaid who had a romantic comedy releasing this week. A romantic comedy, it seemed prudent to add, that costarred Jenny's husband of ten years.

Not Emma's ex.

Emma squinted at his face and couldn't suppress another shudder. Emma had long suspected Ben of cheating, but she always rationalized that she had no real proof. They were so far into the wedding plans. They'd been together for so long. They had been college sweethearts.

Her list of excuses seemed endless.

But almost seven months ago, Emma had arrived at the office only to realize she'd left some important papers behind. She texted Ben, hoping he hadn't left for work, but it was close to ten in the morning and he didn't respond, so she headed back to their apartment. She opened the door to see Ben and Jenny engaged in some very…*experimental* positions.

What ensued was a mess. Jenny didn't even bat an eye. In fact, she asked Ben if they could meet at her hotel later, to finish the job, to which he agreed, and Jenny gave Emma a sickening girlfriend-to-girlfriend smile before reminding her of client confidentiality.

Emma was too shocked to respond. But, when she finally was able to react (and Ben had put some clothing on), Emma threw him out of the apartment. He accepted it with minimal fuss.

Or so she thought.

A couple of weeks later, Ben was waiting for her when she got home.

"How did you get in here?" she demanded, stepping into the apartment.

"I can't get my deposits for the wedding back."

His voice was so controlled. Emma felt a frisson of fear race down her spine, but this was Ben. She'd known him forever. He wouldn't hurt her. Physically, anyway.

"Consider it payment for breaking my heart. Get out." She held the door open and gestured at him to leave.

He casually walked toward her, then slammed the door shut and pinned her against it, making her cry out in surprise.

"I don't think you heard me, Emmaline. *I. Can't. Get. My. Money. Back.*" His eyes, once so warm and loving, were brittle and hard.

"You're hurting me!" she squeaked, trying to twist from his grasp. He held firm.

"Don't pretend you don't know, Emmaline. I need that money. It's mine. And I owe some very big people—very important people—a lot of cash. Now, because you were so"—he slammed her against the door—"damn"—he slammed her again—"stingy"—

another crash against the door—"with your bank accounts, I can't pay them back. And they'll kill me, Emmaline."

Emma couldn't breathe. This was Ben! He was an insurance agent, for crying out loud! Who could be trying to kill him?

He released her suddenly, then stepped back. "You're going to give me the money. I want twenty thousand by Thursday."

She gasped. "Ben, I don't have—"

He was back on her in an instant, crushing her. "You have a very nice life insurance payout," he sneered, his lips inches from hers. "Remember? I set it up myself. And I know I'm still your beneficiary, Emma." His eyes turned to ice. "I'll use it if I have to."

Emma felt the threat all the way to her soul, and she choked back a sob. This was not the Ben she'd known, the Ben she'd loved for so long.

This was a monster.

She nodded, unable to form words, and he pushed her to the floor, where she fell in a heap. He opened the door and stepped over her, then turned and looked down at her in disgust. In a low voice, he added, "You've made things very difficult, Emmaline. If you run, I will find you. And it will be deemed an accident. I'll make sure the payout happens quickly and efficiently." He smiled coldly. "You'll have a lovely funeral. Not that anyone would show up. I'm all you ever had."

He pulled the door shut, and Emma lost her stomach.

Emma was shocked back to the present when someone knocked on the conference room door. "I have this booked for a client meeting!" a voice called apologetically.

Emma swallowed hard and stuffed the incriminating images back into the envelope. She would get them to the shredder immediately.

Ben had been sentenced to a year and some months in jail, and Emma had hoped when he came out she'd have a plan.

A glance at the unexpected envelope in her shaky hand had her wondering if she might want to start planning.

* * *

At some point, her wineglass emptied itself.

Emma gave it a small frown. It had been doing that all night, but she refused to be bothered by it. She just refilled it from the bottle that was sitting obediently next to her on the small table on her tiny little terrace, in her tiny little corner of New York City.

She squinted at the bottle before she put it down. It was mostly empty—when did that happen? She must've swigged—er, *sipped*—more than she thought. She couldn't bring herself to care, though. After the day she'd had, coupled with not taking a night off in forever, she deserved some down time.

Her clients' social lives had replaced her own years ago. She put every ounce of herself into being a great publicist. She could smooth over any situation her clients found themselves in. Her years of dedication (okay, not taking a vacation or a full weekend in the entire seven years she'd been at Price Publicity) gave her contacts all over the city—reporters, journalists, magazine editors, restaurant owners—but her biggest successes came from social media. Her coworkers always turned to her for the best ways to spin something in 140 characters or less, inventive hashtags to offset negative press, and clever Facebook statuses that made light of serious situations. And she also possessed a good ear for warning bells, which helped her notice the bad vibes before a disaster struck.

However, as she sat on her little terrace, looking out over the crowded street below, she wished she were anywhere else, for the first time since she had arrived in the city years ago. It was a never-ending barrage of busy lives, all colliding in a few square miles. And her job never let her go—"regular business hours" was code only for one's physical presence within the Price building, because the clientele at Price Publicity tended to make rather serious mistakes at all hours of the night.

She took another swig of wine as her phone rang.

"'Lo?" she answered, peering into the wineglass.

"Emma—we have a crisis."

Emma took another swallow of her wine before answering her boss. Her tongue felt a little fuzzy. "Josh, I'm not working tonight."

"Are you drunk?" he asked. Emma could almost see his brow furrow, as if he couldn't possibly fathom the prim and proper Emma Perkins getting drunk. By herself.

On a Wednesday night.

"Nooo," Emma snorted.

"Oh my God. You *are* drunk."

"Why are you calling me, Josh?"

"Because you need to be in the office tomorrow morning at seven. I was checking my email—"

"You really do work too much," Emma interrupted.

"So says the pot to the kettle," Josh snickered. "Listen, a hi-pri came into our inboxes almost an hour ago. We've all been waiting for your response."

Emma's fuzzy brain tried to snap to attention at the mention of a high-priority email, but it just wasn't working right. "From who?" The only client who would warrant a high-priority email was the one in the incriminating photos.

She took another large sip to block out the memory.

Josh's voice was serious. "Mr. Price."

Emma stood up quickly, choking on her wine. Putting a hand over her eyes to stop the spinning, she managed, "Mr. Price, as in, Mr. Price, the CEO?"

"That's the one."

She swallowed hard. Mr. Price gave everyone a BlackBerry so he wouldn't have to call them—in his opinion, every employee at his firm was on call for him all day, every day, through email. He reserved the phone for his clients.

Josh continued, "Emma, stop drinking and get yourself together. Mr. Price wants to see us in his office at seven tomorrow morning. There's a potential new client—he's so wealthy he eats money for breakfast. And he's demanded you and only you, and he's refusing to deal with anyone else...even Mr. Price."

"Oh, God," Emma groaned.

"Exactly."

Mr. Price loathed when clients refused to deal with him directly.

Especially the exceptionally wealthy ones. And if they requested someone outside the top tier of management, Price wanted detailed, in-person reports three times per week for the length of the contract. If she didn't deliver results in the form of a contract extension, there would be hell to pay.

Who was she kidding? Her life was already a living hell; it wasn't like it could get much worse.

"Okay, respond to that email for me? I'll be there. Tell him I'm with a client right now or something."

"Done," Josh replied, the *tap-tap-tap* of a keyboard audible over the line. "I'll meet you outside the office at six thirty."

"Okay," Emma said with a sigh, ruefully pouring the contents of her wineglass into the plastic potted palm on the terrace. "I hope I'm not hung over tomorrow."

"Tonight, take two aspirin and drink an entire glass of water before you go to bed," Josh instructed. "I need you alert, Perkins. In the morning, you're going to drink a small glass of orange juice. No coffee."

"What?!"

"Trust me, Emma. Keep it simple, right?"

Emma smiled a little. That was her mantra for her clients— keep it simple. Simple press releases, simple statements, simple truths—or lies, as the case warranted.

If only real life worked like that.

"Good night, Josh. I'll see you in the morning."

"Six thirty, Emma."

Emma hung up, morose. Work always came first; everyone always needed something from her. But that was how her world worked—she gave, everyone took, and she was paid for it. Emma squared her shoulders and reminded herself that she didn't need anything else from anyone. She had herself, and that was enough. It had been that way for years before Ben, and she was committed to being that way for years to come. She had her job, her health, and her true passion.

When Emma was small, maybe seven or eight, her father had

given her a giant toy castle. It was enormous, one of the spectacular dollhouses they sold in department stores, and it sparked her imagination like no other toy. Her mother gave her a tiny princess doll, and an entire garrison of knights to protect it. Emma usually made the princess rescue the knights, which made her mother laugh. The tinkling sound was full of joy; she always said how proud she was that her daughter was willing to save herself from any evil princes.

It was Emma's clearest memory from her childhood, aside from the day her teacher led her into the principal's office, where a police officer told her that her parents had been killed in a car accident.

When the time came for her to move into her grandparents' house, she left the castle and the toys behind.

But in college, something propelled her to take a medieval studies class, and in it, she found peace and a rediscovered love of knights in shining armor, which led to a major in Medieval Thought and Antiquities. It was her passion, and even though her job was demanding, she made time every month to write an article or two for various obscure publications. Articles that she told no one about, and even wrote under a pseudonym. It was her last shred of that girlhood dream, and she didn't want reality to ever intrude.

She blinked back the prick of tears. Her reality was anything but valiant knights. No, hers only included the evil prince. She was grateful her mother wasn't alive to see what a failure she'd become.

Emma shook herself from the direction of her thoughts, refusing to start a pity party that would no doubt have her reaching for another bottle of wine. She couldn't go down that path, not when she had an important meeting in the morning about some hotshot client. She looked up at the sky, wishing she could see the stars, but in the city, all she ever saw was the kind of star who demanded more and more of her.

Her phone buzzed with a text from Josh, reminding her to take the aspirin. Emma headed inside the empty apartment, trying to ignore the loneliness that threatened to overwhelm her.

* * *

"Ms. Perkins." Paul Price clasped his hands tightly in front of his protruding belly. Although she tried to avoid looking directly at it, Emma always found herself staring at his shirt, her eyes locked on the bottom button as it strained against the hole. She wondered, if it *did* pop off, whether she'd have to dodge left or right.

Mr. Price cleared his throat, and Emma's eyes snapped up to his. *Caught.* She mentally chastised herself and resolved to pay better attention.

"You're certain there's no prior connection to this client?" Mr. Price asked.

Emma slid a glance to the clock that hung on the wall behind Josh, who was also forced to sit through this meeting. It was barely past eight a.m. She wasn't sure how much longer she could hold out before asking for coffee.

She carefully folded her hands in front of her and rested them on the polished mahogany conference table in the center of his cavernous office. "Mr. Price, I promise, I have never heard of Aidan MacWilliam. I don't understand why he called you on your personal phone, nor why he's refusing to work with any other publicist but me."

Emma had to admit, she herself was curious as to why Mr. MacWilliam sought her services. On paper, she was just like all the other midlevel publicists at the company. While she did have a growing list of well-known clients, she knew she wasn't yet at the level where the elite people of the world would seek her out. And, glancing at the file in front of her again, Aidan MacWilliam seemed to fit into that category.

"Perhaps he knows your work," Mr. Price concluded, interrupting her thoughts.

Emma doubted it, but didn't say it aloud. Publicly, her name wasn't attached to anyone—clients rarely told each other about a great publicity manager, for fear the attention would be taken from them and placed onto the newer, bigger client. Plus, according to Mr. Price, this client was from Ireland. Price Publicity, LLC's entire client base was mostly American, with some Asian companies.

Mr. Price heaved a great sigh, as though he had finally thought his last thought on the subject, but ruined the effect when he added, "MacWilliam wants you. He stated very clearly that his situation is a private one, and that he wouldn't discuss it with anyone but you. So." He cleared his throat meaningfully. "You'll accept him as your new client, but I want daily updates as to what he wants, how you're going to provide it to him, and how we can use this to promote the company in the public eye." He dismissed them both with a wave of his hand, and Emma quickly followed Josh out of the intimidating office.

In the kitchen area, as she stirred the sugar into her cup of coffee, Emma leveled a stare at Josh. "So you're telling me that this guy—MacWilliam—calls up the biggest publicity name in New York City *on his home phone* and simply demands that he wants *me* as his PR manager?" She tilted her head skeptically.

Josh casually leaned against the counter, sipping his own cup. "You heard Price. MacWilliam is a wealthy, reclusive man." He picked up the folder and pulled out the dossier. "He wants what he wants, when he wants it—not unlike the majority of our clients. Hmm. No online presence, no paper trails, no reputation smears, not even an angry ex." He looked at her soberly. "After what happened with Kincaid, this should be a walk in the park. Maybe it's just what you need to get your mojo back."

Emma blinked back the sudden prick of tears, humiliation swamping her; Josh was the only one who knew of her situation, as she'd put the paperwork in months ago to be removed from the Kincaid account. "I'm sorry. My personal life shouldn't affect my professional one."

Josh smiled sympathetically. "I know you're suffering. A broken heart is—"

Emma threw her hand up. "Whoa. Let's get one thing straight. I am not brokenhearted over losing that cheating, lying jackass. Absolutely not. I'm upset that I didn't see it coming. But I am *not* upset that I am free from a loveless *waste* of a relationship."

Josh blinked. "Okay then."

"Now. Back to MacWilliam. You agree that this doesn't add up, right?"

"There are plenty of eccentric folks out there," Josh replied, clearly relieved that her outburst was over. "And he specifically requested that you be the one to assist him. And, as you know, the wealthiest clients get what they want. We deliver it."

"So you want me to meet with him tonight, take him to dinner, see what this is all about?"

Josh shook his head. "No. Well, maybe. First, you'll meet with him here, this afternoon. I want him to be well aware that we have a face to his name. Safety first."

Josh was a good guy, and he was always ensuring his team's security. No one could have meetings outside the office without documenting them first—and in such a large city, Emma was grateful for it.

Josh continued to pore over the paper in front of him. "Oh. Here's something. Looks like he plans to check out the auction that we're handling."

Christie's was having a special auction that the publicity firm had been hired to promote. A collection of pristine, rare, and expensive medieval artifacts had been placed for auction by an anonymous source, and it promised to be one of the most glamorous events of the year in New York City. Tickets just for the chance to view the artifacts were priced in the thousands. Emma was dying to see pictures, but all items and descriptions were under lock and key. No one was allowed a sneak peek until twenty-four hours prior to the event. And even then, you had to present a cashier's check in excess of ten thousand dollars at the auction house for access to the artifacts.

She wouldn't be seeing those anytime soon.

"Emma!"

"Sorry," she replied automatically, once again caught lost in her thoughts.

Josh sighed. "You need to shake this funk. Maybe MacWilliam is the client to do that."

"Well," Emma capitulated with a small smile, taking the folder labeled *Aidan MacWilliam* from his outstretched hand. "I don't have any Irish clients."

"You do now."

* * *

Emma straightened her skirt and smoothed her hair. Mr. MacWilliam was waiting for her in Mr. Price's office.

"Dibs," Heinous Heidi murmured as Emma passed by her cube. Emma paused despite her better judgment. "Excuse me?"

Heidi smirked. "After Mr. MacWilliam meets you and realizes his mistake, I call dibs on his account. Price already signed off."

Two interns popped their heads up from their cubes.

"Holy hell, Emma. Did you see him? I know we get lookers in here all the time…but *whoa*."

"He is so unbelievably hot!" the other chimed in breathlessly.

"Down, girls," Emma replied with a slight smile. Her expression became frosty as she turned back to Heidi. "Looks like you'll have to fight for him."

Heidi gracefully crossed her endless legs and sat back slightly, giving Emma a perfect view straight into perfect cleavage. She gave Emma a Cheshire Cat smile and almost purred when she replied, "Oh, Emma. I don't fight for men. They fight for me. I'm sure you can relate…oh. That's right. You've never had anyone fight for you. In fact, if memory serves, you don't have anyone anymore." She snickered.

Emma felt the blow exactly where Heidi wanted it to land, but she struggled not to let it show.

Intern One's eyes were enormous, and she slunk back down to her desk, but Intern Two seemed not to realize the viper's den into which she was staring. Heidi glanced up at her and raised an imperial, elegantly threaded brow. "Get me a grande cafe mocha, no sugar, no whipped cream, extra dry, with half skim, half 2 percent milk. Extra hot. *Now*, Thing Two."

The girl scrambled off her chair amid loud crashes and a few gasps as she rushed to do Heidi's bidding. Heidi gave a last look to Emma before turning around, effectively dismissing her.

Emma bit her tongue, her ears steaming, and continued on. No matter how many times she told herself she was a better person than Heidi, it really didn't matter. When you sleep with the boss, you get the best contracts. And Emma refused to sleep with her boss.

At least she doesn't have a corner office, Emma consoled herself. Heidi's cube was just as small as her own.

Gayle, Mr. Price's sixty-something personal assistant, gave her a wink as Emma approached the office. "The heavens are smiling on you today," she whispered as she pressed a button. Mr. Price's door unlocked, and Gayle waved her in. "If you do nothing else today, enjoy that eye candy. We're all jealous you get to spend time with him in close quarters!"

Emma's mouth dropped open. Where had all the professionalism of the world gone? First the interns, now Gayle? Well, on second thought…the interns were college girls. Emma expected that kind of behavior from them. But Gayle? She was a grandmother, for heaven's sake! Emma gave her a bemused look, then took a deep breath. Letting it out slowly, Emma breezed into Mr. Price's office as though she met with high-profile clients on a daily basis.

"Ms. Perkins?" The lovely accent changed her name to *pair-kins*, his deep voice resounding in her chest. She saw him sitting at the same table she spent her morning at, the view of Central Park in the distance behind him.

And her mind went completely, utterly blank.

Aidan MacWilliam stood with an easy grace, and her eyes went wide.

The man was her darkest fantasy, all dressed up in a tailored Armani suit and tie. Searing green eyes, framed by unfairly dark lashes, stared back at her, and a slight smile played at the corners of his lips. His jaw and cheeks looked to be carved from granite— hard, smooth, perfect. His nose had a slight crook in it, as though it had been broken before. His shoulders were enormous; she dimly wondered if he played football. She simply stared up at him, her mouth dry, before realizing he was holding out his hand.

She dumbly grasped it, her eyes refusing to blink as if they didn't want to miss out on a second of the raw masculine beauty before her.

"Hello," she managed. "I'm Emmaline Perkins. From Price Publicity."

She mentally slapped herself. Of course she was from Price Publicity! They were standing in Mr. Price's office, for crying out loud. Emma felt the heat creep up her neck; she wouldn't blame him if he walked out, told Gayle he'd changed his mind due to her utter lack of intelligence and sweaty hands.

Instead, he smiled at her, his white teeth flashing as her knees went weak. "Aidan MacWilliam. Pleasure, Ms. Perkins." He raised her hand to his lips and, very chastely, kissed her knuckles.

She swallowed hard. She wasn't sure if it was the way he said her name, the way he kissed her hand, or the intoxicating combination of both.

Apparently taking pity on her scattered wits, he waved her over to the table and waited for her to sit before folding himself into what had moments before appeared to be a normal-sized office chair. Now it resembled something closer to a child's toy. He leaned back, crossed an ankle over a knee, and nodded to the large white binder sitting on the table in front of her.

Emma glanced at it, then back at Mr. MacWilliam. It almost hurt to look at him. Gayle's advice popped into her head—*eye candy overload.*

"I'd like to get to know you a bit, see if we can work together," he said.

Emma's brows knit. She wasn't sure what she'd expected from this meeting, but an interview was not it.

He stood and offered her a bottle of water from the small cooler against the wall. She shook her head, and he helped himself to one. His lips wrapped around the opening of the bottle. When he ran his tongue over his bottom lip, Emma mentally shook herself out of her daze and bit the inside of her own lip, hard.

Stop! she chastised herself. *He is a client. And you are committed to being single for*...she paused in her thinking, then mentally shrugged. *You're committed to being single for a while. Sure, he's sexy, but he'd be a rebound.* That was all this was—a healthy reaction to another male. A wave of relief washed over her. She could corral her rampaging hormones; all she needed to remember was that he was a client, nothing more.

"Have you ever seen a léine?" he asked, returning to his seat.

Emma blinked, thrown by the question. "As in an Irish kilt?" *Whatever happened to questions like, "Tell me about a time you excelled"?*

He grinned. "I'll forgive you that because you're an American. For reference, the Irish don't wear kilts; those would be the Scots."

She placed her elbows on the table and folded her hands together, her hackles rising. If there was one thing she was not, it was uneducated in Irish history. "I'm aware that the Irish do not wear kilts, Mr. MacWilliam. However, there is no word in the English language that would properly convey what a léine is, which is why I drew a comparison to something similarly worn by a well-known people."

His smile grew. "Duly noted. Language barriers are difficult. It would be easier if the world spoke in Gaelic."

She tried not to snort. "Gaelic is no cakewalk."

"Are you familiar with it?" he asked. In Gaelic.

"A bit," she replied, also in Gaelic.

He raised a brow, impressed. He reached down next to his chair and pulled a large leather satchel onto the table. Carefully, he withdrew a léine—*holy moly, that looks authentic!* she thought wildly— then slid it over to her.

"Have you ever seen one of these, Ms. Perkins?" he asked again.

Reverentially, she held the blue cloth in front of her. Silver threads shot through it in a checked pattern; the material was thick, soft, and warm. She carefully studied the thread and the weave, then stood and carefully shook it out. She spread it on the table, assessed, then turned it around and assessed again. It looked like a long tunic with flaps of fabric at the shoulders. She wrinkled her forehead in concentration; she couldn't figure out how those pieces fit into the overall purpose of the garment.

"I have, but only in pictures." She met his eyes. "Do you know how this particular léine would've been worn?"

Mr. MacWilliam watched her, his thumb and forefinger playing with his bottom lip as though he were deep in thought. Without answering, he stood and shed his jacket. He placed the léine over his head and wrapped the extra fabric around himself. The complicated knots he tied at the front and even the back puzzled her, but once she saw it on him she almost clapped with glee.

That was most definitely a medieval style of dress.

Aidan stood, completely at ease in a medieval piece of cloth and a modern-day suit. The dichotomy was jarring; if his hair were longer and he shed his trousers, Emma could almost picture him riding across a forest, low on horseback, sword strapped to his back...

"It looks as though it's from the 1400s, maybe the 1500s, I would guess," she said without hesitation, erasing the image from her mind. She was a sucker for anything of medieval or Celtic history, and as such they were usually the subjects of her articles. Although it was nice to fantasize about it, college courses were about as close as she could—and wanted to—get to the Middle Ages.

"Very impressive, Ms. Perkins," Aidan said, approval written all over his features. "Mid-1400s."

"I've never seen a replica of such high quality."

He unfastened it as quickly as he'd put it on and tossed it onto the table. "It's not a replica."

She gasped. "What? Good gracious, you just threw it! Shouldn't it be behind glass? How is it so well preserved?"

A ghost of a smile touched his lips. "I believe I was asking the questions."

She blanched, horrified that she'd actually reprimanded a potential client for handling his own belongings.

"I am relieved to find that you are interested in artifacts," he replied wryly. "Are you aware of the upcoming Antique Armory auction?"

"Of course," she replied quickly, then cleared her throat. "Some of our clients plan to attend."

"Perfect. Are you free for dinner tonight?" he asked, stuffing the léine back in the satchel.

She bit her tongue. Hard.

"I have reservations at The Colcannon and would love your company. We can continue our discussion there, after you've had a chance to go through this information." He nodded at the white binder. "I trust I've passed muster with your office, as no one's interrupted us."

Her face gave away her guilt. She hadn't had a client call the firm out on its in-office first meeting policy before.

"Don't think another second on it, Ms. Perkins. I'm fully satisfied that this firm shows a high regard for its employees' safety." He held out the binder, but as she went to take it, he gripped it tightly until she met his gaze. "I must have your word that this is for your eyes only, Ms. Perkins. No one from your team—legal or otherwise—can view it, or dinner, and all else, is canceled."

Emma nodded, though his insistence on secrecy gave her pause. "I didn't get any of my questions in," she pointed out, feeling the need to lighten the moment. Aidan MacWilliam was clearly a take-charge type.

His face softened, and he chuckled. "All right, then. I enjoy rain, sunsets, and whiskey."

She laughed. "Not those kinds of questions. But okay. I'll see your rain, up your sunset by a sunrise, and exchange your whiskey for wine."

"Your beauty is outmatched only by your wit, Ms. Perkins."

The cadence of his words washed over her, and she allowed herself to relax a fraction more.

"Keep up the compliments and I think we'll suit just fine," she said with another laugh. "All right, Mr. MacWilliam. I'll keep your contract terms secret. For now."

"For now," he acquiesced. "I'm taking you as a woman of your word." He released the binder, and she felt the thrill of a small victory. "I'll pick you up here, or at your place?"

"I'll meet you there," she deferred.

He pursed his lips, but didn't argue. "One more question."

She waited expectantly.

Aidan picked up his suit jacket. "What's the best piece of advice you give your clients about answering questions?"

"Never answer a question with a question," she said immediately. "It just invites more questions."

He smiled, and she felt as though she had passed another unquantifiable test.

"Wise. Perhaps you can walk me out," he said as he shrugged his jacket back on and picked up the leather satchel. He tossed his empty water bottle into the recycling bin and gave her a conspiratorial wink. "My way in was fraught with predators."

"Ah. Of the female sort? Perhaps you need a bodyguard more than a publicist." Emma couldn't help but let out another laugh.

He gazed at her. "You have a lovely laugh, Ms. Perkins. I hope I get to hear it again soon." He opened the door for her, then followed her out.

They were almost immediately waylaid by Heidi.

"Oh, Emma, *there* you are!" she exclaimed in her sultry, I-just-adore-you falsetto voice. She placed her hand upon her chest—more of it was showing than earlier—and gave a small shake of her head. "I've been looking all *over* for you. The deadline for the *New York Times* piece about your client came and went, and she just tried to cancel your contract!" Heidi placed a hand on Emma's arm and lowered her voice. "Don't worry—I wrote something for her a couple of years ago, and once I polished it up a bit, it did the trick. Account and reputation saved! But really, that's the third time you've let her down this month!"

Emma's jaw hung so far off her face she wasn't sure if she'd be able to scrape it off the floor.

"Oh! I'm so sorry, you're with a client. I didn't mean to intrude." Heidi held out her hand and batted her eyelashes. "Heidi Swanson, publicist of the year for Price Publicity."

Aidan's eyes never strayed past Heidi's face, and Emma gave him major points for that. Heidi's chest was so fluffed it was a wonder she didn't float away.

"Aidan MacWilliam." He shook her hand briskly. Despite having just been at complete ease with him a moment ago, Emma felt a frisson of intimidation at his stony expression. "You understand that your blatant attempts to discredit Ms. Perkins do you more harm than good, Ms. Swanson?"

"Oh, you misunder*stand*, Mr. MacWilliam," Heidi hurried to explain. "Emma and I work together; we're on the same *team*."

"MacWilliam! Pleasure to finally meet you!" Mr. Price boomed as he approached. "Is your meeting over so soon?"

Fraught with predators. She couldn't have stated it better herself.

"Price," he replied in the same tone he had used with Heidi. He turned his full gaze to Emma, and though his face remained hard, his eyes softened toward her. His voice firm, he stated flatly, "Under no circumstances can anyone see the contract." His eyes never left hers. "Absolutely no one. Just you, or the entire agreement is off."

"Duly noted," Emma replied, biting the inside of her cheek. Aidan MacWilliam was proving himself to be a very insightful client, and she had the sudden urge to ensure she kept him.

Heidi sputtered, and Aidan's eyes crinkled slightly at the corners, as though he were enjoying ignoring her as much as Emma was.

"Right, right, Ms. Perkins only," Mr. Price assured him as he tried to steer him back toward his office. "Do you drink? I have a delicious brandy. Vintage, very good stuff. Care for a glass?"

"He prefers whiskey," Emma interjected, then pressed her lips together quickly. She hadn't meant to say that.

Aidan caught her eye, and he let her see the humor lurking beneath his stern exterior.

"I have other engagements," he said curtly. He gave Emma another kiss on the knuckles (she fought the urge to swoon again), then shook Price's hand before stepping into the elevator. He didn't acknowledge Heidi.

As soon as the doors closed, Heidi flipped her hair. "He carries a man-purse. Who does that?"

"It's a medieval satchel," Emma said, not troubling to hide her disdain. She didn't bother to wait for a reply before saying to Mr. Price, "I'm meeting him for dinner tonight to discuss the contract. I'll need the afternoon to review this binder, and you heard him. I think it's best if I leave the office for a while to review this."

Mr. Price didn't object as she turned on her heel and left, a huge smile lighting her features as Gayle pretended to be busy (and gave Emma a very tiny thumbs-up as she passed) and she made her way back to her desk.

Aidan MacWilliam was definitely an interesting character...*and*, she admitted to herself, *quite a nice piece of eye candy*. She grinned again.

CHAPTER 2

Aidan MacWilliam was not a man to leave things to chance, but some things were beyond even his control—specifically, Ms. Emma Perkins. She wasn't at all what he was expecting, which was laughable now that he'd met her. He'd been prepared to go into battle—her reputation, his cousin Colin informed him, was for a well-earned steely countenance. She was a talent that her current company hadn't yet fully exploited, and Colin hoped to steal her away before they did so.

Aidan had to admit, he hoped he could pay attention to the job at hand. Colin had tasked him with determining if Ms. Perkins was as effective in person as his latest client swore she was. Celtic Connections needed only the best for the head of its PR department, but Colin didn't want to post the position publicly for reasons unknown to Aidan.

As they were family, Aidan didn't question him. He simply agreed to meet with the woman, conduct the interview in an unassuming way, and report back to Colin with his impressions.

First impression? Smart. Ms. Perkins was a quick thinker, and witty, too. She was also, he admitted without hesitation, quite beautiful. Her hair was a dark honey blonde, and her eyes were not easily forgotten. The stunning shade of blue, almost violet, was unlike any color he'd ever had the fortune of seeing. Her professional demeanor was well practiced; if he hadn't been watching for it, he wouldn't have noticed her subtle, admiring glances.

He chuckled to himself. There wasn't much he didn't notice about Ms. Perkins.

There weren't any pictures of her online or in print—none

on the web, her company's website, or even social media. Aidan had had his own contacts do some preliminary research on her, but she kept the lowest profile he'd ever seen—aside, of course, from his own. He wondered if that was what made her so good at her job—her clients' "misdeeds," as she called them, were fixed almost immediately. Most people didn't even know a transgression happened at all, or it was turned on its head into something positive.

He finished buttoning his shirt and pulled on his most comfortable pair of jeans. His suit was gone; he had showed Emma his friendly business side (and, unfortunately, a little of his not-so-friendly business side thanks to the large-breasted bit of evil in her office), and now he needed to get more personal. Trustworthy; less like a business arrangement, more like a friendship.

Aidan looked around for the hotel key card and cursed. Back home, his security system consisted of a very sharp sword, not that he had to make use of it very often. In fact, he mused, spying the key card on the granite counter in his suite's large kitchen, the last time he'd had the pleasure of using it was when Colin had visited him in Ireland and they'd engaged in a bit of sport in the back garden.

His fingers flexed. It had been far too long since he'd enjoyed the sound of steel upon steel. He couldn't wait to have his old sword back; none other had quite the balance to it like that one did.

He flipped off the light and grabbed his black leather jacket from the back of the dining room chair. His suite at the W Hotel was enormous—certainly bigger than his modest cottage in Ireland. The suite boasted two floors of living space. The dining room held a large, polished table with six chairs. The kitchen was modern and sleek, and all black and chrome. A living room and powder room completed the first floor, and the upstairs held two bedrooms, each with its own full-sized washroom.

Opulence. Even after all these years, he still hated it.

Colin had insisted on making the hotel reservations. Pompous arse, he knew how much Aidan loathed lavishness, which was no doubt why he'd booked the swankiest room possible. Their relationship was more like brothers than cousins, and Aidan took great pleasure in the thought that he would get his revenge somehow.

Aidan put his thoughts aside and grabbed his satchel, which was stuffed with treasures sure to make Emma's unique eyes light up like a Christmas tree. He could only imagine what her response would be. That feistiness and her quick wit would be a boon in the upcoming days.

If she agreed to it.

He frowned. Wayward thoughts weren't going to be of aid. He needed to remain focused on his end goal—determine Emma's abilities, get the sword from the auction, and get back to Ireland before Colin could set him up on a date with some new client. Colin had held off so far, but Aidan could sense his cousin's growing impatience with his determination to get back home. Despite that, Aidan hadn't any desire to be Celtic Connections' latest match. He liked his solitude, he liked his peace, and he loved how it grated on Colin's nerves.

Aidan closed the door behind him and hit the elevator button, sliding his arms into his jacket. He needed to keep his wits about himself, and refocus on the task.

His cell rang, interrupting his thoughts. "Are you downstairs?"

"You bet yer arse I am, and I got another one of those parking tickets," Cian MacWilliam barked from the other end. "Shite, mate, you'd best have a plate ready fer me at Paddy's. The bobbies aren't big Irish fans and they didn't like me threatening them."

The elevator dinged, and Aidan grinned at the man standing in the lobby, who doubled as his driver tonight. "They don't look kindly upon brutes threatening them with swords. I'm surprised you didn't get yourself thrown in a cell for the night."

Cian tightened his jaw as he shoved his phone into his pocket. "I would've liked to see them try."

Aidan clapped a hand on his back. "Try to bring the temper down. I've got myself an important meeting, and I would appreciate it if you could turn on the charm. I know you have it in there somewhere."

"She best be a looker," Cian grumbled.

Surprised by the small jolt of possessiveness he felt, Aidan shoved his hands into his pockets. "Doesn't matter much, mate." They walked toward the nondescript gray sedan with a neon orange ticket on the windshield. "This is business, not pleasure."

Cian spat out an obscenity as he slid the ticket from under the wiper. "I'm in sore need of some pleasure."

Aidan rolled his eyes as he pulled open the door. "You can have your fun when we get home. Let's get going already."

Cian started the car. "I've been waiting eight long years to get home. Another twenty seconds isn't going to change anything."

Aidan pulled out some papers from his satchel. "It will if you don't pay attention to the road. Drive on, Cian."

Cian's sigh was deep, but he acquiesced. "Aye, my laird."

* * *

At seven o'clock precisely, Aidan stepped into another world. He was damn proud of this restaurant; he had designed it himself and handpicked the chef from his home country. He hated all the fuss that went with opening a restaurant, so his chef, Paddy, took all the recognition. It was part of their agreement—Aidan remained a silent partner, fronting the money and vision while Paddy created the delicious fare and became the face of the establishment. Aidan preferred it that way. His privacy was worth much more than what the restaurant brought in.

Gregory, the efficient (if stodgy) host, led him through the public dining room, which was anchored to the left of the entrance by a wall-to-wall hearth. The back of it was blackened with soot, and the logs inside it were charred. A stack of logs and peat moss leaned haphazardly against the surround, drawing the eye to the stonework on the walls that looked as though they had stood in place for hundreds of years. The arches that broke the space into clustered areas looked smooth from time instead of a builder's tools. The tables were crammed together in typical New York style, and the patrons clamored to be heard over the sounds of the open kitchen and bartenders slinging drinks. It was stunning in its authenticity—and if there was anything Aidan was a full expert on, it was medieval taverns.

Gregory led him through a heavy curtain, and when it fell closed behind him, the noise lessened considerably. Emma sat at the table, her golden hair piled atop her head in a haphazard knot, secured with two sticks that looked as though they'd be useful in a fight. Her face glowed in the candlelight, and her eyes brightened when she saw him.

"Mr. MacWilliam, hello," she said warmly, standing as he came closer. He took her hand again and kissed the back of her knuckles, careful to linger a fraction of a second longer than necessary. He caught her blush.

"Thank you for meeting me here," he said. He handed his jacket to Gregory and said, "We'll have whatever the special is tonight. Send back a bottle of Jameson and one of pinot noir"—he looked to Emma, who nodded her assent—"then we're not to be bothered except by Cian, who will tell the staff of any needs we may have."

"Very good, sir." Gregory waited for Emma to sit, then fanned her napkin over her lap. Aidan waved him away, and as soon as the curtain dropped, she sat back and admired the room.

"This is a beautiful restaurant," Emma said, smoothing the napkin over her lap. She glanced closer at it, then held it up. "Look! This is the same design as the front door!"

He'd been very specific in the creation of that door. The stained glass was thicker than regulation, and looked as though it had been pulled from the Book of Kells—intricately designed images surrounded a capital *C*. Throughout many of the details, smaller instances of the letter *M* were interwoven, with leaves of ivy snaking their way around each line of the letter, a sword slicing across it. The linen napkins had that same *M* embroidered in a light silver, in the corner. He was pleased she noticed it.

"Impressive," she admitted. "Very impressive."

"Hmm," he replied, stroking his chin. "You could be talking of many things. My command of the English language? No, no...we already covered that." He furrowed his brow in mock concentration, then snapped his fingers. "Ah. You must mean my memory. When a woman says she likes something, it behooves a man to pay attention."

Emma regarded him curiously. "Actually, I was talking about your *command* of the staff here. What is it about you that makes them snap to attention? Is it your presence? Your authoritative voice? Your good looks?" she teased.

"Or," Aidan replied dryly, "it could be that I'm the owner." He took pleasure in the way her mouth dropped open into a perfect little O. "Which brings me immediately to business. What did you think?" He jerked his head toward the binder, which sat between them on the table.

Emma toyed with the edge of the tablecloth. "That innocent little binder holds a whole lot of information, Mr. MacWilliam."

"Aye," he agreed. He kept his breathing even and his face impassive, but he couldn't control his heart as it sped up slightly.

"At first, I couldn't believe what I was seeing," she admitted. "I was quite surprised."

"Surprised?" he asked.

She took a sip of her water. "Yes. Very surprised. It's not every day I'm handed a binder that contains not just a lengthy and very thorough contract for publicity management, but also an entire lot of medieval artifacts up for auction."

"I wonder what you *are* handed every day," Aidan mused.

"Nothing like this," she replied dryly. "The point is, I thought it would be easy enough for me to search for these items online. Imagine my surprise when I couldn't find any of them."

"Surprise. There's that word again," he murmured. The server entered with the bottles of whiskey and wine, and Aidan waited for him to pour. Emma gave her nod, and the server left as quietly as he had come.

Aidan raised his glass. "To our partnership."

"I haven't accepted yet," Emma reminded him, although she did tap her glass against his. "In fact, I'm quite interested to find out how you obtained these images. This auction is closed until twenty-four hours prior to its start. And, as this binder wasn't made in the last hour, I have to wonder how it came to be in your possession."

Aidan peered at the binder. "Did you sign the contract?"

"No."

"Then I'm afraid I can't tell you how it came to be in my possession." He watched her struggle with herself for a moment as he enjoyed another sip of his drink. He smiled in appreciation. The more expensive whiskeys be damned; Jameson was a fine display of Irish excellence.

"I need to have my legal team—"

"Absolutely not."

She leveled a stare at him that had, perhaps, made lesser men quake. "I am not a lawyer, Mr. MacWilliam. You're asking me to sign a legal document, one that I don't fully understand. That's unfair and wrong."

Colin would appreciate that mindset. Aidan reached across the table and opened the binder. "Then let's go over it, line by line," he suggested. He motioned her to move her chair around to him, and she complied, albeit grudgingly.

"Go ahead. Ask me your questions."

"You're not my lawyer," she pointed out.

"Do you trust me?"

Emma narrowed her eyes and bit her lip, and Aidan wondered if she would be brave enough to tell him the truth. After a moment, she shook her head.

"No. I don't trust anyone."

She was reinforcing his good opinion of her with each word she uttered. Colin would be lucky to add her to his team.

"Smart," he replied. "But in this case, incorrect. I'll take you through this contract." He opened the binder. "If you have any lingering questions, we'll see what they are and determine, together, if you can take them to your legal team tomorrow. And if I misrepresent anything, you can certainly terminate the contract based on that. See? It says so right here, first paragraph."

She pursed her lips, and Aidan waited, slightly nervous. He wanted the chance to get to know her. Not because he was intrigued by her intelligence and her sly wit, he hurried to assure himself. No, it was because Colin was right—this woman was perfect to head up a team overseas. He had to get her to sign on first with him, then with Colin.

"All right," she finally agreed. "Let's go over this together. But I'm not promising anything."

He smiled fully at her and set to work.

* * *

Emma couldn't help but notice that Aidan's intense gaze hadn't left her face as they discussed the contract. It was almost unnerving how focused he was. She tried to suppress a shiver of awareness; the thought of that focus on her in a different situation made everything south of her belly clench.

She didn't bother telling herself to stop with the inappropriate fantasizing; she knew she was a lost cause.

He flipped the binder to the back and slid it all the way in front of her. "If you were given the ability to purchase one item from the lot, what would you choose?"

She frowned. Surely he realized she could never afford one of the relics; just the starting bids were higher than her monthly income. "I don't like to play pretend, Mr. MacWilliam. I deal in facts."

"I enjoy hypotheticals, Ms. Perkins, so humor me, if you would." He gave her an encouraging smile, and her heart turned in her chest. "If money were absolutely no object, and you could purchase any one object in here, what would it be?"

She decided to play along, and once again looked through the various pieces—helmets, coins, a jousting stick, a writing desk, wax seals, even a piece of fairly well-preserved fabric. She was only pretending to notice the items, though—she spent more than two hours drooling over the various pieces earlier in the afternoon. About halfway through the pages, she stopped and studied the picture of a silver sword boasting a large green gem in the hilt, with an intricate pattern etched on the handle. She squinted to see the pattern in greater detail. It was fuzzy, but from what she could tell it looked like the letter *M*, twisted up with vines, and a sword stabbing through it lengthwise.

She pointed to it. "This."

Aidan stroked his chin, regarding her thoughtfully. "Are you sure?"

She frowned at him, again feeling as though this were a test. "You asked, and this is my answer. This sword, had I all the money in the world, is what I would buy."

"Why? The large gem? It would make a beautiful pendant."

She was horrified at the thought of desecrating such a pristine relic. She wondered again what he was after.

"No, Mr. MacWilliam. While the gem is very beautiful, what strikes me as special is the etching. If you look closely, you'll see it's a letter, entwined with foliage of some sort, and pierced with a sword." She paused, and realization dawned. She held up her napkin. "That's the same *M* as this!"

Aidan's eyes burned into hers, his voice low. "What would you do with such a sword, lass?"

Captivated by his intensity, Emma's breath hitched. "I'd use it to learn about its original owner."

Apparently, her answer was what he'd wanted to hear. He let out a breath, then gave her a blindingly brilliant smile. Emma tried not to react, but when he smiled like that, her heart stopped and her breathing quickened. She desperately tried to get hold of herself. The man was way out of her league. He was too charming, too smart, too wealthy. More than that, he was a client. She had no business lusting after him.

He was saying something, and Emma tried to shake off the remnants of that smile and focus back on his words instead of his firm mouth.

"I need your love of medieval antiquities, Ms. Perkins."

"How do you know I love medieval artifacts?"

He blinked quickly. He opened and closed his mouth. "It's clear that you have a keen eye for valuable artifacts. You chose the most expensive and rarest item in the lot." He signaled to the man standing just inside the doorway. "Cian, have them bring the main course."

He was diverting attention, and Emma's BS flag went up, but years of experience in her field made her hold her tongue.

"And I need you for another reason as well. You have a reputation for saving your clients from themselves." Aidan turned his attention back to Emma, and she frowned.

"You need me to save you from yourself?"

His laugh was hollow. "I'm so far beyond saving, but I'd like that to stay between us."

She sighed. "Mr. MacWilliam, let's be honest. What, exactly, do you want from me?"

His face remained impassive. "I thought we just went over it. I need you to represent me at the auction tomorrow night."

"Your anonymity is guaranteed at the auction house. All you have to do is use one of their proxy-by-phone in-house bidders. You won't have to show your face, and the public, without any visual, won't be able to trace you."

He shook his head. "No. I need to *be* there, to ensure the lot is as expected. But I can't bid for myself."

She raised her eyebrows. "Why not?"

His expression grew serious. "As far as anyone knows, I'm in Ireland. And I need it to stay that way."

She leaned forward and lowered her voice. "Are you in trouble of some sort?"

"Nothing you need to be involved with. But I prefer it if the only ones who know I'm here are you, your boss, and my clansman."

She glanced over at the man standing by the door. "Him?"

"Aye."

"Okay," she replied slowly. "So, if you're not going to bid in this auction, why are you here?"

"I didn't say I wasn't going to be a bidder." He drained his whiskey glass. "I said I wasn't going to be bidding *myself.*"

Her eyes widened. "You can't mean for me to do so in your place?"

He nodded wordlessly, his expression determined.

Emma swallowed hard. "I…" she trailed off, unable to formulate her jumbled thoughts. "This isn't…"

He tipped his glass toward her. "Either you accept the contract or you don't."

She carefully—regretfully—pushed the binder away. "I don't think I can sign this after all."

Aidan merely lifted a brow.

"You've put me between a rock and a hard place, Mr. MacWilliam." She felt a keen disappointment; she really liked him, and working with him would've been a welcome breath of fresh air from her normal sort of client.

He gently nudged the binder back toward her. "I realize that and I'm sorry for it. But you're the most qualified to help me. And I've taken provisions within this agreement against any ramifications to your career, plus the additional offer to pay ten thousand dollars immediately, deposited directly into your bank before the auction tomorrow night."

What he was offering was insanity, pure and simple, but what she said was, "This is all very strange. Price would never accept a client paying me directly."

"If Price wants his commission, he'll do as I say," Aidan replied mildly.

"Mr. MacWilliam, a very large percentage of Mr. Price's clientele plan to attend this auction. Some are flying in at the last moment, others are using proxy bidders. If I act as *your* proxy bidder, as you stipulate in this contract, and I outbid another Price client on an item—"

"All items."

She choked. "What?"

He topped off her wineglass. "All items, Ms. Perkins. We're obtaining the whole lot."

"That's millions of dollars!" she burst out.

"I estimate about three million," he replied without inflection.

Three million dollars? Emma couldn't imagine having that much money to spend on dusty artifacts, no matter how amazing their history.

"Mr. MacWilliam, I can help you find a proxy bidder—"

"There isn't any time, Ms. Perkins," he interrupted. "It's you or me. And I am paying your firm a hefty sum to ensure that it's not me."

He folded his arms and leveled a stare at her.

"All right, Ms. Perkins. You want honesty?"

She nodded cautiously.

"I believe you hold a rather expensive degree in medieval studies."

"Medieval thought," she corrected as the color rose to her cheeks. He must know about her articles—but how?

He dismissed the difference with a wave of his hand. "Your knowledge of the time period is exactly why I wanted you as my publicity manager. Your thesis was on medieval Ireland from the early 1400s through the 1600s. I read it, and enjoyed it."

"You read it?" she replied incredulously. The piece—which was over a hundred pages of meticulous research, images, historical documents, and interviews on the actual interclan politics of the time versus what was passed through storytelling—was her pride and joy.

And she was certain that not even her master's committee read it all the way through.

"I'm not an antiquities dealer," she clarified quickly. She tucked a stray hair behind her ear, and an idea struck. "I can, however, put you in touch with a very well-known one here in the States."

He smiled as if amused. "Only you, Ms. Perkins. Your knowledge of medieval artifacts is impressive, and I need someone to bid for me tomorrow night. This will allow me to see how you work under pressure, if I'm to hire you on an extended contract."

She tamped down the urge to scream. "I don't have what you say you need. You must realize that I am successful in PR because my clients know I'm invisible. That means I don't make the news, and I don't make a spectacle of myself. Publicly bidding for a client of Mr. Price's would probably get me fired. I can't afford that."

Aidan sat back and braced his hands on the table. Large, calloused hands that seemed more suited to a hard day's labor than signing business documents. His voice rumbled in his chest. "I would make it more than worth your while."

Emma's mouth went dry. How did he make that statement sound so alluring and sexy? She couldn't allow his charm to work its magic on her, though; she wasn't going to go all doe-eyed and simpering, which was no doubt what the man was used to. "I've worked very hard to get to where I am in this company, and I can't throw it away for five months' rent."

Aidan shrugged. "I'm not asking you to, but if you must think on it, please do. You have until the auction, after all. But might I draw your attention to the amendment?" He gestured to the binder again. "Read it carefully, lass."

She bit the inside of her cheek and turned to where they'd left off. She read aloud: "In addition to the fees set forth by Price Public Relations, Ltd, the Client (*Aidan MacWilliam*) does hereby agree to the additional sum of $38,453.67, paid directly to the Undersigned (*Emmaline Perkins*) with the sole purpose of relieving debt incurred through student loans for the knowledge sought by the Client. The Client also agrees to pay one (1) year of royalties to Price Public Relations, Ltd, for any clientele lost from the direct result of this agreement, providing the Undersigned is fully employed for at least one (1) year following any incurred clientele losses."

Emma couldn't believe what she was reading. How did he get a copy of her thesis? Furthermore, how the hell did he know her loan balance?

And why wasn't she more freaked out by it?

She tried to calm her racing thoughts, but one pushed in front of all the others: Instinctively, she trusted him.

And look where instincts got you, she reminded herself sternly. *A death threat from a man you thought you knew better than you knew yourself.*

She met his eyes, but couldn't form any words.

He flashed his secret smile at her again. "I make it my business to know everything about someone as important as you, Ms. Perkins. If you decide not to sign, I have a backup plan. But I really, really hope I don't have to use it. You're my Plan A, and I like you a lot more than my Plan B."

"I can't help you." She had never before told her clients no. And she knew Price would be livid when she told him that she failed to secure MacWilliam as a client. She took a deep breath, then looked him straight in the eyes. "If you want honesty…I'm not willing to give up my career for a fat payout."

"Admirable," he murmured. "I can respect that."

Emma resisted the urge to reply, and instead took a long drink of wine.

"However."

Damn. There was always a "however" from clients.

"I give you permission to speak to Price about this. If he signs off on it, will you do it?"

She blinked.

He waited another heartbeat, then leaned forward. "Ms. Perkins."

"You want me to tell him what, exactly?" She waved at the binder. "That contract is for me to join you at a social event, presumably to help you navigate the American auction world. While it's not exactly common practice, it isn't anything that requires this level of secrecy." She paused. "Unless there's something you're not telling me."

He stroked his chin, silently watching her with keen eyes.

She sat back with a *whoosh.* "This is all a test, isn't it? You want to see how far I'll go to give you what you want before you tell me the real reason why you selected me to be your rep."

She saw the smile form on his face before he schooled his features. "As you refuse to sign any contract with me, I'm afraid I can't answer that. You have until the auction, Ms. Perkins. My offer stands until then. But before you join me, you'll have to sign the papers."

"I'm sorry this can't work out." She placed her napkin on the table.

"I rarely make mistakes, and I know you wouldn't be a mistake. I suggest you sleep on it. Let's meet tomorrow at your office in the morning to discuss it further." He handed her a business card, and she tucked it into her purse. He continued, "For now, let's enjoy our dinner. I'd love to hear what you think of it. I've had Paddy prepare the house special. Have you ever had colcannon?"

She stared at him a moment, unsure if he was serious. After all that discussion, and all he did to get to her, he was willing to let her walk? She frowned. She shouldn't worry about him; Mr. MacWilliam seemed more than capable. And he mentioned a Plan B. Surely he had things in hand.

Glancing down at the plate in front of her, her inner history geek barked out a laugh. Colcannon was a staple of the *late* medieval Irish diet—boiled potatoes and cabbage mashed together and flavored with shallots and cream or butter.

"Technically, this is not a medieval dish," she replied. "Why would you create a 1400s medieval atmosphere, then name the restaurant after a dish that doesn't even show up until the late 1600s?"

He laughed. "That knowledge. *That* is why I sought you. Don't devalue it," he demanded when she started shaking her head. "It's why only you will do. I'll settle for only the best. Very few people in the world would notice a mere two hundred years' difference, Ms. Perkins."

She rubbed her temples. She had never met anyone as forthright, yet enigmatic, as Aidan MacWilliam. She could usually read people very well, but the things that came out of his mouth were beyond unpredictable.

"I let Paddy name the restaurant, and he loves that dish," he explained. "The medieval decor is a nod to my past."

"You can trace your family to medieval Ireland?" she exclaimed, amazed and slightly jealous all at once.

His expression darkened. "You could say that, aye."

His voice was so deep, and she couldn't break eye contact even if she wanted to. She was in way over her head with him, and damn the man if he didn't know it, too.

Suddenly, his phone rang, and he held it up apologetically. "I have to take this. Excuse me?"

"Of course," she replied automatically, relieved at the interruption. Whatever was going on, she had to get a grip on herself.

* * *

Determination etched on his face, Aidan ignored the call and walked through the kitchen, onto the street behind the restaurant. After a quick sweep of the area, he pulled his phone from his jacket and stared at it, weighing his decision. He hit "call" on the number he'd just missed, and the person on the other end picked up immediately.

"So?"

Aidan barked out a laugh. "You're a right bastard, you know that?"

He could hear Colin's smile as he replied, "I do. So is she as perfect for the job as I expected her to be?"

"Even more so. She is properly annoyed at me right now," Aidan responded. "But she's brilliant, has strong ethics, and would do the job admirably."

"What do you have to do to close the deal?" Colin asked.

"I'm not sure yet," Aidan admitted. "I'm still working that out. By the way, who is the client that referred you to Ms. Perkins? Maybe name-dropping would aid here."

Colin cleared his throat. "Client?"

Aidan went on alert at Colin's tone. "Aye, cousin. You told me the lass was referred to you by one of Celtic Connections' clients."

"You must have misheard me," Colin said matter-of-factly.

"And I wonder what you said that I so misheard?" Aidan leaned against the brick wall, giving a nod to a man who blew by him on a bicycle, the scent of Chinese takeout following him.

"I said I found her in the Celtic Connections database."

Aidan's eyes narrowed. "No, you didn't."

Colin's voice became downright jovial. "Oh, I'm sure I did. She popped up in my database while I was searching for potential matches for a client, and I thought she'd be a perfect match. You know. For the company."

Aidan snorted in disbelief. "I know your game, Colin. You think to *match* me? You really *are* a right bastard."

"I would never match without consent," Colin declared. He ruined it with a chuckle. "But if she's as amazing as you think she is, get her to sign on with you, then introduce us and I'll do the rest as far as getting her on my team. You'll be on your own when it comes to wooing her."

"No one will be wooing anyone," Aidan countered.

"Hey, man, that's your decision to make. But get her to sign on. I really do need a PR manager, and none of the folks I've interviewed have given me a good reason to hire them. I'm in over my head with all these press releases, trying to get the London office set up." Colin paused. "I need someone who I can trust. Do you think she could be that person?"

Aidan rolled his eyes. "Damn you."

Sounding relieved, Colin laughed. "Then finish the job, lad, and get the woman to my office already."

Aidan tucked the phone back into his pocket and gritted his teeth.

He should've known that Colin wouldn't have sent him to New York City just to scope out a potential hire. But then again, he'd been so disconnected from everything for a while—his world had seemed rather gray and boring lately, and he'd welcomed the opportunity for a change of scene.

And heading back into the restaurant, Aidan privately acknowledged that Ms. Emmaline Perkins was the brightest spot he'd seen in longer than he cared to admit.

He cursed Colin's matchmaking tendencies again. He would pay for this—but right now, Aidan had bigger issues to work out.

Such as not allowing the lovely, feisty woman currently waiting for him at their table to walk out of his life quite yet.

CHAPTER 3

The next morning, Emma stared at her computer screen in disbelief, as though the negative balance in her bank account would somehow fix itself.

So far, it remained in the red.

The bank representative she spoke with was very nice. She said it looked as though someone had withdrawn all of Emma's money. Because it was a debit transaction, the representative explained, they'd have to look into it before reimbursing her. That could take up to ten business days. And the charges had overdrawn her checking balance, so it pulled out her entire savings as well.

That warranted its own investigation, which could take up to three months.

But, the overly cheerful representative informed her, they'd certainly look into it just as soon as they could, and she'd receive a letter in the mail about the decision five to ten business days after the decision had been reached...

Emma had nineteen dollars and seventy-two cents to her name, because that was all that was in her wallet.

She tried not to panic.

Ben had ruined her credit when he went off the deep end. All her credit cards had been joint accounts with his; they'd been together since college, after all, and it had never occurred to her to open her own separate accounts.

Someone must've stolen his cards. How else would her money have disappeared? There wasn't any way to withdraw money from jail.

Her rent was due in three days, her electric bill was already overdue because she'd forgotten to pay it last month, and all she had in her kitchen was half a gallon of milk, a box of cereal, and a bottle of soy sauce.

And now she had to worry that someone had stolen the identity of her ex, whom she had never taken off her account? She was going to have to call the credit bureaus and make sure her own identity was safe.

Emma dug around in her purse for her cell phone, but her fingers instead closed on a smooth, firm rectangle. She pulled it out and stared at it for a moment, then absently twirled Aidan MacWilliam's card between her fingers, remembering his offer. Ten thousand dollars, direct deposited to an account...she could certainly go grocery shopping.

She wouldn't be evicted.

She would have enough money to live for more than the next couple of months. She didn't have anyone to ask for a loan, and her landlord was not an understanding sort.

She glanced down at the card again:

Aidan MacWilliam, Entrepreneur
Ireland

She rolled her eyes. Informative business card.

She flipped it over and read the phone number he'd scrawled, surprised it was a local one. Then again, Aidan MacWilliam was a surprising man. There was much more to him than he let on. A person didn't become as successful as he was simply by being handsome.

Actually, she knew that to be patently false. She knew of quite a few people who were successful because of their looks, but none of them matched her almost-client's intellect and business savvy.

She pursed her lips, then grabbed her phone and dialed the number.

"Good morning, Ms. Perkins."

In spite of herself, she smiled. "How did you know it was me?"

"No one in New York has this number. Have you changed your mind?"

"Perhaps," she replied briskly, trying to infuse her voice with professionalism. Instead, it came out kind of breathy and panicky.

"Are you all right?" he asked, concern lacing the words. "Would you care to meet for breakfast instead?"

She glanced at the clock—8:30 a.m. Oops.

"No, thanks, I already ate. I apologize about the time. How about ten? That will give me enough time to speak with Mr. Price."

"Sounds perfect. I'll see you then."

She hung up, feeling slightly better, but not by much. *My day couldn't possibly get any worse*, she assured herself.

* * *

Emma's words came back to haunt her not an hour later as she stared, horrified, at yet another computer screen. She couldn't blink and her stomach was in knots.

And she wasn't on her bank website anymore.

"Emma—snap out of it," Josh said briskly. He was perched on her desk, rubbing his temples. "We need to fix this. We need some time to come up with a plan."

"We don't have time," Emma managed to choke out, trying desperately to tamp down the rising tide of panic. "I…I didn't…I mean, why would I?"

The incriminating pictures she had shredded just yesterday were now splashed across every online entertainment news site.

And her name was attached to them.

"I know you didn't release these photos, but…" Josh read the headlines from the screen. "Kincaid gets Kinky with a Convict." He scrolled down. "Cheater, Cheater, Kincaid's a Beater."

"Oh my God," Emma groaned, burying her face in her hands.

Josh continued to read. "The man in the pictures, identified as Benjamin MacDermott, was allegedly engaged to Kincaid's publicist, Emmaline Perkins of Price Publicity—"

"Please stop," Emma moaned, the feeling of nausea intensifying.

"Perkins—my office—now!" Mr. Price barked as he strode by

her cubicle. She looked up at Josh in misery. Even Heinous Heidi kept her mouth shut as Emma passed her desk.

Emma and Josh followed him into the office, and she managed not to flinch when he slammed the door behind them. She met Josh's eyes and was grateful for the support—although even he couldn't get her out of this mess.

"Let's review the facts," Mr. Price said, his voice steady (which, Emma noticed, was in distinct opposition to the color of his face). "Your fiancé—"

"Ex-fiancé," Emma blurted out.

He gave her a withering look. "—was caught with Jenny Kincaid. She has affairs all the time—her husband doesn't give a rat's ass, so no divorce necessary. However, the reason why we were hired was to keep evidence of these affairs out of sight. Ms. Perkins, you realize that Mr. and Mrs. Kincaid have a movie coming out...a movie where they fall in love and live happily ever after?"

"Yes," she replied miserably. She knew where this was going.

"You can imagine the calls I've been receiving this morning for a statement as to Mrs. Kincaid's activities. If it were just a rag, we could control this. But it's not, Ms. Perkins. It's much bigger than that, because these photos have gone viral. Completely viral... in fact, 'Kinky Kincaid' is the top-trending phrase online. The Kincaids—*and their lawyers*—are on their way to the office now," Mr. Price exploded, slamming his hands onto the table. "The movie's producers—*and their lawyers*—are also on their way to the office now!"

"We can spin this," Josh said. Emma was afraid he might rub the skin off his head, he was kneading his temples so hard. "It's not our fault Kincaid can't keep her hands off every living male. It's not the end of her career. We can fix this."

"I'm so glad you have such confidence," Mr. Price said sarcastically. "Need I remind you, her actions are precisely why we are in business. Our asses are on the line here. Linda, Heidi, and Jessica are calming down other clients as we speak. But this is only part of the issue at hand." He redirected his focus back onto

Emma. "You are being accused of deliberately releasing materials to humiliate and defame Mrs. Kincaid, as it was your fiancé she was screwing."

"What?" Emma nearly shrieked. "I most certainly did not!"

"Her lawyers are going to come in here and try to slap you with a lawsuit." His eyes hardened. "You have worked here for a long time, Ms. Perkins. That is the only reason why our lawyers will step in on your behalf. That suit won't see the light of day…but you know what has to happen next."

"A personal lawsuit? They think Emma gave out the pictures to destroy her fiancé's reputation?" Josh asked. "That's just stupid. She'd ruin her chances of ever working in this city—or anywhere in PR—ever again."

Emma was having difficulty breathing. *This isn't happening.*

"We don't have time to fix this," Mr. Price said, ignoring Josh completely. "The movie cost over two hundred million to make; if they don't make that back and they decide to attribute it to this scandal, we're done. What we will do, however, is damage control. I have my *best managers*"—Emma felt the dig keenly—"working to fix the Kincaid crisis, which may in fact be a lost cause. But the rest of our clients will not be, and we need to reassure them of that. My business is at stake here, Ms. Perkins. I have clients calling, worried that they are in danger of being personally targeted by my staff." He stood up straight and delivered the killing blow. "I will make an announcement to our clients that this *unfortunate event* will be dealt with swiftly and severely. You have fifteen minutes to gather your belongings and get out of my building. You're done here."

• • •

Emma stood outside her office building, clutching her heavy cardboard box, fighting back the sting of tears as she stared up at what used to be her floor. She was humiliated, angry, and a little scared of the future…everything that she'd sworn, on the day her grandfather died and she was left without any family, she would never allow herself to be.

"Ms. Perkins?"

Emma nearly jumped out of her skin. She spun around, the contents of her box rattling forcefully. "Mr. MacWilliam! What are you doing here?"

He frowned slightly at her as he closed the door of the car behind him. "We have a meeting to discuss the contract?"

Emma bit back a curse. How was she to tell him that there wouldn't be anything further, because her career was over? She decided to just spit it out. He had a Plan B. He'd said so last night.

She took a deep breath, uncomfortably aware of her decided *lack* of a Plan B. "I'm no longer employed with this firm. I'm so sorry, Mr. MacWilliam; you'll have to find someone else." Her voice shook, and she almost dropped the box. "I'm sorry," she repeated.

"Emmaline," he replied, concern etching his features. "Take a breath. What happened?"

She gave him a bright, false smile and clutched the cardboard tighter. "Just a small mishap. I'll bounce back. Just need to take a break, is all."

"Are you all right?" he asked. His eyes looked darker and more intense than they had last night; she prayed that he couldn't see through her brave façade. Brave being that she wasn't allowing the tears to fall, although they were blurring her vision.

"I'm sure I will be. I really do have to go—I don't want to be here when the lawyers arrive." She made to move past him, but he put his hand on her arm, effectively freezing her to the spot.

"I'll take you home."

Emma just barely resisted the urge to melt into the stability he radiated. She was in uncharted territory; she'd always known where she was going, and how she was going to get there. But at this moment, she was adrift in a sea of unknowing…she had to get away before she embarrassed herself further and broke down in tears in front of him.

"I'll be okay," she repeated. She wanted, more than anything, to lean on someone. But she didn't know this man, and she had too much pride to simply cry on the first available shoulder.

It didn't matter that she really, really didn't want to do it on her own anymore.

"Emmaline—get in the car." Aidan tightened his grip on her arm and took the box from her with his other hand. "Let me take you home." She didn't protest as he all but pushed her into the vehicle. "Cian—change of plans." She gave the driver her address as Aidan reached into a small cooler and withdrew a bottle of water. "Drink. You look like you're going to faint."

Obediently, she took a sip. "Thank you," she said automatically. "And I am sorry that I can't represent you."

"Why not?" Aidan asked, motioning for her to keep drinking.

Briefly, she explained what had happened, and when Aidan didn't say anything, she took it as confirmation that he realized the severity of the situation. As they pulled up to her apartment, he grabbed her cardboard box off the seat. "I'll carry it up. You still look as though you may fall over."

Fall apart was on the tip of her tongue, but she agreed with a nod. The elevator was broken, and she didn't feel very steady on her feet.

"Thank you for the ride," she said as they trudged up the stairs.

"You're entirely welcome." He shifted the box in his arms.

She opened her apartment door and let out a shriek. At once, Aidan pinned her protectively against the wall, the contents of the box scattering across the hallway. He drew a dagger from somewhere, and she felt a flash of fear course through her body…but his focus was on the inside of the apartment, not her throat.

"Stay here," he commanded. "Cian, good timing, as ever."

"You left your purse," the driver explained. He held her purse in one hand and a dagger in the other.

What the hell?

She glanced into her apartment again, her heart in her throat. The entire thing had been turned upside down; every drawer in her tiny kitchen had been pulled and emptied on the floor. Remnants of her breakfast bowl lay amongst the trash, which had also been emptied, and a knife protruded from the middle of her kitchen table. The cushions to her couch were gone and her television was smashed into thousands of pieces all over the floor.

Cian took Aidan's place in front of her as Aidan went straight to her bedroom; the door was wide open. She glimpsed her clothes all over the floor, and gasped when her eyes landed on her bed. Someone had taken a knife to it; the sheets were shredded and there was a gash in the mattress where the springs were showing.

A moment later, Aidan came out of the bedroom, closing the door behind him and sheathing the dagger in his boot. "'Tis safe. No one is here." Cian stepped away from her, and she didn't even bother to move.

"Your day is not enviable," Aidan finally said, looking around. He frowned, then yanked the knife from the center of the kitchen table and pulled the note from the blade.

"I'm back. You have two days to get me more money," he read.

Emma's mind spun. Everything—her money, her job, all her possessions—was lost.

Where, exactly, was she supposed to come up with more money? And when did Ben get out of jail?

She shook her head once, then covered her face. She didn't bother to stem the tears as they fell through her fingers.

CHAPTER 4

Aidan thanked the policeman as he left the hotel suite, and glanced with concern at Emma. She sat on the sofa, toying with her necklace, and stared blankly at the gas fireplace in the wall.

"His parole officer promised me he'd call if Ben was up for early release," Emma said to no one in particular. "He promised. Swore it, even."

Aidan silently sat down in the armchair directly across from her and steepled his hands against his chin.

"Because Ben had made direct threats against my life," she added, her eyes rooted to the flames as they danced. "I guess I didn't think he'd try to ruin me first. If he had the power to take all my money, why didn't he just do that and disappear? Why does he have to come after me like this?"

"Some men—and I hesitate to use that label in association with your ex—enjoy the feeling of power."

Her eyes swung to Aidan's. "He wasn't like this when we were together."

Aidan didn't respond.

She continued, her voice hollow. "I've lost everything. First he took my money, then he ended my career." She met Aidan's eyes, her own haunted. "And now he's taken my safety."

Aidan's chest constricted. "He has not, Emmaline. Not if you don't allow it."

She laughed incredulously. "Allow it? All I want is to be free of him. But there's no escape. I think he proved that rather effectively, don't you?" She jerked her head toward the door where the policeman had exited. "I don't even have a place to live right now. I don't know where he is, or what his next move will be. Don't you see?" She choked on a sob. "He holds all the cards!"

Aidan hated the stark desolation in her voice. The woman was twisting him in knots, and despite having known her for less than a day, his gut told him she needed protection—but that she wouldn't readily accept it.

What disturbed him more than having gut feelings about a woman was that he had a deep and primitive need to be the one to protect her.

"He doesn't hold *all* the cards," Aidan replied carefully. "I still need you. Tonight."

* * *

The blatant sensuality in his words jolted Emma from her dark place. She blinked, then realized Aidan was talking about the auction.

"I don't think I'm the right person for this," she faltered. Her brain was on overload—was it really only a couple of hours ago that her boss had fired her? And then her apartment…it was a strange kind of relief that Aidan had been with her when she'd discovered it. He took charge, giving her the space she needed to process the events—without being asked. He ensured her safety, filed the police reports, and made her eat something.

It was a nice feeling to be mother-henned over.

But that couldn't last. The thought of cleaning up her apartment exhausted her, and angered her—which gave her enough of a reality check to acknowledge that she couldn't rely on this man's hospitality, no matter how freely it was offered. She'd done that once before, and look where that had landed her.

"I'll make you a deal," Aidan offered. "New contract. Same terms as before, but you get the commission—not the firm. You go to the auction and obtain the relics with me. Then, you stay here until I can have your apartment cleaned up. And change your locks," he added darkly. "Definitely change your locks…maybe add a couple more."

"My world is a mess right now," she said, shaking her head.

"Then join me in mine for a while," he replied softly.

Emma wasn't sure why he was so insistent on helping her. Before she could work out another way to refuse his offer, he held up a single finger. He rose from the chair, then reached for his leather satchel. He carefully withdrew a dagger and presented it to her, hilt first.

Her breath caught, and her face lightened. "Oh…this is a medieval dirk! A real one—look at all the nicks on the blade!" She reverentially ran her fingertips over the highly decorative hilt. "It's so beautiful…" She handed it back to him, and her fingers grazed his hand.

The electricity nearly knocked her over.

With one hand, Aidan gently took the blade from her loose fingers, and with his other hand he very gently cupped her chin and raised her head until her gaze collided with his. He studied her for a moment, then directed his attention to her lips, looking very much as though he wanted to kiss her. She watched, breathless, as he moved a fraction of an inch closer, and his eyes traveled back up her face. He blinked slowly, as though hesitant to miss a second of the moment, and Emma's heart beat loudly in her chest. Her lips parted, and she involuntarily licked them, drawing his eyes back down. Her breath hitched.

A sudden bolt of nerves jolted through her, and she stepped back quickly, nearly knocking a lamp off the side table next to her.

Embarrassed, she tried to shake off the haze of desire as she stepped out of his reach.

He didn't move. "I'll teach you how to use it. Consider it a fringe benefit of working for me."

Emma quickly scooted farther away from Aidan. "Mr. MacWilliam, not to be rude, but…trust me when I say that you don't want any part of this. My life is in shambles at the moment." She stood quickly, searching for her purse and coat. "I have to be going. I'm sorry I can't help you."

Aidan closed the distance between them and placed the blade on the table next to the lamp. "Where will you go?"

Emma spied her stuff on one of the chairs in the elaborate dining room and attempted to walk over to it casually. She had a sinking suspicion she may have lunged, but she needed to get out of there. "Oh, I'll be fine." *No, I won't.* "I have some friends I can stay with." *No, I don't.*

She was going to end up on a bench in Central Park. *Out in the open, where Ben can find me and finish the job.*

She tried to swallow her fear. The police officer had assured her that once they determined it was in fact her ex who broke into the apartment, her restraining order would be approved quickly. Most likely Monday morning, even. That just meant she had to stay alive until then, of course.

"Emma." His use of her nickname stopped her. "You're safe with me."

"I beg to differ, Mr. MacWilliam."

He held up both his hands. "Please. Stay. I'm leaving right after the auction to go to Boston. The hotel room is yours as long as you need it—a month? Two months? It's under my name, and no one knows where you are right now."

Emma snorted. The only person she could trust was herself— she knew better than to accept what he was proposing. Aidan's offer surely had strings attached, and she couldn't afford to be his marionette.

"Thank you for the offer. Truly, I appreciate it, but I'll be fine." She had to leave immediately, and the overwhelming urge to accept his aid was frightening her. Hadn't she learned her lesson the last time she'd blindly trusted someone? "I'm afraid I'm not the right person for your job, Mr. MacWilliam." The suddenly stuffy air choked her, and she swept into the dining room, anxious to leave. She nodded stiffly to Cian, then ran out the door.

* * *

Cian let out a low whistle. "Well, ye blew that one good an' proper, my laird."

Aidan glared at him. "We can't let her go without protection. MacDermott is out for blood. That woman is in trouble," Aidan growled as he headed toward the door.

By the time he reached the elevators, Emma's had already left. He hurried into the second elevator, dragging his hands through his hair. If she got to the street before he made it downstairs, he might never find her again. His stomach did an inexplicable flip at the thought.

He pushed all thoughts aside when the doors opened onto the lobby. As he strode toward the front desk, intent on asking the concierge which way Emma had gone, he saw her hurrying down the front steps.

He darted after her, weaving between well-dressed couples and tourists alike. He slid to a stop in front of the glass double doors, yanked one open before the doorman knew he was there, and dashed onto the steps. Emma disappeared around the corner of the building, and Aidan's rising panic pushed him into a run.

He had no doubts that Ben MacDermott would continue to terrorize Emma. He'd known his fair share of men just like him— men who had nothing to lose, so they derived what power they could by using violence and fear.

His father, rot his soul, was proof of that.

The hair on the back of his neck stood up, and Aidan went on full alert. His instincts never proved him wrong, and right now they were screaming.

"Emma!" he called, alarm in his voice. She was walking fast, but he ran after her, dodging pedestrians and skateboarders. "Emma, wait!"

She spun around and glared at him. "What?" Immediately, she held up her hands. "I'm sorry." She swallowed hard, her eyes glistening with unshed tears. "I'm trying not to lose it," she whispered. "But—"

Aidan saw the gun pointed at her, and he didn't think. He lunged at her, cutting her off midsentence, and glass shattered around them into a million pieces. He covered her body with his, cradling her head in his hands, and protected her from both the falling shards and the chaos that erupted around them. People ran and screamed, nearly trampling them in their desperate bid to get away. Almost immediately, sirens sounded and horns blared, but through it all, Aidan remained wrapped around her, a protective cocoon, ensuring nothing touched her.

If he wanted to, he would have killed her. The man had taken careful aim, and there should've been no time for Aidan to knock Emma out of the way. Aidan understood the intent behind the bullet...it was a warning shot.

Emma was in far more danger than he initially realized.

"Are you okay?" he asked, his voice low in her ear. She nodded jerkily, and he carefully pulled back, wincing as the glass slid off his back, balancing on his knees on the pavement. He helped her to her feet. "We have to get out of here," he said. "I don't care to spend my night with the bobbies, explaining anything." Aidan frowned at her ashen face, then tucked her under his arm. He glanced back. He didn't get a good visual of her ex's face, but he damn well knew he was close to them. Too close.

"I think someone tried to shoot us," Emma said, her hands shaking.

"Let's not wait around to give him another shot, then," he replied as he steered her toward a taxi. He nearly pushed her inside, following close on her heels, and instructed the cabbie to drive east before heading back toward the hotel. Aidan locked first Emma's, then his own door. Once they were out in the traffic, one of a thousand other yellow taxis, Aidan pulled out his phone, sent a message to Cian, then turned to Emma.

"I'm having a bad day," she blurted, her voice breaking.

"I know," he said.

Emma burst into tears. He pulled her into his arms and let her cry, not caring about the makeup on his shirt, or the wet stains on his lapel, or the alarmed looks from the cabbie. He just held her and hoped it was enough.

• • •

"I'm not a crier," Emma repeated once they were back in the hotel room, this time to Cian, who held out a fresh tissue toward her.

Cian merely nodded, looking as though he wished the whole business were over and done with, then quickly left the room.

Emma leaned back on the couch and glanced at Aidan. His expression was deadly serious, his frown fierce.

"I'm not your problem to solve," she said quietly.

"You're not a problem, period," he replied, just as softly.

"Mr. MacWilliam—"

He snorted. "I think we're past formalities, Emma. Call me Aidan."

Emma felt a headache coming on strong, and she glanced at the clock. "All right, *Aidan*. I couldn't help you even if I wanted to."

He quirked a brow. "Really."

She folded her arms. "Really. The auction you want me to help you with is in less than six hours. I have no clothing to wear." *I have no clothing at all*, she reflected morosely.

"Why are you so unwilling to accept aid?"

"Why are you so willing to give it?" she shot back.

Aidan's expression turned thoughtful. "That's the question, isn't it? You don't trust my motives."

She remained silent, refusing to incriminate herself.

He thought for a moment. "I rarely make mistakes."

She snorted. *Wealthy and full of himself. Well, he'd fit right into my former client roster.*

He raised a brow but continued to speak. "My instincts have saved me more times than I care to remember. And my instincts are telling me that you're the right person for this job."

"Is the position of Aidan MacWilliam's publicity manager so difficult to staff, then?" she quipped.

He smirked. "You'll never know unless you take the chance." His phone rang then, and he reached over to silence it. He rummaged in the satchel at his feet and withdrew the white binder.

His phone rang again. Clearly annoyed, Aidan grabbed it and looked at the caller ID. He flashed her an apologetic grimace. "I have to take this. Excuse me?"

She chewed her lip as she watched him leave the room, considering her reasons for turning down his offer.

Well, first, you don't know this guy. He could be a crazy psycho. After all, Ben showed no outward signs for years!

Although, she reflected, Ben refused to go out with her friends. He never stopped her from going with them, but after a while she found that she preferred his company, so she stopped going out.

He might not have stopped you, but he would act hurt that you chose your friends over him, and you'd feel guilty every time. And you "preferred" not to deal with his attitude more than you ever "preferred" his company.

She hated that she allowed her friendships to disappear. She wasn't even sure she could find any of the women anymore; most had married or moved away. She'd been lonely in these past few months, but with the demands of her career, she hadn't found the time to look anyone up.

So what if Ben maybe displayed some odd behavior? You don't need anyone's help! You're not a charity case!

But Aidan had made it very clear that this job wasn't charity—he claimed he needed her services, and even before her worst day of all time began, he'd made it obvious that he only wanted her representing him.

That has to count for something, right?

Emma wasn't sure if she was talking herself into or out of his help.

"I apologize about that," Aidan said as he strode back into the room. "Business never stops."

She gave a weak smile. "What's your Plan B?"

His brows knit. "Sorry?"

"Yesterday, you said you had a Plan B. What is it?"

"Go alone," he said simply.

She blinked. "That's your big Plan B?"

"I never claimed it to be something outrageous."

Emma fought a smile. "So you didn't."

"What's your Plan A?" he asked. Then, his eyes twinkling, added, "Assuming, as I'm wont to do, that I'm Plan B?"

Without meaning to, she laughed. She clapped her hands over her mouth to stem it, but it was no use. The entire day had been something out of a bad dream, and she realized with a start that she needed something to focus on.

And the gorgeous man in front of her, presenting her a kind of redemption, was definitely something on which she could focus.

She chewed her lip, considering. She reminded herself that Aidan was not Ben. He hadn't any reason to offer her a job other than that he needed her services. And, Aidan was offering her a way to earn her way out of the situation she was in, which she appreciated. She hated to be a charity case, and he seemed to understand that.

And, of course, what came with that offer was hard to pass up: money, a safe place to stay, and medieval artifacts.

A reluctant smile tugged at her lips. "You assume wrong, Aidan. You're actually my Plan A. I'm willing to take the chance."

* * *

"That's good news," Colin said grimly, his eyes focused on the computer screen in front of him rather than Aidan's face on his phone.

"Aye, don't jump around with excitement," Aidan agreed dryly.

"Sorry." Colin turned his attention toward the video chat. "Things here are blowing up. I've got a new client who's an absolute arse. We've sent him on four dates, and each of the women have come back with a 'hell no' response when asked if they'd be interested in a second one."

"Ouch."

"Yeah, the guy's a real Prince Charming. He's taken up entirely too much of my thought processes for today. It really is good news that Perkins is open to a new opportunity, though."

Aidan nodded. He wondered if Colin had done any searches on Emma as of late. Her name was attached to the day's biggest scandal—and not in a good way. She was painted as a scorned woman, out for revenge on her ex and whomever he'd cheated on her with—some Hollywood actress. Aidan didn't read much past the headlines, and it seemed as though Colin was too busy to notice anything amiss with his potential new hire.

"I hope she's good with public speaking," Colin was saying as Aidan tuned back into their conversation. "If she's going to work here, I'm going to need her help with the press conferences in the UK. They love their telly over there. Is she doing any public speaking while you're in town?"

Aidan paused. "I don't think so."

Colin sighed audibly, his face revealing a bit of the stress he seemed to be facing. "Damn. The media relations are only part of it—I also need someone to stand next to me as a spokesperson. Maybe I should just go with the last woman I interviewed up here. She's not the nicest person, but she'd get the job done."

Aidan shrugged, but inwardly, his pulse kicked up. "Let me see what her event calendar looks like. Maybe she does have something, and I'm just not aware of it."

"I hope she does." Colin raked a hand through his hair, then turned the phone's camera to his computer screen. The display of meetings in his email calendar made Aidan's head spin. Colin sighed. "Do what you have to so I can contact her directly. I need some help."

* * *

"You don't have to do this."

"I don't want any employee of mine to show up to a white tie event in casual attire," he replied dryly, echoing the words of Tess, the stylist.

"Listen to the man," Tess said brusquely. "I'm set for now. I have your measurements and I'll send over the dress before tonight's event. Do you have hair and makeup set up?"

Emma's eyes were wide. "Um...no?"

Tess *tsk*ed and gave her a disapproving stare. "Shall I arrange that as well? I have a few contacts and could try to find someone."

"That's not—"

"Yes," Aidan interrupted Emma. "Please do. Put it on my bill."

Tess's eyes turned speculative as she looked between Aidan and Emma.

"This is too much money for one night," Emma protested, her face reddening. "Honestly. There's probably a million charities your cash could support instead."

Tess placed a firm hand on Emma's arm. "In my experience, the more you struggle, the more they spend. He's a big boy. Let him spend his money how he sees fit."

Aidan winked at the woman, who had to be at least twenty years his senior, and she waved her fingertips at him as she breezed out of the suite.

He leveled a stare at Emma and watched in satisfaction as her protest died on her lips. "You agreed to this."

She folded her arms and pursed her lips.

"You signed the contract," he continued.

She huffed out a sigh and raised her eyes to the ceiling.

"You gave up any and all rights to the next twenty-four hours of your life."

Her mouth dropped open. "I did not!"

He chuckled. "Just checking your hearing."

Emma shook her head in apparent frustration. "I get that I need appropriate attire tonight. But I don't need you to purchase me a new wardrobe!"

He looked at the cardboard box sitting on the floor. "Your belongings beg to differ."

While Emma was sequestered with the stylist in the extra bedroom, Cian had salvaged what he could from her apartment, but there was little to be saved. Almost all of her belongings had been destroyed; the only things untouched were whatever was at the laundromat, which Cian had picked up on his way back to the hotel. And, judging by the size of the box, it didn't look like she'd sent much in her last drop-off.

She growled at Aidan, then rubbed her forehead with the tips of her fingers. "I had enough clothing to last me until I'm paid."

He shrugged and remained silent. He got the distinct feeling that if he told her the real reason why he wanted to buy her clothing, she'd run so fast out the door he'd never catch up to her again.

Hell, even Cian had raised a bushy brow when Aidan demanded Neiman Marcus's best personal shopper to be sent to his suite posthaste, but he wouldn't be deterred. When a lass came under a laird's protection, he took care of all her basic needs. Food, clothing, shelter. And whether or not she knew it, having signed that contract, Emmaline Perkins was now under his protection, and, until he reunited with his brother, Aidan MacWilliam was the laird.

For the first time since being separated from Nioclas, Aidan's chest didn't tighten at the thought of him. His driving need to return home seemed slightly dulled.

Emma's mutinous face snagged his attention, and he frowned at her concern over his bank account. He tried another approach. "I want you to look a certain way while representing me."

She guffawed. "Oh, right. Because my usual business attire is inappropriate?"

"You'd be better in business casual."

"Since when are jeans business casual?" she asked, her jaw set.

"Since I declare them to be," he answered, folding his own arms. "Isn't it bad form to argue with your new boss?"

She scowled at him, realizing the futility of her argument. "But—"

"Call it a cultural thing," he drawled. "And, if that doesn't work for you, then think of it as a uniform."

She gritted her teeth, and after a charged moment, she ground out, "Thank you." Then, because she apparently couldn't seem to help herself, she added, "All of this is unnecessary, but I'm acquiescing."

"So gracefully, too," he murmured, and took an inordinate amount of pleasure at watching her face suffuse with heat. "You're quite welcome, anyway." He sat on the sofa and checked his watch. "I have some business to do this afternoon. Feel free to make use of the suite. Full telly lineup, movies, the whole thing."

She half smiled. "Thanks, but I'm not big on television. I'll figure something out."

"You're welcome to use the iPad if you'd like." He pointed to the device in the kitchen. "Order a book? Play a game of some sort?"

She looked interested, and he took it as a good sign. "What's on it?"

"Not much, but you can download what you wish." He retrieved it and handed it to her.

Her eyes, glued to the screen, were enormous. She raised them to meet his, and Aidan felt something shift in his chest.

"You have access to the Book of Kells on this?"

He shifted uncomfortably. "Aye. It's publicly available through Trinity College."

She shook her head as she swiped through the pages. "Not in its entirety," she breathed. "I would know. I look for it online all the time. This is amazing—thank you." And this time, the sincerity of the gratitude, plus the warmth from the true smile she bestowed upon him, knocked him flat.

His breath caught and his chest tightened at her beauty. Her brilliant blue eyes sparkled, bringing him back to carefree childhood mornings spent on the seashore. The rosy color in her cheeks was the exact hue of the small flowers that dotted the Irish countryside; her honey hair, tendrils of which had escaped her hair tie and now framed her heart-shaped face, danced like fairies as she moved her head.

She looks like home.

• • •

Curled up in the corner of the couch closest to the fireplace, Emma held her teacup between both hands as her eyes drank in the images on the device in front of her, which she'd propped on the arm of the sofa. The firelight danced in her hair, illuminating the lighter strands and shadowing the darker ones.

Ensconced in her reading, Emma didn't hear the brisk knock at the door, and she almost dropped her teacup in surprise when a man breezed over to her and fell to his knees. Aidan rose and stood behind the couch. He rested his hands on it, his face schooled into a blank mask.

"Ooh, your cheekbones are exquisite!" the man declared in a thick French accent, grasping Emma's chin and turning her head from side to side. He slid his fingers over a piece of hair that had escaped her ponytail. "Oui, oui. The natural curl in your hair is delightful. I'll fix it, though, don't fret, *ma chérie.*"

"I didn't realize I was fretting," she replied, leaning back a little.

He leaned closer to her, closing the small distance she had created. "I am Howard. I will make your inner beauty shine for your gala tonight. Where will this amazing transformation happen? Here, or another room in this *magnifique* hotel?"

"Um…maybe one of the bedrooms?" She shrugged and looked at Aidan. *Is this guy for real?* she wanted to ask. She noted the humor lurking in Aidan's eyes, and her lips quirked at the corners in response.

"I believe your evening preparations have begun," Aidan deadpanned.

"Indeed they have, monsieur!" Howard declared, standing with a flourish. "I shall make her into a breathtaking swan."

"You can't improve perfection," Aidan murmured. "But you're certainly welcome to try."

Before Emma could form a response, Howard led her to the stairs, explaining that Tess had already sent him pictures of the dress that was on its way to them.

* * *

"My laird?" Cian stood by the door, his face incredulous as the door upstairs slammed shut. "Did you just…"

"It was a compliment, Cian, nothing more," Aidan replied as he sat back down to the spreadsheets and contracts on the table.

Cian snorted, and Aidan rolled his eyes. "By the saints, I've complimented women before. 'Tis not so strange."

"I've not heard such flowery sentiments leave your mouth since we came to the future," Cian replied, considering. "'Tis interesting, is all."

Another knock at the door saved Aidan from replying to *that* insight. "That'd be the dress, I suppose."

"Aye," Cian concurred, his eyes twinkling. "Merely frosting for the *perfect* cake, no doubt."

Aidan grabbed the nearest report and flipped it open, refusing to take his clansman's bait.

CHAPTER 5

Two very quick hours later, Emma felt a little like Julia Roberts in *Pretty Woman* (*well*, she amended, *minus the whole prostitution thing*). She looked at herself in the mirror, smoothing her hands down her sides for the umpteenth time, unable to believe her own reflection.

The cerulean blue, one-shoulder, floor-length Valentino gown shimmered as she moved, and strappy, blinged-out sandals gave her an extra three inches. Howard had tamed her hair to within an inch of its life. It was twisted around her head in a complicated but oh-so-elegant way, and dotted with small silver pearls. On each wrist she wore a set of four thin silver bracelets, and an additional small diamond bracelet of the same size ("to give an elegant touch," Tess had declared). Emma's earrings, also silver, were inlaid with tiny diamonds, and each had a small silver pearl drop.

I could really get used to job perks like these, Emma thought, feeling the giddiness rise inside her. She let out an excited breath and grabbed the matching clutch on the counter. *If only for tonight*, she amended quickly, remembering the entire wardrobe set to be delivered tomorrow morning. Tess refused to divulge the amounts, but from the designer names she was dropping, Emma had a sinking suspicion the numbers were in the thousands.

She glanced around the bedroom, giving a last-minute check that she had everything she needed. The suite was incredible. Every inch of it was decorated to a standard she'd never seen. It was truly a home away from home. *Yeah, about two thousand square feet larger than my home.* It must have been amazing to live this way every day. Perhaps Aidan's home in Ireland was even bigger.

A crash made her look to her right as she stepped off the bottom stair; Cian was staring at her, openmouthed, and a cup was rolling on the floor at his feet. Aidan was on the phone, his back to her as he stared out over the Manhattan skyline. He turned at the sound of the crash and, catching sight of her, ended his call abruptly.

"You look stunning," Aidan said, striding forward. She noticed he was in a tux; his bow tie was slightly askew. It made her smile.

"Thank you," she replied as he reached her. Self-consciously licking her lips, she reached up and straightened the tie, then felt her cheeks flush. She ignored the reaction; he was a client again. She was just making sure he appeared professional.

"Ready?"

"*Réidh.*"

A slow smile crossed his features, and Emma blushed. She quickly explained, "Like I said in the office, I only know a little Gaelic. I've tried to learn it for years, but it's one of those languages that I think I'd have to be immersed in to fully learn."

"Perhaps I can afford you the opportunity in the future," he replied smoothly, causing her heart to jump in her chest. "But, for now, we must go; I want you to have a good look at the items before the auction begins."

"Have you seen them in person yourself?" she inquired as they stepped out.

"Aye."

"Which item do you want the most?"

He didn't answer her immediately. As he slid into the limo behind her, he immediately removed his jacket and rolled up his sleeves before reaching for a champagne flute. "The sword."

"Why do you want all of them? Why not just go for the sword?"

He smirked at her. "Because, until about seven years ago, they were all mine to begin with. I've come to take them back." He offered her some champagne.

Emma's mind raced as she silently accepted the glass. *How did he amass millions of dollars' worth of artifacts? Why did he sell them? Why does he want them back now?*

He started to laugh—a wonderful, rich sound that jolted Emma out of her own thoughts. "Emma, lass, if you wonder any harder, your eyebrows will fall off your face." He relaxed, stretching his long legs out in front of him, and rested his chiseled arm across the back of the seat.

She took a sip of the champagne to avoid responding. He was grace, sex, and alpha male personified. And she was not above admitting that he was overwhelming in a tux.

"I had—and have—a very large assortment of artifacts from the Middle Ages. I sold many of them once I realized they were actually worth something. With the help of some very trusted sources, I found investing to be a rather interesting way of making money."

"So, other than restaurants and medieval artifacts, what do you invest in?" she asked, rolling the champagne flute between her fingers.

"I have a swordfighting school outside of Galway. That's gaining in popularity with all these Hollywood types. Also some green technologies and real estate."

He was looking at her so intimately, so intensely, she thought she might combust on the spot.

"Fascinating," she murmured, her mind racing. How was it that she'd never heard of him before? He was stunningly handsome, richer than Croesus, and unmarried. How had he avoided the paparazzi?

"No." He leaned forward, his green eyes narrowing slightly. "What's fascinating is what is going on in that beautiful head of yours. You're overthinking something."

She drew her eyebrows together, a protest on her lips.

"Emma. I'm good at spotting a lie, so don't waste your time with one."

She put the champagne down and sat up a little straighter. "All right, then. I can't figure out how you've avoided the spotlight," she admitted.

"And?"

At his raised brow, she reluctantly added, "And you are overwhelming me with your generosity. I'm in a completely different place than I was yesterday, and I'm not adjusting very well."

Aidan placed his elbows on his knees and rested his chin on his hands. Shaking his head slowly, he replied, "Emmaline Perkins, I had no idea you thought so little of yourself."

"That's not it at all." She bristled, immediately defensive.

His smile was slow and seductive. "First, there's never reason to be nervous—or defensive—when you're with me. I understand and accept that you don't trust me yet—you shouldn't trust anyone except yourself right now. Second, I don't know anyone—man or woman—who would have dealt with your situation with as much grace; your entire world has been turned around, yet here you are, the consummate professional, going into the most anticipated auction with the world's wealthy elite, as if you've been doing it the whole of your life. After being sacked, then ransacked…here you are. Funny, witty, refreshingly direct, beautiful, poised, and confident." He sat back and raised an eyebrow at her. "Swan. How apt."

"Swan?" she asked, thrown.

He nodded slowly. "What your makeup man said earlier. You are indeed a swan. Elegant grace, gentle beauty. But when you try to scare it, it fights back with everything it's got."

Emma simply stared at him, transfixed. A delicate shudder ran up her spine.

Aidan glanced out the window as the car slowed. "Smile for the cameras, Emmaline. Show the world that it can't take you down."

He opened the door before she could formulate a response.

* * *

"Go for one-twenty." Aidan's voice, low in her ear, was confident and calm, contradicting the nerves jumping within Emma. She raised her small paddle as inconspicuously as possible, but, as she was quickly learning, there was no such thing as inconspicuous at an elite, closed auction.

"We have one hundred twenty thousand dollars. Do we have one-twenty-five?" the auctioneer asked. "One-twenty-five. Do we have one-thirty?"

"Yes," Aidan said in her ear, clearly enjoying her discomfort. "Doing great, Emmaline. Keep going. Our competition has some sweat on the back of his neck, so I think we're close to his breaking point."

Emma nodded, her palms damp. This kind of money was unlike any she'd seen. Aidan had already dropped over a million dollars. But this—the sword with the same etching as was on The Colcannon's door and napkins—was what he'd come for. While they had perused the artifacts before the opening bid, Aidan had confessed that it was a special sword his late brother had given him.

Before Emma could offer her condolences, his face had shuttered, and he'd moved on to the next item.

"We have one hundred thirty thousand dollars. Do we have one-thirty-five?" the auctioneer called. Her competition kept his paddle firmly in his lap, and Emma felt a rush of jubilation. *We did it!*

"One-fifty," someone suddenly called out from the back.

Emma turned in surprise, her gaze falling on the back wall, which was lined with telephones. One of the men on the phone held his paddle high.

Aidan swore, then apologized. "Keep going, Emma." She raised her paddle, and the bidding continued. "I'm going to get that sword, come hell or high water."

And, two hundred and fifty thousand dollars later, Aidan MacWilliam was once again the proud owner of an authentic, mint condition medieval Irish sword.

She couldn't *wait* to touch it.

Aidan excused himself to speak with the auctioneer, and she sat back in her chair, letting the breath whoosh from her body. Someone tapped her shoulder, and she half turned in her seat…and came face-to-face with her as-of-that-morning ex-boss.

"I don't know what you think you're doing." Mr. Price's smile didn't match the anger in his low voice.

"Mr. Price," she managed to say.

"Surprised that I'm here? Why? Many of my clients are here; it's a great networking opportunity. Of course, it's going to be nearly impossible to convince anyone that you haven't been plotting this for quite some time. I don't know what you're trying to accomplish. You will not ruin my business, Perkins. I've already made it known that you were fired, and this just puts the nail in your coffin. Scheming to outbid my good name? I'm happy I fired you before this came to pass. And I'm even happier that you'll never work in PR again. Even you must know it's a rookie mistake to go against me. Everyone who tries, loses."

"Paul."

Mr. Price started as Aidan returned, his body radiating disdain.

"Threatening my publicist, are you?" Aidan asked.

Mr. Price stuttered, his eyes becoming slits. "You stole her?"

Emma opened her mouth to explain that you can't steal someone who's been fired, but Aidan beat her to it.

"Stole her? Like she's some sort of commodity? Shame on you, Price. No, I saw a talented young woman who'd been set up to fail at your company. And I've asked her to join mine. That's not stealing. That's making your poor business decision my best one."

Price snickered. "She'll screw you over too, MacWilliam. You just watch."

"I'd suggest you watch your language, as there are ladies present," Aidan replied coolly.

"None I can see."

Emma's mouth dropped open, and she gave him a scathing glance. "I pity your clients. They have no idea what they're really getting from Price Publicity," she said in a voice just loud enough to be heard by everyone in the immediate vicinity.

Barely containing his rage, Price glared at her. "You will never work in PR again, Perkins."

"She already does," Aidan snapped, his patience clearly gone. "Leave her alone, or I'll make you wish you'd never met her."

"I already do," Price spat, then turned on his heel and stomped off.

And Emma knew, with sudden, complete clarity, that it was over. Even when she said it to Aidan, she believed that she'd be able to rebuild her career with another firm, in another city. But Price Publicity had far-reaching hands. If Mr. Price didn't want her in PR, he would smear her all the way to China. She would have to find a whole new career.

The enormity of it slammed into her. She'd have to start over. Again.

"Emma, turn around," Aidan commanded. "Good. Don't say a word to that bastard. He's not worth your time."

But he's worth my career. It's all I have.

As if he were reading her thoughts, Aidan said softly, "You're not alone in this, Emma. I've got you."

Emma shook her head hard and slid out from the row. She needed to get some air—and control of herself.

* * *

Aidan watched Emma go and knew she had hit her breaking point. He tried to follow her, but people were flooding the aisle as they headed to the dinner that was set up in another room. Her shoulders were rigid, her bearing stiff, and she disappeared from view.

And she was unprotected. His heart beat faster; perhaps Emma wasn't thinking of the man who was intent on harming her, but *he* certainly was. And if MacDermott somehow figured out she was here, she was a sitting duck.

He almost slammed into Cian in the foyer of the auction house. "Where is she?"

"I thought she was with you."

"She left," Aidan replied grimly. "We've got to find her."

"I'm right here," Emma said softly from behind him. He spun around, taking swift note of her appearance. She looked unharmed but upset.

Aidan resisted the ridiculous urge to pull her into his arms, digging his fingernails into his palms. "Price is an arse."

"Ass or not, he is a powerful man. He promised me I would

never work in PR again, and I realized I would have to start all over again. And he's right."

Aidan shook his head in disgust. "After tonight, you'll have more than enough money to start over, doing whatever you want."

"I really do enjoy my career, Aidan."

He frowned. "I see. I'll make some calls, see what I can do for damage control—"

She held up her hand. "Aidan, please. I know damage control better than most people, and this situation is unsalvageable."

"I thought nothing is unsalvageable in publicity."

"It is if the most powerful man in the business makes it so." Emma sighed. "I'll figure it out tomorrow. I've had enough of today to last a lifetime."

Aidan studied her thoughtfully. "All right. For now, let's settle the payments and head back to the hotel."

She nodded, a small, sad smile gracing her lips, and allowed him to usher her ahead.

• • •

Later that night, Emma stood in her room, wrapped in a fluffy white robe. She dumped the cardboard box of her clothes onto the lushly made bed.

One box. A single box contained the only items that hadn't been destroyed in her apartment. Only the small load of laundry she'd hastily dropped off at the laundromat the other day. She had very little of value, monetary or sentimental. After her grandparents died, Emma was left with all their belongings—as well as their debts, funerals, and a myriad of other expenses. She was forced to sell everything to pay for it all. She had no inheritance from her parents—all they left to her had gone to her upbringing.

All she was left with was memories.

She grabbed her dark pink SAVE A HORSE, RIDE A COWBOY nightshirt from the pile and tugged it over her head, allowing herself a false sense of comfort from it.

Though she would've preferred to hide in the hotel bedroom all night, she needed something to drink. She glanced in the en suite bathroom and amended that—she needed something stronger than tap water.

Mentally girding her loins, she opened the door and walked downstairs to the living area, but she stopped short at the sight of Aidan, who was sound asleep on the couch. He'd turned the gas fireplace on, and the light danced off his features as he took long, even breaths. He still wore his tux, although the jacket was slung over the arm of the couch. His bow tie hung, untied and uneven, around his neck, and his shirtsleeves were rolled up to his elbows. His forearms were huge—solid muscle, relaxed in sleep, covered with a dusting of dark hair.

He was the most beautiful man she'd ever seen, but also the most complicated. Did they really only just meet yesterday? She felt as though she'd known him for much longer.

Or perhaps she'd just had the longest day of her life.

She studied him. He was a throwback to another era. Gallant, protective, almost…chivalrous.

She mentally rolled her eyes. That word was only in her mind due to the overwhelming medieval artifacts she'd been privy to that night.

And what was his relationship with Cian? He was more than just Aidan's driver and bodyguard. They seemed to be friends, and he called Aidan "my laird" frequently. Perhaps it was an Irish thing, to call someone "my laird" out of respect. She certainly hoped Aidan didn't expect her to call him that. Although she had to admit, the power in that title was rather sexy.

Emma mentally shook herself. Even though she held onto her sanity by a mere thread, she could allow herself a small, harmless crush on the man who'd saved her from an undesirable situation. It was probably even natural.

She carefully eased herself into the wingback chair and watched him sleep. She openly admired his jawline, wondering why he hadn't been chased down by a modeling agency. His five o'clock shadow was making a spectacular appearance, giving his face an even harder edge.

She watched his chest rise and fall rhythmically. His chest was rock solid—there was nothing soft about him, but when they'd left the auction house he'd held her hand gently, as if he would break her. When leading her into the hotel, he had rested his palm against the small of her back, just enough pressure to move her forward without any effort. His hands were rough and calloused, as though he spent hours every day splitting wood with an axe, yet his manners were suave and sophisticated, something she'd expect from a businessman.

He was a mystery, and Emma wasn't sure she wanted to solve it. She would have to move to a new place. With the amount of money Aidan deposited into her account that evening, she could go anywhere she wanted, at least for a little while.

"Emma, if you don't stop thinking so hard, I won't be able to finish my nap," Aidan said without opening his eyes.

She gasped. "I didn't know you were awake!"

"I didn't want to interrupt your inspection," he replied. "Did I pass?"

She crossed her arms and he opened one eye.

"I guess not," he said, a small smile playing around his lips. He stretched, and Emma tried not to stare.

A small laugh escaped her mouth, and she clapped a hand over it to stop the completely inappropriate giggles.

"I'm glad you can find humor in my failings," Aidan replied dryly.

"Laugh or cry," Emma giggled, slightly hysterical. "The sum total of outlandish incidents in my life, prior to yesterday, numbered exactly zero. But since I met you, it's been one catastrophe after another. I must admit, your job offer came at a fortuitous time."

Aidan shifted uncomfortably. He leaned forward, placing his elbows on his knees. He pressed his clasped hands to his mouth for a moment, then said hesitantly, "This was left at the front desk for you." He reached behind the couch and picked up a bulky envelope from the end table.

Emma frowned. "Who could that be from?"

He didn't look at her, but instead dumped the contents of the envelope onto the coffee table between them.

She drew a sharp breath. She leaned forward and gingerly picked up the charm bracelet that lay in the middle of the mess.

Aidan placed his elbows on his knees, then clasped his hands and rested his chin against them.

"Ben took me to a jeweler about a month before we broke up. He asked me to pick out some pieces that I liked, for my wedding present," she explained shakily. "This is the bracelet I chose."

She glanced at the charms scattered on the table and the bile rose to her throat. "Oh, God."

Aidan sifted through the charms. A revolver, a knife, an axe, a sword, and a bottle of poison glinted in the firelight. Emma dropped the bracelet as though it had burned her. Horrified, she met Aidan's steely eyes. "He means to kill me."

"Not on my watch."

"You can't be with me every moment," she whispered, fear choking her.

"I damn well will be. But we're still going to need some backup to protect you."

"Backup?" Emma whispered. "As in, a security guard?"

He ignored her question and instead grabbed his phone. "Cian. Alert the hotel that absolutely no one comes up here. I want guards in the elevators." He hung up, and a smile suddenly broke across his face as he noticed her shirt. "Ride a cowboy?"

She flushed. "Um…"

"I'm all about the message," he drawled, "but I hear knights are better."

"I'm not having this conversation," she declared, wishing she'd thought to put it on inside out.

"Emma, you are one surprise after another, you know that?"

"Yeah. I get all the best surprises," she muttered, her eyes shooting to the jewelry littering the table. She stood and began to pace.

He swept the pieces into the envelope and crumpled it in his hand. "What do you want to do about this?"

"He'll find me no matter where I go," she whispered, wrapping her arms around herself. "In a city of millions, he tracked me here. He has eyes everywhere."

"Are you sure about that?"

"I wish I could say no, but my gut tells me otherwise."

Aidan crushed the envelope a little more, and Emma could hear the charms break. "Then we have two options. One is to involve the police again."

"That wasn't the most effective route." Emma hated the tremor in her voice.

"Nay. The other option is to test your theory out." He looked up at her through his lashes, his eyes a clear green. "We see how far he's willing to go."

"To what end?" she asked.

"He'll never stop unless we make him."

"This isn't a *we* issue. This is my battle. I'll have to confront him. Or get him the money."

Aidan raised an eyebrow. "And you think, knowing whatever it is that you may or may not know, that he'll just let you off the hook when you pass him some money?"

She chewed her lip. "Maybe?"

"Well, before you try that out, perhaps we can try mine first. Come to Boston with me, Emma."

"Boston?"

"Aye. It's close enough that we can make it there quickly, and far enough away that he will have to make an effort to find us." Aidan's gaze speared her. "At this point, Emma, what do you have to lose?"

My life, she thought morosely, her eyes drifting to the now fully compressed handful of trash in his hand.

If she stayed, he'd find her.

If she went, perhaps he'd give up and leave her alone. Boston was a nice city. It wasn't as big as New York City, but hadn't Ben just proven to her that size didn't matter? Perhaps distance would.

She nodded slowly. "Okay. I'll go."

He stood and Emma tried—and failed—to look away from the sinew in his bare forearms. "We'll leave tomorrow. Do you have anything else you think Cian might have missed at your apartment?"

She sighed heavily. "Possibly. Things like my passport, birth certificate—the important papers are in a safe, in a special compartment in the closet. One can only hope that Ben didn't see it."

"We'll stop there after we retrieve the items from the auction," Aidan said. He stretched again, then winked at her when he caught her staring. "Sweet dreams, Emmaline."

Her eyes widened, and she glared at his retreating back. *He set me up!* Well, at least she could enjoy the view from behind as his punishment. Or her reward.

He cast a glance over his shoulder and tossed her a megawatt smile, and her heart skipped a beat.

Only when he ambled leisurely up the stairs did she realize she'd been caught staring again.

Damn that man!

CHAPTER 6

The next morning, just as he was stepping out of the shower, Aidan opened his door to insistent banging. "What do you want, old man?"

"The bellman's here with breakfast," Cian said grouchily. "He won't leave; he's just standing there like he's daft."

Aidan secured the towel around his waist and sighed. "He's waiting for his tip, you fool." He grabbed his wallet from the nightstand and walked out, digging through to pull out a twenty-dollar bill. Handing it to the bellman, he thanked him, then walked to the door and closed it behind him.

"Good morn—oh!" Emma's face turned scarlet, her eyes locked on his chest.

"Good morning, Emma. I trust you slept well?"

"Ah, um. Oh. Yeah. I, uh." She licked her lips and managed to drag her eyes up to his, and she colored even darker. "I'm sorry. What?"

Aidan couldn't resist the smug smile that crept along his face. "I asked if you slept well."

"I do. I mean, I did, yes," she said quickly. She averted her gaze, and it fell on the table behind him. "Is that breakfast?"

"Aye. Are you hungry?"

She murmured something incoherent, and Aidan stifled a laugh. "I'll just go put some clothes on. You look very refreshed today."

She glanced down at herself and managed a real smile. "Yes, thank you. The clothes from Neiman Marcus arrived this morning. I admit I've never owned anything this comfortable." The soft denim jeans fit her perfectly, hugging her curves in all the right places. The long, open cashmere sweater, a deep navy blue with silver threads woven through it, flattered her already lovely figure, and the white shirt she wore accented her breasts to perfection. She was barefoot, her red-painted toenails peeking out at him from the hem of her pants. "Tess certainly thinks blue and silver are my colors."

He didn't say anything, but Cian cleared his throat meaningfully.

"I'll pay you back for them," Emma said.

He shook his head as he walked back to his room, calling over his shoulder, "No, you won't. But the thought is appreciated."

"I'm not a kept woman!" she called out after him. Then, embarrassment coloring her tone, she added, "Oh. Good morning, Cian."

Aidan chuckled as he loped back to his room. He sobered, though, when he thought of taking her outside the relative safety of the hotel suite.

The thought made something in the vicinity of his chest burn.

"We'll leave straight after breakfast, if you're amenable?" Aidan remarked a few minutes later as he grabbed a roll.

She choked on her orange juice, and gratefully accepted the napkin from his outstretched hand. "Okay. I can head into the apartment and salvage what I can while you finish up at the auction house."

"No," he replied easily.

She didn't fight him, and he considered it a small victory.

The silence stretched.

Finally, Emma asked, "If I wanted to stay here, would you try to force me to go with you? To Boston?"

Aidan considered for a moment. He could tell her the truth, but he didn't want to alarm her. "No."

She visibly relaxed. "Thank you." Silence again. Then, "I have a condition."

He poured himself a cup of coffee. *As if that would change anything, lass.* "Oh?"

"Yes. Separate hotel rooms, and I pay my own way."

"If you prefer," he replied casually. *Absolutely not happening.* He needed to keep her close; locks were easily broken. His sword, however, was not. He felt a moment's regret for lying to her. But her safety came first.

"I admit to feeling a little lost here," she said with a small laugh. "I haven't had a morning off in eight years."

"Pretend it's a weekend," he suggested, buttering a thick piece of toast.

"I work weekends."

"Okay. Pretend it's Christmas."

"Believe it or not, I worked Christmas, too."

He stared at her a moment, and he suddenly understood why Price's comments to her the night before had been so upsetting. "You must have truly loved your job."

She smiled sadly. "Not the clients, no. But I loved feeling needed, and people who do bad things always need people like me to fix their screw-ups." She took a bite of her pancakes and swallowed, a thoughtful look crossing her features. "I never stopped to think about how my work prevented them from ever taking responsibility for their actions."

"That can't be all true."

She shrugged. "Maybe not. I worked with a lot of individuals, but I liked working the corporate clients more. I am very good at spinning words, and I have very good judgment." Her gaze dropped to her hands. "Most of the time, anyway."

"Car's ready when you are, my laird," Cian interrupted, joining them at the table.

"Thank you, Cian. We'll be down shortly."

They finished eating in silence.

• • •

While Aidan made arrangements for shipping his items at the auction house, Emma waited in line for coffee across the street. After returning to her apartment earlier, she needed a pick-me-up. Everything was destroyed, but nothing was stolen. It was as though the act was done simply to frighten her. Instead, all it did was make her angry. Thankfully, her safe was untouched, still in its hiding place. Aidan hefted it down the stairs, and Cian loaded it in the car.

Cian sat at a table, looking for all the world as though he were reading his phone, but she knew better. Emma glanced around the line of people in front of her. Seven deep, and the man at the counter had a long and involved order. She wasn't in a rush; Aidan had said he would be about a half hour, as he had forms to complete.

"Excuse me...Miss Perkins?"

A tall man stood next to her, his long dark hair pulled into a neat ponytail at the nape of his neck. It didn't fit with the suit he wore; he reminded her of a Wall Street finance professional gone rogue. He had a small beard, just enough to be called one, and his blue eyes were very dark, the irises rimmed with black. He said in a quiet voice, "We were told that you had money for us. I'm here to collect it."

Emma stared at him in shock for a full minute before realizing the line was moving. She moved up, hoping Cian could see her around the display of coffee that blocked her and the man from view.

"I'm sorry, Mr....?"

"We know you bought a whole lot of stuff last night at a pricey auction," he replied, ignoring her. His tone was clipped. "He told us he gave you two days to get the money, but we don't think you need that much time."

"I, uh—" Her mind went blank, fear threatening to swallow her whole.

"Perhaps you've forgotten the state of your home, Miss Perkins. I would hate to see something worse happen to you."

She blanched.

"The money, Miss Perkins. Bring it back to your apartment within the hour. Leave it on the floor, and you and your new boyfriend won't be hurt this time. We'll give you three minutes to get out of the apartment before we take it."

"Leave me out of this," she replied, her voice barely above a whisper.

"Not my call to make. On the floor, Miss Perkins," he repeated in a low voice. "I suggest you revisit your apartment—*again*—and take a hard look. That will provide a good indicator of your life until I get the money your fiancé owes me."

Ex-fiancé, she corrected mentally. She sucked in her breath, and he turned on his heel and swiftly exited the coffee shop.

Beverage forgotten, Emma started shaking. Her heart pounding, she tried to see if the man—or Ben—was standing outside the building, but there were so many people on the sidewalk, either could've concealed himself easily.

"Excuse me?"

She shrieked, causing people to turn and stare.

An older woman stepped back, affronted. "I just wanted to know if you were in line!" she explained indignantly. With a "hmph," the woman walked away.

Panicked, Emma fled the shop and ran across the street, almost colliding with an oncoming car. She pushed open the doors to the auction house and sprinted to the reception desk.

"Ma'am?" the security guard asked as he half rose from his chair.

"I have to go to your shipment room," she gasped out, her heart slamming into her chest as she heard the doors behind her open. She didn't look back for fear of seeing the man from the coffee shop. "Please, right away, it's an emergency."

"I'm sorry, but that room is occupied at the moment. What's the nature of the emergency?" he asked.

Before she could answer, a hand landed on her arm and she spun around, a scream catching in her throat.

"Ms. Perkins, who was that?" Cian steadied her. "In the shop, the man. Who was it?"

"I have to talk to Aidan right away!"

Cian's bushy white eyebrows drew together in concern. "About what, lass?"

"The man from the coffee shop." Aware that she looked like a madwoman, she tried to slow her breathing. "Did you see him?"

"Aye. Tall fellow with the hat. I saw him leave, but I didn't see him speak with you." He frowned. "He waited until you were out of my sight. He probably knew I was there with you." Cian nodded once to the security guard. "Come with me, lass. Aidan will be out in a moment. Until then, you can stay with me, in the car."

She allowed Cian to escort her back outside. She attempted to see if the man was still watching her from somewhere, but there were just too many people. Cian helped her into the car before getting in the driver's seat. He locked the doors. "Tell me what happened."

She related the events to him as he drove them around the block. His kind eyes flicked to hers in the rearview mirror more than once, his concern evident.

"Do ye think he was the man who sacked your apartment?"

"Yes," she replied without hesitation. "He suggested that I look at my apartment again, and told me it was a 'good indicator' of what my life will be like until I give them the money." She quickly related the other details of the short conversation, her voice shaking as badly as her hands.

Aidan walked out of the building with some packages; Cian pressed a button to open the trunk. A moment later, the trunk slammed shut and the back door opened. "Did you drink your coffee already?" Aidan asked, nodding at her empty hands.

"Emma was approached," Cian said before Emma could respond. Quickly, Cian filled Aidan in on the events of the last half hour.

Aidan's jaw hardened. "Are you all right?" he asked her, his voice clipped.

"Yes. I think it's worse than I thought, though."

Aidan's eyes narrowed. "The story you gave to the police officer—you said you didn't know why he threatened you."

"No, I said that he'd shown violent tendencies in the past," she replied wearily, dropping her head into her hands. "He's tied up in some serious stuff, I think. And now, he's got people after me!"

Aidan gave a nod to Cian, who pulled out into traffic.

"Best let the whole sordid tale out, lass. I need to know what we're up against here."

In all her years of living in the city, Emma never once felt the fear coursing through her veins as she did now. Could she really trust this man? Her history with men wasn't exactly a testament to her good judgment.

"We've got a long ride ahead," Aidan reminded her.

"Boston isn't all that far. What if he's following us?" she exclaimed suddenly, twisting her head to peer out the back window.

"He's not. Cian made sure of it."

"How can you be sure?" she asked, her voice high.

"Emmaline. The incident in the coffee shop will never be repeated."

"You can't know that." She glanced out the window, wondering if Ben or one of his minions was close.

"I can, and I do. Trust me, things will settle once we're in Boston. No one knows you there."

"Like the Witness Protection Program?" she wondered.

"Better," he said. "It's the Aidan MacWilliam Protection Program."

• • •

"Emma, be reasonable."

Emma remained silent. She was being perfectly reasonable— Cian had dropped them in front of a building that, while beautiful, was clearly *not* a hotel.

"You'll like Colin. He's nice, and has plenty of room," Aidan coaxed.

"I don't like relying on the charity of others, Aidan. I said I'd pay for my own hotel room. And I don't know anything about this man," she added.

He smiled humorlessly at the jab. "You know enough about me." They stood outside the building; Aidan's hands were jammed into the pockets of his leather jacket and Emma's arms were crossed. He gently grasped her elbow and led her toward the door. "His name is Colin O'Rourke. He's my cousin. We're close. And we're going in, Emma. It's cold."

"I'm not cold, thanks to this ridiculously expensive jacket," she replied, narrowing her eyes.

"It's a safe place," Aidan replied firmly.

She reluctantly gave in (she had no choice, as she was in the middle of an unfamiliar city with a madman after her), and walked up the stairs without further comment.

Colin opened the door, a smile on his face. "Aidan! Long time no see, bro!"

Emma stared. Colin O'Rourke looked as though he just stepped from the pages of a J. Crew catalog. His dark blond hair was casually swept to the side, and his tee shirt clung to enormous, muscled shoulders that tapered into impressively built biceps. Low-slung, well-fitted jeans hugged his long, lean legs, and his eyes were a chocolate brown that actually sparkled. The dimples in his cheeks were so deep Emma almost fanned herself.

"Emma Perkins," she finally managed, holding her hand out. Colin shook it, grinning.

"A pleasure, Emma. I'm Colin O'Rourke, and welcome to you, as well. I'm happy you agreed to come with Aidan; I've been very interested in meeting you." He had a very slight Boston accent.

"Colin…" Aidan started, a warning in his voice.

Emma couldn't tear her gaze away from Colin. "Have you?" she asked faintly.

"Of course," Colin said, nearly shutting the door in Aidan's face. "He's never brought a woman to meet the family before."

"Oh, it's not like that," Emma hastened to inform him. "I work for Aidan." She glanced around; they stood in a foyer with stairs to her right. A doorway to her left revealed a living room, with a comfortable-looking couch and set of armchairs. In front of her was a hallway that led to the kitchen.

"We all work for Aidan," Colin replied dryly, bringing her attention back to him.

"No, really," she protested. She turned to Aidan. "Didn't you explain to him?" She noticed his stormy expression and frowned.

"Not yet," Aidan replied, shrugging out of his coat and tossing it onto the couch. "I've been waiting to see him in person." He embraced Colin. "Remember your place, O'Rourke. It hasn't been all that long since I trounced you in a wrestling match."

"No need for a pissing contest," Colin replied agreeably, slapping him on the back. "So she works for you?"

"Indeed she does. She's exceptionally good at her job."

Colin slid a glance to Emma, then replied lightly, "That's good news."

"I'm sorry for barging in on you like this. I insisted we stay at a hotel, but Aidan refused."

Colin flashed his thousand-megawatt smile at her (she wasn't immune—her stomach turned to jelly) and shook his head. "I would be insulted. I have plenty of room here. It's a four-bedroom brownstone, and I only use one of them. Well, actually, I have another houseguest, but there's still plenty of room even with him here."

"Not O'Malley," Aidan groaned.

Colin frowned. "Do not ruin any of my furniture. If Bri ever found out you destroyed something valuable, you'd be toast."

Aidan's face changed to suspicion. "First, if that means what I think it means, we will indeed be staying somewhere else. And second, I doubt I'll see Bri, as you won't take me to her."

Bri? Who's Bri?

"You know it's not that easy," Colin protested mildly. "And if you need my help, as you mentioned last night, I think staying here is the safest bet, right?"

Aidan glanced at Emma, who was desperately trying to pretend she wasn't interested in what they were saying, then asked Colin, "Where is he, then?"

"He'll be down momentarily. Emma, let me take your coat. Would you like something to drink?"

"No, thank you," she replied. "Um, where's Cian going to stay?"

"With Aidan," Colin replied, as though it were obvious. "I'll put you in the adjoining room."

"There's no need to go to all this trouble," she insisted. "Cian didn't think we were followed. I don't mind a hotel and Aidan can stay here—"

"Methinks the lady doth protest too much," a deep, lilting, Irish-accented voice behind her said. Emma let out a small scream and whirled around, and, for the umpteenth time that day, her heart nearly stopped.

The man before her was tall—taller than either Colin or Aidan—and all she saw at first were impossibly large arms, crossed over an equally large chest. Her eyes traveled up to a face that would stop traffic—a chiseled jaw, covered with a day's worth of dark stubble; a small cleft in his chin; smooth lips; a strong, patrician nose. Hard planes, cheekbones to die for, almost jet-black hair, and eyelashes that should've been illegal on a man. They framed the most beautiful set of hazel eyes Emma had ever seen.

Her mouth dried.

"O'Malley," Aidan said tensely.

"MacWilliam," he replied jovially. He stepped off the stair and held out his hand to Emma. "Reilly O'Malley. Call me Ry."

"Emma, uh…Emma…"

"Perkins," Aidan growled between his teeth.

"Right. Perkins," she echoed as Reilly brought her hand to his lips. "Are you another cousin?"

Reilly met Aidan's eyes, and his smile widened. "Aye."

Did all the gorgeous man genes in the world fall to your family, Aidan? she wondered, slightly dazed.

"Probably not all of them," Colin replied, not bothering to hide the smile in his voice.

Emma clapped her free hand over her mouth and felt the blush creep up her neck. "I didn't say that aloud, did I?" she asked, horrified.

"Think nothing of it," Reilly said easily, not letting go of her other hand. "The only one here whose head would get bigger is your friend Aidan's, and he doesn't seem to be paying any attention."

"Emma, I'll show you to your room," Aidan spit out, taking her hand from Reilly's and tucking it protectively into his arm. He shot Reilly a look and only glowered harder when Reilly laughed at him.

Emma didn't say anything as they walked down the hall. She was more than humiliated and tried to rationalize her behavior. *I've been under a lot of stress. I was threatened today. I'm tired from a really long drive.*

But she couldn't really lie to herself. These three men—four, if she included Cian—had more testosterone in their pinky fingers than Ben did in his entire body, and it scrambled her wits. She sneaked a peek at Aidan, and she swallowed hard. Colin's all-American good looks and Reilly's sex appeal still paled in comparison to the dark, mysterious man walking next to her.

Good thing she worked for him. Getting involved in anything other than a professional relationship with a man like him would overwhelm her. She was sure of it.

Besides, she reassured herself, *I would never involve myself with a client, so it's a moot point.*

"You'll be sleeping here," Aidan said gruffly as he opened one of the doors. "It has a lock. I suggest you use it."

"Are your cousins a danger to me?"

He met her gaze. "They wouldn't lay a hand on you."

"Then why would I need the lock?"

He closed his eyes for a moment, then looked directly at her. "To keep me from laying a hand on you."

Emma must've looked as confused as she felt, because he closed his eyes again, muttered something incomprehensible, then, without warning, cupped her face and kissed her.

• • •

She smelled like sunshine and heather.

She tastes like home, Aidan thought.

Emma's lips parted in surprise, and Aidan took the opening, running his tongue along her bottom lip, invading her mouth, tangling her tongue with his. He deepened the kiss, drank in her sigh, and felt a flash of triumph as her body melted into his. She wrapped her arms around his neck and pressed herself against him, and his control nearly snapped. Without breaking the kiss, he backed her into the room and kicked the door shut behind them. He walked her backward to the bed and laid her down on it, pressing his own body into hers. Feeling her passion rise for him, he hungrily kissed her neck, her ear, the sensitive spot beneath her earlobe, and she moaned his name.

"This is a bad idea," she whispered, even as she tightened her grip on him.

He eased from the kiss, unwillingly, and sat up, his breathing ragged.

"What was that for?" she whispered, her hand touching her lips.

So that every time you look at another man, you'll remember that you're mine.

"I don't know," he finally said. He stood. "Lock the door, Emma."

He closed the door behind him and waited to hear the lock click. It didn't matter that when he kissed her, he felt a whisper in his soul, telling him she was his forever. No. He should not have given in to his impulse. She was a woman in trouble, and he was a bastard for taking advantage of her vulnerability.

He snorted to himself. Vulnerable though she might be, she would probably never admit it out loud.

"You can't claim every pretty girl who turns your head," Reilly grumbled as Aidan flopped onto the couch in the front living room.

Colin, in one of the armchairs, put his booted feet up on the coffee table. He smirked. "I'm interested to know how you got her here. And so willingly, too."

"Those new Docs?" Reilly asked, leaning in to admire the shoes. "They're nice. Good quality."

"Thanks. Got 'em on sale," Colin replied, admiring them. "Normally I hate getting new shoes, but these were a great find. No need to break them in."

"If you ladies are done comparing shopping notes?" Aidan cut in, annoyed.

"Looks like she's got under his skin," Reilly noted.

"Shove off."

"Don't see what's got his knickers in a twist," Reilly said to Colin, who shrugged, still admiring his new Doc Martens.

"I'll go real slow so the dim-witted one here can keep up," Aidan said with a roll of his eyes. "I got my sword back."

Colin raised his eyebrows. "Nice. How much did that run you?"

"Wouldn't you like to know. That's not the important part." He switched to Gaelic, in case Emma came downstairs, and quickly relayed her situation through to the threats in the coffee shop that morning.

Colin let out a whistle. "She's in some serious trouble."

"And you stepped in, the white knight, waving your sword," Reilly stated.

"Sounds slightly dirty when you say it that way," Colin snickered.

"By the saints, you arses, the lass needs my help!" Aidan nearly shouted, his knuckles white.

Colin sat up, dropping his feet, and even Reilly sat straighter.

"Holy hell," Colin breathed. He looked at Reilly in shock. "He's claimed her."

"I've done nothing of the sort," Aidan sputtered.

"My laird," Cian said, descending the stairs. "With all due respect, ye've given the lass food, shelter, and clothing. All she owns now is MacWilliam colors, and she's under your protection. Methinks it fair to say—"

"Don't," Aidan growled.

"Sorry, MacWilliam," Reilly guffawed, "but it looks like you found your mate."

Aidan stopped short of tackling Reilly as Emma came down the stairs.

She paused at the door. "About before—"

"No worries, lass," Reilly said.

"Don't worry about it," Colin added.

Aidan just watched her, his fingers gently pulling his lips.

"Okay, well, thanks," she said, clearly at a loss.

"Do you play cards?" Colin asked suddenly.

She cocked her head. "Depends on what you're playing for."

"Money and bragging rights," Colin answered.

She looked thoughtful.

"They'll wipe the floor with you," Aidan warned.

She raised her eyebrows at him. "You playing?"

"You bet."

"Deal me in," she decided firmly.

"Have a seat, Emma Perkins," Reilly laughed. "I think I like you."

As she settled next to Reilly, Aidan began to worry that his teeth would grind themselves into powder before the night was through.

CHAPTER 7

The next day, a loud crash greeted Emma at the bottom of the stairs. She paused and peeked around the corner.

Aidan was on the floor, wrestling with Reilly. Two grown men, wrestling as though they were children in a schoolyard fight.

Emma rather hoped Reilly would win their skirmish. Emma still wasn't sure what to make of that kiss, and Aidan had scowled at her the entire night. It was so at odds with everything he'd done and said to her since they first met, and she wasn't sure who she was angriest at—Aidan, for being such a jerk, or herself, for letting her guard down.

Either way, she made the firm decision that they were in a strictly professional relationship now.

Aside from the fact, of course, that she was staying in his cousin's house, hiding from her crazy ex.

She had to figure out a way to free herself from Ben MacDermott.

Shaking her head, she carefully sidestepped the two men as they crashed into the back of the lovely leather couch. From what she could see as she skirted past, Aidan appeared to be bleeding from his lip, and Reilly was sporting a nasty bruise under his eye. They also seemed intent on beating each other to a pulp. Emma rolled her eyes.

She didn't understand boys when she was younger, and things hadn't gotten any clearer now that she was grown.

Emma felt much more comfortable after last night's games, when she'd soundly trumped all of them at poker, Texas Hold 'Em, and even Go Fish. She'd had a good time, despite the remnants of whatever that kiss was between her and Aidan. Plus, Aidan didn't even pretend to like Reilly, which made Reilly flirt all the more outrageously with her. It was interesting to watch.

Reilly's head popped out from the living room. "Good morning, Em—oof!" He disappeared again.

She found Colin in the kitchen. He stared intently at a laptop, muttering to himself in Gaelic. She had a sudden thought that she might have landed in a house of lunatics.

Well, she tried to rationalize, *that isn't any different than my typical clientele, really.*

"Good morning," she said, sliding into the chair beside him.

"Morning, Emma. Sleep well?"

As well as I could, knowing that the man who kissed my socks off was sleeping only a door away. "Yes, thanks."

Another loud crash was heard from the living room, followed by what she was sure were curse words in Gaelic. Colin didn't bat an eye as he added, "They don't even try to get along. Haven't for years."

"I see," she replied, her most charming smile in place. "Last night, you mentioned your matchmaking business, and I realized I signed up for it a few months back." She grimaced. "I thought I was ready to jump back into dating, and I saw an article in the paper, so…Anyway, when did you take ownership?"

He cleared his throat. "About, um, eight years ago."

"It's done very well," she replied. "Some of my clients used Celtic Connections. They did so with great success."

"I'm happy to hear it," Colin replied. Another crash. "Coffee?"

"Sure, thanks," Emma said. Another thud, followed by grunts.

"Whenever you hop back on the dating circuit, let me know," he offered, sliding her a steaming cup. "We have great matching profiles when you're ready to settle down. Serious inquiries only."

She took a sip and frowned thoughtfully. "Thanks. But I don't think marriage is for me." But even as she said the words aloud, her heart hurt. Ben would never allow her peace enough to date, let alone marry.

She also wasn't fool enough to think that she could entrust her heart to anyone ever again.

"You'd make an excellent wife, I'm certain of it," Reilly drawled, entering the kitchen with Aidan.

"Are you offering to make her one?" Aidan growled to Reilly.

Emma choked.

Reilly laughed at Aidan, who was wiping the blood from his lip. "Down, boy. Emma, excellent job at the cards last night. Beginner's luck?"

"Perhaps," she murmured, reaching for her coffee.

"Ah. A woman of many secrets. Well, that's fine by me," Reilly replied, helping himself to her coffee before she could get to it. At her protest, he flashed her a mischievous grin. "Ah, love, we're all family here. We share everything."

"Not everything," Colin interjected mildly, watching Aidan attempt to reign in his temper.

"Aye," Reilly agreed. "Not everything. But most things."

"Do you always tease him?" she asked. Reilly just shrugged, and Colin laughed.

"One of the reasons they act like children is because they love each other so much," Colin explained.

"Hardly," Aidan growled.

"So how, exactly, are you related to each other?" Emma asked. "None of you look anything alike."

Colin cleared his throat. "Our family tree has, um, many branches."

"You all have different last names. That's interesting. Are your mothers all sisters?" she asked.

"We're more like second or third cousins," Colin said carefully, and Emma's BS radar went on full alert.

"Second *or* third?" she replied.

"Right. Many branches," Colin reminded her.

"Right," she echoed. She poured herself another cup of coffee, since Reilly was still drinking hers, as they swiftly changed subjects and began to (loudly) discuss the state of affairs in Ireland. Reilly, who owned a cottage near Dublin, was arguing with Aidan about the property taxes, and Colin just continued to stare at his laptop.

They were trying too hard. She'd seen it hundreds of times with clients; she wasn't fooled. She wondered what the real story was—she'd only asked a simple question about their family history.

She caught Aidan's eye and raised her eyebrow. He stood abruptly, cutting Reilly off midsentence. "Emma, come with me. I don't want your sweet self tainted by any more time spent with O'Malley."

"You wound me," Reilly replied. "Is Cian around today?"

"No." Aidan didn't elaborate.

"Actually, I have some questions for Colin," Emma cut in. "I'd like to know more about your matchmaking business. Did Aidan ever fill out a profile?"

Colin was clearly caught off-guard by the question. "Well—"

"Why is that important?" Aidan interrupted.

Emma took a sip of her coffee. "Because if I'm going to do my job successfully, I need to know what information about you is out there. Is his application still in your database?" she pressed Colin.

He looked bemused. "Of course."

"How secure are your firewalls? Have you had any hacking attempts recently? Has your client information ever been put at risk? What safeguards do you have in place in the event of such an occurrence?"

"Still not seeing the importance here," Aidan cut in irritably.

She raised an eyebrow. "Let's say a patron at The Colcannon decides that he had a terrible experience there. He digs around and finds your profile on Celtic Connections. He can glean all sorts of personal details to use in whatever way he thinks of to damage your reputation. If we know what information is publicly available, and what information is privately available, our case against him will be stronger in court, and we can mitigate the damage. So, I want to know how secure your information is on Colin's database."

Aidan's mouth hung open in surprise. "Oh."

Colin inclined his head, his expression impressed. "I'll take you through it all this afternoon in my office."

"I thought you said the office was 'organized chaos,' and that not even the housekeeper would touch it," she teased. "Maybe we'd better stay in the kitchen."

"Unnecessary," Aidan said swiftly. "We can discuss it later, but for now you can rest assured the information in that application is no longer in Celtic Connections' servers."

"You wiped my servers?" Colin exclaimed. "You don't have permission to do that, MacWilliam!"

"Colin's overprotective about the business," Reilly murmured in Emma's ear. "He loved Brianagh—the original founder—very much and he promised to take care of it for her. You'll see a temper tantrum now."

Colin and Aidan weren't paying attention to her and Reilly; Colin stood nose-to-nose with Aidan and was shouting all sorts of things at him in rapid-fire Gaelic. Emma caught "Brianagh," "fool," and what she thought were a few choice words directed at Aidan. Aidan didn't shout back, but she could see the muscles on his neck bunching.

"How, exactly, are they related again?" she asked again, watching the spectacle with interest. Never having any siblings or cousins, Emma had never had the opportunity to argue with such enthusiasm before. All her relationships were businesslike; she'd never blown up at anyone like that before. It was fascinating to watch.

"Technically, Aidan is Colin's uncle. Many times removed," Reilly replied, draining the coffee cup.

"Really? You want to pull that out already?" Colin asked incredulously, turning on Reilly.

Emma's head spun. How could that be? "Uncle?"

"Uncle Aidan, that's me," Aidan responded. "It's a convoluted tale, lass, and I'm hardly traceable to Colin through bloodlines. Irish families—we're enormous by default. No need to worry, though. His reputation is so clean, I think if anyone did associate us, it would be only for the good of my *brand*."

The reminder hit its target—Emma was his employee. She ignored the little stab of pain in her chest. He was right, of course. She had to remember that she was not a part of this family, or any family. She relied on herself, and while these interactions were interesting, they were not her concern. She gave a brief nod.

"We are done here," Aidan said sharply. "Emma—get your coat. We're leaving."

"Save your commands for Cian," Reilly snapped. "You're not her laird."

"No, I'm not," Aidan snapped back. He leveled a stare at Emma. "I am her employer. And it's business hours. So let's go."

"Where, exactly?" she asked, folding her arms.

"To my restaurant."

"Another one?" Stunned, Emma watched him leave the kitchen.

"You really know how to put him in a bad mood," Colin remarked, punching Reilly lightly on the shoulder.

"It's a talent," he agreed. "One which you seem to share lately."

"Emma, before you go," Colin said as Emma stood, "Aidan, Ry, and I have all had a chat about it, and it's going to take a little time to get your apartment all fixed. Also, we're concerned about your safety. We'd really like you to stay here. Long-term."

She started to protest, and he hurried on before she comment.

"It's not entirely altruistic. I was hoping you might spend a little time helping me with Celtic Connections. We're trying to expand overseas, and I'm not sure how to present the business in foreign markets. I wonder if you might be willing to help with that, offering some advice."

"That's really kind, Colin, but…" She shook her head uncomfortably. Aidan must have put him up to it, and she wasn't sure she liked it.

"This isn't for pity," Reilly assured her. "Colin knows what you did with that software company that expanded from California to Japan."

"True," Colin confirmed.

Despite herself, she grinned. "That was a fun account. I never got to go to Tokyo, though."

Unsurprisingly, Heidi had gone in her place, after Emma did all the work of closing the account and creating storyboards, presentations, and contacts in the States. Now that she was out of the environment, Emma really saw how much she'd done for Price Publicity and how little she'd gotten in return. She had a momentary flash of relief that she'd never have to enter that office again.

"I have to see if it would cross any contract lines," she replied. "But if it doesn't, then I'll help you out. Thanks."

Colin gave her a nod, a lock of his hair falling over his forehead, and she couldn't help but smile at him. Colin O'Rourke was an all-American heartbreaker, and nice to boot. It worried her a little that she wasn't even the least bit interested in him.

"EMMALINE!" Aidan boomed, exasperation in his voice. He appeared in the doorway again, wearing his black leather jacket over his gray polo shirt.

Her mouth went a little dry, and, irritated, she knew why Colin just didn't do it for her.

He wasn't Aidan MacWilliam.

* * *

Later that day, while Aidan was holed up in the office with Reilly, Colin introduced Emma to the third floor of his massive house. The entire floor was one large room that spanned the length of the brownstone, with the same honey maple wood floors as the rest of the house. The stairs from the second floor led directly into the enormous space, which managed to be light, open, and airy, yet comfortable and welcoming. A gorgeous, highly detailed light blue oriental carpet lay nearly wall-to-wall. The two armchairs were overstuffed, and a basket full of thick fleece blankets sat near a stone fireplace in the wall. The gas insert gave that end of the room a cozy feel.

The best thing about the fireplace wasn't its ambiance, though.

What made her heart beat faster were the shelves surrounding it. She gazed upon the titles lining the walls and felt a little like Belle did when the Beast showed her his library. She was surprised to find a myriad of subjects—just from her first glance, she saw historical texts, literary fiction, and a bestselling thriller novel.

Her eyes traveled to the bright double window at the back of the room, and she noted the inviting window seat. It was padded in a fabric that complemented the blue decor, with oversized chair pillows propped against it.

"This is amazing!"

"When Bri lived here this building was split into two units. I inherited this from her, and when the neighbors wanted to sell, I bought and renovated the whole thing into a single-family home. At the very least, I needed a place to store all Bri's romance novels," he said with a roll of his eyes. "That girl had so many, it's no wonder she started a matchmaking service."

Never before had Emma so wished she had a family like this one. All the men were still so devoted to their family member, years after her death. Emma felt a flash of sadness for them all. The more she learned of Bri, the more certain she was that they would've been friends.

Of course, she'd have been meeting her under really strange circumstances, so who knew what the woman would've thought? *Hi, I'm Emma. I work for Aidan, but every time I look at him, my knees get a bit wobbly. It's okay, though, because we're not a thing, that'd be unethical. Oh, and I'm on the run from my ex, and I'm just going to crash here with your family until I figure out what I'm going to do.*

Yeah. That'd go over well.

"…in here," Colin was saying.

She blinked at him and ceased her imaginary conversation with a dead woman. Quickly, she promised herself to work on a real social life once she'd sorted her current mess out. "Sorry, I was woolgathering. What was that?"

He waved her further into the room. "I was saying, feel free to hang out in here. It's a great place to lose yourself for a while."

"You're right. And thank you." She paused. "So, if the first floor has the kitchen, living room, office, and a bathroom, and the second floor has four bedrooms…"

"Two of the bedrooms have their own bathrooms," Colin informed her. "Aidan's room and the one that's unoccupied. Something's up with the plumbing, so I'm not using it until I can get someone to fix it."

"Okay, so four bedrooms and two bathrooms. Then you have this floor, which is incredible…what's on the fourth floor?"

He grinned. "My master suite."

Images of what that must look like flitted through her mind, but before she could ask, he said, "I can show it to you next, if you like."

She blushed.

"Anyway," Colin said, taking pity on her, "please feel free to make use of this room. Until your apartment is ready, I want you to feel at home here."

"Thank you," she replied, glancing around again. She couldn't wait to get started—she spied a copy of *Buile Suibhne*, her favorite late medieval Irish tale, and she was itching to get her hands on it to read the translation.

"The stairs over there"—he pointed to the opposite end of the room, to a matching balustrade—"go straight down to the kitchen. Feel free to bring anything up here."

She nodded, and Colin gave her a salute before loping down the stairs.

Hurrying over to the gold book, she carefully pulled it down and grinned at the cover. She loved every single thing about medieval Ireland. Though she'd also studied the politics and religious theory, she loved the folklore and stories best. *Buile Suibhne* was by far her favorite—a violent, temper-driven pagan king who's cursed by a bishop, who ultimately finds salvation when he converts to Christianity.

The sociological truths buried in those pages made her head spin with excitement.

She carefully opened the cover and turned a page. Then another. And another, and another…and realized they were completely in Irish Gaelic.

She frowned. She didn't recognize some of the words.

She went to flip to the copyright page, but there wasn't one. She realized with a start that she was holding a very old copy of the original text in its original language, and she had nothing better to do than wrap herself in a fleece blanket and sit on the window seat.

Her day was looking like one of her best ever.

She placed the book on the seat, then decided she needed sustenance. She knew herself; once she cracked open that book in earnest, she wouldn't move, even if the house was on fire. Temporarily quashing her inner history nerd, she headed downstairs.

Thirty minutes later, Emma sat on the comfortable window seat, *Buile Suibhne* forgotten in her lap.

She was frozen to the spot, absorbed by the spectacle happening three stories below her, in Colin's tiny back garden. At first, she tried to look away. When her eyes wouldn't comply with her demands, she tried talking to them sternly, to convince them that she was doing nothing better than spying. She even attempted to close her eyes, but it was pointless.

After all, she was watching two incredibly beautiful, shirtless men swordfight—*with medieval swords*—directly below her.

She could appreciate Colin's strength and grace. His arm muscles bulged and flexed with each parry. A large, dark tattoo wound about each of his upper arms, and they seemed to dance with each thrust. The sound of his laughter was almost as loud as the ring of metal against metal. His chest was rock hard, leading to a tight six-pack that she suspected was actually more like an eight-pack. A light dusting of hair covered his chest.

Her eyes, once they'd fully scoped the male beauty that was Colin O'Rourke, strayed to Aidan. And once they landed on him, they wouldn't move.

Never before had she had such little control over her vision.

Emma drank in every detail of him. Every well-defined muscle in his chest, arms, stomach, and back rippled as he parried. He looked as though he'd recently spent time in the sun. Aidan's face was tightened into lines of concentration, but every once in a while he'd throw out a laugh and her heart would kick into high gear. He was taller than Colin, and there wasn't an ounce of fat on his body. Broad shoulders gave way to a muscled back.

Amazing. She'd never noticed how attractive a man's back could be.

It seemed they were verbally sparring as well, though she couldn't hear them. The harder one laughed, the harder the other fought. Aidan's forearms bunched with each clash of the blades, and he also had tattoos around his arms, similar in style to Colin's. She couldn't make out the details, but it looked like Celtic knots or some sort of vines.

She continued to shamelessly admire Aidan from the safety of the library. His chest was sculpted, with incredible pecs that flexed menacingly with his swordfighting. His stomach had more muscles than she thought humanly possible, and just the sight of his obliques inexplicably sped her breathing. From this height, she could just make out a happy trail, and she suddenly had an intense desire to follow that trail wherever it would take her.

Emma almost slapped herself. She was being fanciful and ridiculous. *Get a grip!* she chided herself. *Work ethic, Perkins. Dig it out from the under that avalanche of lust.*

She refused to think of the kiss last night. He was way out of her league, anyway. He was wealthy, model-gorgeous, knew how to wear a medieval léine, and was, she admitted, a great kisser. The man did things with his tongue that made her—

She blew out a breath slowly. *Do. Not. Think. Of. That.* Apparently, after convincing her they didn't exist, her hormones finally decided to make an appearance in her life. She was not appreciative of their timing.

When the two men finally paused for a water break, Emma decided it was time to stop ogling and get down to her reading.

The trouble was, history didn't hold a candle to her present day.

. . .

"Ow!"

Emma shook her hand and glared at the fancy espresso/latte/coffee device in Colin's kitchen. It had looked harmless when she first approached it, but the moment she touched the damn thing, it spit and hissed like a caged wild animal.

Because she was the first one up today, she thought it might be nice to make coffee. Colin always seemed to have some ready for her and anyone else who wanted it, so she padded down the gorgeous white-and-oak stairs, her steps muffled on the beautiful oriental stair treads. Her bare toes sank into the thick carpet in the main hallway on the way to the stunning chef's kitchen, and she marveled at the house's cleanliness.

Except the office, she reminded herself with a chuckle.

She placed her hands on her hips and returned her attention to the problem at hand. She never actually saw Colin make the coffee; she wasn't sure where to put the grounds.

She glanced at the maple cabinets above the caramel-colored granite counters and let out a sigh. She didn't even know which one would contain coffee.

She spied a little red lever on the angry machine and the box of English Breakfast tea on the counter. After a quick search, she located the coffee mugs and placed a bag in one. She placed her cup under the spout and had her finger on the lever when a rumble of laughter from behind stopped her cold.

"I wouldn't use that one, lass." Aidan walked into the kitchen, dressed in a black tee and running shorts, a towel around his neck. "That starts the foamer."

"Foamer?" she echoed, carefully removing her hand.

"Aye. I don't know why he doesn't have a normal pot, like the rest of mankind."

She looked down at her cup. "Well, perhaps I won't have any tea, either."

"Either?"

She placed her cup back in the cabinet. "Well, at first I thought it would be nice if I made coffee for everyone, since Colin always has it made for everyone else. When I hit the on switch, it spit at me and burned my hand."

"It spit at you," Aidan repeated, a smile playing at the corners of his lips.

"Yes," she said firmly, "it spit at me. Then I realized that I didn't know where the coffee was, so I gave up that plan. I saw the tea and thought I'd make a cup, but, well, you know how that went." She glared at the machine. "I don't like this thing."

Aidan walked around the island between him and Emma slowly, and she suddenly felt like prey.

Was there a word for prey that wanted to be caught?

No, no, no. Stop it. He's just going to show me how to—

He stopped directly in front of her, his body inches from hers, and slowly leaned in. Emma's breath hitched, and her body went on full alert, her senses hyperaware of him. His clean scent filled her nose, and his nearness made her knees turn to jelly. When her eyes locked on his clean-shaven face, it took every fiber of her being not to rise up on her toes and run her tongue along his jawline.

His eyes met hers, and she saw it—raw hunger. As he raised his hand slowly, she parted her lips, hoping for a second taste of Aidan MacWilliam.

The sound of something rustling above her head forced her to look up.

Aidan brought a bag of coffee down to the counter and trapped her between his arms.

She couldn't move. She didn't *want* to move.

They stood like that for a long moment before he shook his head a little, as if questioning his sanity, before he placed his hand on her jaw, tugged it open, and melded his firm lips to hers. Her eyes fluttered closed of their own accord, and she was suddenly enveloped in his arms, his hand stroking her neck. He cradled her head and flicked his tongue to hers. She wrapped her arms around his shoulders and brought them up to his neck, as he kissed her gently, carefully, as though she would break.

She sighed softly and leaned into him, and he growled into her mouth. Aidan kept one hand in her hair, his fingers gentle, and pressed his other hand into the small of her back, bringing her body flush with his. He deepened the kiss, devouring her in the best of ways. Emma felt cherished, branded, and hot all over.

She pressed into him harder, and he slid his hand up her spine, sending chills throughout her overheated body. She ran her fingers through his hair, surprised at its softness. He drew her attention away from wandering thoughts, though, when, without breaking the kiss, he grasped her waist and lifted her onto the counter. He angled her head and kissed her as though his life depended on it.

She lost all coherent thought.

His hands were on her back, her shoulders, her hair, her legs. She dragged her hands up his abs, feeling the ridges of muscles and flesh; she wanted to tear his shirt off and kiss him everywhere, all at once.

"Ahem."

Dimly, she registered that someone was standing on the other side of the island, and she tried to disengage from Aidan.

"Kitchen's closed," Aidan said, his voice rough. He rested his forehead against Emma's.

"Let me know when it's open, all right? I need some coffee before I start working," Colin replied, the grin in his voice unmistakable. A few seconds later, a door opened and closed.

They looked at each other for a moment, breathing hard, and didn't say anything. Aidan flicked his gaze to her lips, and kissed her hard and deep before pulling away. "I won't apologize for that."

More confused than ever, she glared at him. "I don't know whether to slap you or...or..."

His green gaze locked on her for another moment, and he let out a sudden chuckle. "Christ, Emma, what you reduce me to. Kissing you in my cousin's kitchen."

"That felt more like ravishing," she snapped before she could stop herself. She slid off the counter.

He brought his body against hers once more, and she cursed herself for freezing in place. He leaned down, his mouth on her ear, and ran his tongue along it. "Then you've never been properly ravished," he whispered. He wagged his eyebrows at her, and she pushed away from him. He chuckled.

"I hate it when I miss a good joke," Reilly said, walking in. He was dressed similarly to Aidan, in shorts and a tee, holding a towel and a water bottle. His jaw hardened when he saw the two of them together. "You look like you're ready for our exercise this morning, MacWilliam. And your lady friend looks like she may be in need of a guardian."

"Give it a rest, O'Malley."

"I'm a Protector," Reilly said, as though that were some sort of explanation.

Emma wrinkled her brow. "What do you protect?" she asked.

"All sorts of things," he replied. "Lasses, mostly."

She arched a brow at him.

"Wolf in sheep's clothing, lass." He threw a nod toward Aidan, who gave her a quick grin and headed out the back door.

"Is it safe to enter?" Colin asked, poking his head in the kitchen. He gave her a dazzling smile and noticed the bag behind her. "Ah. I see you found the coffee."

She threw up her hands and stomped toward the stairs, leaving Colin scratching his chin in the kitchen.

CHAPTER 8

Aidan ran along the street, barely breaking a sweat. Reilly kept pace easily and, perhaps more importantly, silently. Aidan did not want to discuss the events of his morning, and certainly not with Reilly.

They made their way through the streets of Boston's Back Bay, and Aidan couldn't help but notice the signs of spring. The trees showed their green, and some residents had already filled their flower boxes with colorful tulips, daffodils, and peonies. It was pleasantly cool.

And still, Aidan couldn't shake the tension from his body.

"Were you able to find anything out?" he finally asked.

Reilly slowed. "Aye."

Aidan matched his pace. Reilly had contacts in places Aidan couldn't reach; his network was vast. And despite their contentious relationship, Aidan would always fight to the death for Reilly, and the feeling was mutual. They'd been through so much together that they couldn't not have genuine respect for each other, despite the constant needling.

Reilly avoided a large crack in the concrete. "We were followed here. He hasn't figured out where we're staying, I don't believe. I've not yet determined how desperate he is to get to your Emma."

"I wonder what he thinks she can give him?" Aidan slowed his pace further.

"Money?"

"I believe he drained her account."

"So he took her money and destroyed her apartment," Reilly mused, then stopped to take a drink. He swallowed and continued,

"And, of course, the bastard threatened her. Do you think he laid a hand on her?"

"She didn't say," Aidan replied, the hair on the back of his neck rising. "If he did, he'll pay for it."

Reilly slanted a glance at Aidan, and they both realized at the same time that the feeling on their necks hadn't anything to do with the thought of Emma being manhandled.

The weak morning sunlight glinted off a sharp switchblade, aimed point-blank at Aidan's throat.

"Where's my fiancée?" the knife-wielder demanded, his voice low.

Aidan gave Reilly a look, as though to say *Is this lad serious?*, and that was enough to set the man off. He rushed Aidan at the same time another man came at Reilly from behind.

Aidan caught Ben MacDermott by the wrist and wrestled him to the ground. He sucked in a breath when the man's foot connected with his shin. He felt the knife tip graze his chest, and his anger flared. Aidan slammed MacDermott's wrist against the hard concrete and felt the satisfying crunch of bone. MacDermott's knee came up, and Aidan easily deflected it, clucking his tongue.

"Playing dirty, Benjamin?"

"She belongs to me," he grunted as cradled his wrist. "Wherever you take her, wherever you hide her, I will find her." He spat in Aidan's face.

Aidan wiped the spit from his eyes and realized too late he'd given Ben an opening—he received a swift and painful head-butt to the nose. Blood spurted immediately, and Aidan's patience snapped.

"Not likely, Romeo. She's under my protection now."

He gave a swift jab to the man's Adam's apple, making him choke for breath, then flipped him onto his stomach and pried the knife from his hand. Quickly, he slammed the hilt of the knife against Ben's cranium, knocking him out.

Reilly sat on the bench, brushing the dirt from his hands as his assailant lay blissfully unconscious and sported a nasty bruise and broken nose. Reilly gave a jerk of his head at Ben. "Kill him?"

"I wanted to," Aidan growled, slowly standing and shaking out his wrists.

"Why didn't you?"

Sirens sounded nearby, and Aidan clenched his jaw. "He's not worth the punishment here. In my time, a sword to the stomach would end this, and that would be that."

"You know how I loathe agreeing with you, but in this case, you're correct. Let's go, before the cops get here. I have no desire to spend my morning filling out endless paperwork."

Aidan took one last look at the sorry excuse for a man Emma had almost married. His skin was sallow, his frame thin. "I want to haul this lout over my shoulder, toss him in a dungeon, then force the answers out of him. Does he work alone? Are there others who will go after her if he dies?"

"Careful," Reilly murmured, steering Aidan away from the unconscious man. "Your medieval is showing."

* * *

Lying on the couch in the front living room, Emma was so absorbed in the romance novel she'd found in Colin's office (which he swore up and down belonged to his late cousin), she almost didn't hear Aidan and Reilly come in the front door. The soft click brought her awareness to the present and she marked her page before sitting up.

She let out a strangled scream.

Aidan was covered in blood, and his shirt was ripped across his chest. Reilly looked…well, he looked as though he'd just gone for a run. Not even a hair out of place.

"What happened?" she cried, scrambling off the couch and racing to them. She glared at Reilly. "I think your ridiculous fighting crossed a line here, don't you?" She frantically ran her fingers over Aidan's chest and arms, checking for wounds.

He caught her hands in his own. "Emmaline." He repeated her name again, and she looked at him. "I'm fine. We were attacked, but it was nothing. The bugger just happened to hit me in the right spot."

"What about your shirt?" she asked. The tear was long and neatly done, as though someone had taken scissors to it and cut a long line.

"You know, I was hurt too," Reilly interjected.

"I don't see you covered in blood," Emma said in disbelief.

"I'll go have a shower, then," Aidan said, gently disentangling his fingers from hers. "Perhaps when I get out, you can check me for injury."

Emma's face flamed.

She threw her hands on her hips and gave Reilly a quick once-over. "What happened? Random attack?"

Reilly waved her in front of him and she led him into the guest bathroom. He pulled down a first-aid kit from behind the mirror and handed it to her. "I'll let Aidan have the glory of telling you. Go tend to him, but be careful, lass."

"Why do you say that?" she wondered aloud, holding his gaze.

"Because he can't say it himself."

She blinked. "How long have you known Aidan?" she asked.

He answered without hesitation. "Many years."

"And in those many years, how many women have you warned off him?"

He leveled a stare at her. "Not a one."

Her mouth dropped, and she clutched the kit against her chest as he gave her a swift nod and brushed by her.

Talk about mixed signals, she thought as he headed upstairs. She flicked the bathroom light off and glanced up the stairs after him. He warned her to stay away from Aidan, but handed her a first-aid kit, which he himself clearly didn't need.

Aidan, however…

Her brows knit, and she wondered if she would ever understand men.

She wasn't sure she *could* stay away from him. Each time his lips touched hers, an explosion went off inside her brain, and she was powerless against it. Their attraction seemed quite mutual, but he was her boss. She wouldn't lower herself to fooling around with him.

That's what she told herself every time she caught his eyes. And the refrain echoed hollowly in her own mind. And she'd gone back and forth about her ethics almost since the moment she met him.

Never before had she been so tempted by a man. Emma had wasted years on the wrong guy; she'd only dated a couple of people before she met Ben, and that was it. She'd filled out a profile on Celtic Connections, sure—but nothing ever came of it. She had turned down each date they offered her until she set her profile to "inactive." None of the men made her want to take a chance.

If she were honest with herself, she knew there was something between her and Aidan. She would also admit that she would be a fool not to explore it. But she'd been a fool before, and she once again took stock of her life.

On the run, in a strange man's home, lusting after her boss.

Oh yeah. Desirable qualities, all.

She heard the shower stop, and drew a deep breath. Perhaps... perhaps she should take a chance. She never took chances, and thus far in her life she'd merely hung on for the ride.

She was finally ready to take the wheel.

If Aidan wanted to stay away from her, he could. But she wasn't going to stay away unless she received a message from the universe, or heard the words directly from his mouth.

* * *

Aidan rested his head against the tile and let the cool air from the bathroom seep into the shower. His shoulders wouldn't relax, and his thoughts wouldn't slow down.

All because of one blonde, blue-eyed publicist who had stirred more feeling in his chest in a few days than all other women in the whole of his life combined.

He wrapped a towel around his waist and stepped out. He ran his hands through his hair and inspected himself for damage. The small scrape across his chest barely garnered notice; he'd sustained much worse injuries from much larger blades without complaint.

When he was but a boy of twelve summers, he was out riding his favorite horse, Aengus. He'd fallen, and the beast wouldn't let him back on. The creature just kept teasing him—Aidan would get close, Aengus would shimmy away, neighing and blowing. The game went on until Aidan came face-to-face with a stranger who thought Aidan was trying to steal his cattle. Aidan had taken a sword to his lower back, and the scar sat just below his waistline.

Talk about stranger danger. His childhood had been one long lesson in staying alive.

He sighed. In his recent adulthood, he had gone soft. He knew it, and a part of him was grateful for it. A small part, to be sure—he often craved the adventure of his youth. Though the world around him was full of marvels, Aidan's ennui with people grew with each passing year. Most of them were so focused on money and fame they forgot that the true measure of a man's worth was in his clan, in his connections with his past.

His brother would laugh his arse off if he were ever privy to Aidan's thoughts.

When they last saw each other, Aidan thrived on battle and vanquishing enemies. Stealing cattle from other clans so his could eat, protecting Nick and Bri with his life, volunteering for any and all missions.

About two years after he arrived in the future, Aidan began to doubt that he might return to his former life, and so he sought what adventures he could find. Now his vanquishing took place in the antiquities and real estate markets. It was a lot less bloody and filled his coffers more than any battle ever had…yet it left his soul empty.

Pushing his thoughts aside, he threw open the door and stopped short. Sitting on his bed was the lovely Emma, looking both nervous and bold at the same time.

"Needing something, lass?" he drawled, leaning a shoulder against the doorjamb. When his towel slipped a notch, he didn't bother to hitch it back up.

She blinked, her gaze moving from the top of his towel up his arms, over his chest, and finally to his eyes. He felt every bit of her stare, as evidenced by the towel hanging even more precariously over his hips.

She held up a first-aid kit and stuttered, "I, um, thought you might need this."

"And you wanted to deliver it in person?"

"I thought you would dress in the bathroom," she said lamely.

He did smile then. It wasn't a kind smile, or even a welcoming one. It was wolfish, and he could tell she knew it. She swallowed, her throat working, and Aidan took a step toward her. She didn't move, and he raised a brow in challenge.

She raised one back.

Emma Perkins surprised him at every turn, and he'd never felt more alive.

Her gaze zeroed in on his chest, and he just barely refrained from puffing it out to show off a little. The laugh that burst from her lips indicated she'd caught that small flex of his pecs.

"Now that you have me here, ready and willing to be fussed over, what are you going to do about it?" he asked. He advanced toward her slowly, his eyes fixed on hers, which were still fixed on his chest.

"What happened?" she asked, and he glanced down at the red scratch.

"A tiny, insignificant knife. Nothing to worry about," he assured her. He reached the edge of the bed, and her face was level with his hips. The towel hung low, only staying on by the grace of God.

"A tiny knife?"

Aidan saw the worry in her eyes as she rose, alarmed. He pried the kit from her arms, opened it, and pulled out the antibiotic cream. "Aye."

"Reilly's knife?"

He shook his head slowly. "Nay. Not Reilly's knife."

Her face lost some of its color, and Aidan handed her the cream silently. A surge of protectiveness crashed over him as he watched the realization dawn on her…the danger was real and he was involved. He knew there wasn't any point in lying about it.

"Did—was it Ben? Did he try to kill you?" she finally asked.

"He tried *something*. If it was an attempt on my life, it was the weakest one yet."

"Do you often have attempts on your life?" she breathed, her eyes wide with worry.

"Not anymore," he murmured. "We're going to have to leave again, Emmaline. I'm sorry."

"He told you I'm his, then?" she asked. She unscrewed the cap and squeezed some of the cream onto her fingers. "That he owns me, and that he's promised to kill me?"

"Something to that effect, aye."

"Grand," she replied softly, her brows knitting together in concentration as she gently touched her shaking fingertips to his chest.

Electricity jolted through him at her touch, and his muscles jumped. She pulled her hand back quickly.

"It hurts?"

He shook his head, unable—unwilling—to explain his reaction. She began to smooth the cream over his chest more carefully.

Her feather-light touch drove him to the brink of his restraint.

Emma carefully rubbed it into his skin before capping the tube and holding up her hand. "I need to wipe this off."

Slowly, giving her time to tell him no, he pulled the towel from around his waist and gently wiped her hand, dragging the soft cotton over the back of her hand, through her fingers, and over her palm.

She shuddered and closed her eyes.

He raised her other hand and kissed the inside of her wrist, inhaling her scent. Fresh. Clean.

His.

"This is madness," he said, his voice raw. "Tell me to go to hell, Emmaline."

"I can't," she whispered.

He kissed her palm, then took her mouth in a long, deep kiss that seared him straight to his soul.

She traced his biceps, rubbing her hands over his shoulders, and tangled her fingers into his hair. He groaned into her mouth as she pressed herself against him, her body soft, pliant, and completely at his mercy.

She was soft, willing...and completely vulnerable.

The thought was like a bucket of cold water; he broke the kiss and took in her flushed face, lush lips, and dreamy expression.

"Emma," he started.

"No," she said in a low voice.

He felt the stab of disappointment deep and tried to tell himself it was for the best.

"If I only get this one chance," she said, "this *only* chance to have you, to see what this is between us...I want it."

His heart thudded heavily against his chest. He saw honesty in her eyes, and he knew he would deny her nothing.

His lips met hers again, and he vowed to make it the best day—and night—of her life.

With what he and Reilly had planned, it might be all they could have.

CHAPTER 9

Emma couldn't believe it was happening. Aidan MacWilliam, no longer in an almost-too-small white towel, was kissing her like he was a starving man and she was a full-on feast.

All of the deep fear she'd felt a moment ago vanished when his lips moved over hers.

She clung to him tightly, reveling in the feel of his chest pressing against her shirt, dampening it with the water he hadn't bothered to towel off. His tongue shut off her brain, and her body took over. She was all sensation, his hands leaving a fiery trail wherever they touched. He broke the kiss to lift her shirt over her head, and in that moment, she was more than thankful for the baby-blue lace bra in the suitcase he'd brought for her.

She shivered at the raw hunger in his eyes.

Gently, Aidan laid her on the bed, kissing her lips, neck, ears. Her desire was building to a fever pitch. She trailed her hands down his sides, reaching for him, but he caught her wrist and gently brought it back to his mouth.

"If you touch me, this will be over before it begins," he said with a grin, tracing the back of her hand with his lips.

"We wouldn't want that," Emma breathed as he nibbled the inside of the wrist he held.

She cupped his face, and his green eyes intensified. "Emma, I will make this so good for you."

"If your kisses are any indication, I'm in for the time of my life."

"That's just the start, lass."

"Promises, promises," she teased. He arched a brow at her,

then traced her breast with his fingertip, effectively cutting off any further conversation as she sucked in a breath. "Oh…"

He kissed her again, smiling against her lips. She couldn't help but grin back.

"Having fun, Ms. Perkins?" he asked, lazily circling her navel with his fingertip.

"I am," she replied breathlessly. "Can I ask the same of you, Mr. MacWilliam?"

"So far, so good. But I'll let you know for sure when I'm finished," he replied, unsnapping her jeans with a flick of his wrist. He unzipped them, and a slow, sexy smile spread across his face when he saw that her panties matched her bra. "I don't expect to be finished for a long, long time."

In one fluid movement, he pulled her jeans off and kissed her belly. Everything south of her navel clenched in anticipation, and she closed her eyes and dropped her head back.

"Laird MacWilliam!" Someone banged on the door, hard.

Emma's eyes flew open. Aidan ignored whoever was at the door and placed a palm on her stomach, rooting her to the spot. He kissed the inside of her thigh, and a small moan escaped her.

"My laird—they went after O'Rourke as well!"

Aidan's demeanor changed so fast, Emma was still trying to identify what his expression was when he leaped off the bed and strode to the door. She barely managed to cover herself with the bed comforter when he flung the door open.

Sans towel.

"Explain," he barked.

Cian didn't even blink at the nudity. "Colin called. He just arrived here, and is safe but for a scratch on his arm."

Aidan swore and punched the wall next to the door, his fist making an impressive hole.

Emma pulled the comforter tighter around herself, her fear returning in full force.

Cian leaned in and whispered something, and Aidan nodded

grimly. "We leave within the hour. Call Les, get the jet ready. I want to be on Irish soil by tonight."

Aidan shrugged on a tee shirt. "There's something you should know about me."

Emma fumbled with her shirt. It was slightly damp from where Aidan had pressed against her.

"I'm a little…old-fashioned." He slid the zipper closed on his jeans, and Emma tried really hard not to take a moment to enjoy the way they encased his behind.

"I gathered."

"When you signed that contract, you signed on for more than just a job."

Emma paused, her shirt over her face, and thought, *Did I read that contract all the way through?*

"It's not in the document itself," he added as though he read her thoughts.

She quickly tugged her shirt the rest of the way down. "Maybe you could explain it to me, then."

• • •

Aidan looked at Emma, wondering how he would explain it to her without making her think him insane.

Brianagh had taken it well when Nioclas explained it to her. Of course, she was actually *in* the Middle Ages at that point, so perhaps she had a better sphere of reference…

He sighed. "I'm not sure that as a modern woman you'll understand the mentality behind it."

"Modern woman?" she echoed. "That sounds vaguely patronizing."

He sat on the edge of the bed. "Another cultural difference, I assure you. But I'm offering you my full protection."

"Full protection? What's that mean, exactly?"

He scratched his neck. "Well…I take care of you until you're safe."

"What does that entail, though?" she asked, her eyes hardening.

Ah, yes. Independence and trust issues. The lass was stubborn, to be sure, but he found that it didn't bother him.

The thought gave him pause. He avoided stubborn women like the plague; he had too many of those in his clan to ever want one of his own.

Or so he used to think.

"You need to disappear. No paper trails, no way to link your whereabouts—and I can make that happen."

She scuttled backward on the bed. "No thanks!"

He didn't move. "MacDermott won't stop until you're six feet underground, Emmaline."

Her eyes filled with tears. "I know."

"I can keep you safe. You just have to let me."

"I can do it on my own," she whispered. "It's easy enough to disappear."

Aidan regarded her for a long moment, weighing his words. Finally, he asked, "How?"

Emma opened her mouth, then paused. "I don't know yet. But I'll figure it out."

"How?" he asked again.

Aidan's gut twisted with her look of helplessness. It was one he figured she didn't wear very often, if ever. "I don't know," she admitted.

"Let me help you," he said softly. She jumped up from the bed and started to pace. "Like it or not, I'm involved. I have ways to protect you from him."

"I don't want to need your help," she whispered, the tears spilling onto her cheeks. "I didn't ask for this."

"You didn't," he agreed. He stood and stopped her, sliding his hands down her arms to join hers. "But you have it. And I can help you. But you have to let me."

A charged moment passed, and while she silently considered, Aidan said more prayers than he had cumulatively in the whole of his life.

"Okay."

He released a breath. "Your trust isn't misplaced, Emma. You have ten minutes to be downstairs, and we're leaving in fifteen. Grab what you can and I'll buy you more when we get there!" he called over his shoulder as he thumped down the stairs.

• • •

"...a month, maybe more." Aidan was on the phone when Emma cautiously entered the kitchen.

"Let's roll." Reilly bounced on his heels. "I'm ready."

"Reilly loves to fly," Aidan explained wryly.

"I do," he confirmed. "A metal bird in the sky that I control? Oh, aye. Definitely aye."

"Wait. You pilot the plane?"

Reilly smirked. "Private pilot's license."

"Les will be flying this time, though," Aidan said with a roll of his eyes. "He's meeting us at Logan."

"We're really doing this," Emma said, dazed.

"Cian, bring Ms. Perkins's bags to the car," Aidan instructed. "Colin, tell your mother that I'm sorry to have missed her."

"No way," Colin said with a glare. "*You* can tell her when you next see her."

Aidan gave a slight shake of his head, and Colin paused before he nodded back, resigned.

"Be well, uncle."

"You too, nephew. Take care of things if they don't go as planned," Aidan said with a finality that, in Emma's opinion, was a bit unnecessary. Did they say goodbye like this every time?

Well, every family had their weird quirks, she supposed.

"When do they ever go as planned?" Colin replied, and they both grinned like fools before pulling each other into a tight hug. They slapped backs, and Emma looked away when she noticed Colin's damp eyes.

"Emma. I can't thank you enough," Colin said, pulling her into his arms. The hug surprised her; she felt like she'd had more human contact in the last hour than in the last ten years. She awkwardly hugged him back.

"You don't have to thank me," she replied.

"I do." He lowered his voice. "Can you keep a secret?"

"I'm a publicity manager, remember? Secrets are second nature to me."

"God, I hope so," Aidan muttered.

"What was that?" she asked.

"Ready to go," he said, louder.

Colin beamed at her, then whispered in her ear, "In all my years of knowing Aidan, he's never looked so alive. Thanks for letting him take care of you."

She blushed and managed a nod. She was uncomfortable enough realizing that she needed help; it only made things worse when it was acknowledged.

She gave Colin a little wave as they walked outside, where Cian had a black SUV waiting. She slid into the vehicle, and Cian shut the door behind her. She glanced at Reilly, who was sitting in the front seat. When she caught Aidan's eye, he didn't look away. He returned her stare grimly.

"This is not how I wanted to spend my day," he said, surly.

She laughed, causing Reilly to turn around.

"It's for the best," Reilly said pointedly.

"When did you become her sire?" Aidan muttered.

"The moment I met her," Reilly retorted. His eyes softened when he focused on Emma. "You're safe with me, lass."

"But not with Aidan?" she couldn't help but tease.

"Not even close," Aidan murmured so only she could hear. Her pulse fluttered. "Cian, what's our current flight status?"

* * *

They pulled directly onto the tarmac, and Cian drove straight to a private hangar. Before he even had the SUV in park, all doors opened and airport personnel helped Emma out of the car and into the waiting jet. A cheery flight attendant handed her a mimosa, and a uniformed officer checked their passports and luggage.

Even Aidan MacWilliam couldn't escape TSA.

Emma looked around in awe. The jet was lushly appointed; the cream-colored seats faced each other in groups of four, a table separating them into cozy conversational areas. Outlets were everywhere, and she hadn't missed when the flight attendant pressed a button to lower the giant television screen into a discreet compartment in the floor. The minibar at the front of the cabin had a blue light around it, and a door at the back of the cabin stood open, displaying the stewardess's prep station.

Reilly slid into the seat facing her and let out a heavy sigh. "I hate when Les is the pilot."

"Why?"

Reilly pouted, transforming instantly from a man to a boy. "He doesn't let me in the cockpit."

Emma stared for a moment, then burst out laughing. "You're kidding."

"Nay," Reilly said, shaking his head sadly. "He follows the rules all the time. Makes for a stodgy life, if you ask me."

"Stodgy?" she repeated.

"Dull. Boring. Uninspired," Aidan said as he joined them. "Also could describe Reilly on a typical day." To Reilly he added, "Back off Les. He does a fine job of flying this beast, and you could learn a thing or two from him."

"If he let me at the controls, I might," Reilly muttered punitively.

Aidan ignored him. "Mandy's loading the food and we should be in the air shortly."

"Who's Mandy?" Emma asked.

"The flight attendant," Reilly replied, pulling out a book and popping in earbuds.

A flash of something raced through Emma at the nickname, and her eyes narrowed as she remembered the woman who'd handed her the mimosa. The attendant's nametag had clearly said *Amanda*. Not Mandy.

"Easy," Aidan murmured, amusement lighting his eyes. "I've no desire to see bloodshed over a mere name."

"I don't know what you're talking about."

"Mmmhmm," was all he said.

"Mr. MacWilliam, it's a pleasure to serve you again. Would you care for a drink?" Amanda asked, oblivious to Emma's stiffness.

"Please, Mandy, an orange juice would be fine. How's Paula?"

The flight attendant's eyes lit up like the fourth of July. "She's wonderful. I can't believe she's six months old already!" She grinned at Emma. "Paula's my baby. Named her after my husband, Paul." She gave a sheepish smile. "Sorry. I get a bit carried away when it comes to them."

"No worries," Emma managed to say. "Congratulations."

Amanda went off to get Aidan's drink, and Emma refused to look at him.

"Mmmhmm," he repeated.

She ignored him and settled the small sleep mask over her face. Unfortunately, it didn't block out his infuriating chuckles.

* * *

As they flew over the Atlantic, Aidan reluctantly put thoughts of Emma, naked in his bed, aside. He needed to make plans. Contingency plans, in case things went awry.

Aidan pulled out his phone and powered it on. A flood of voicemails, emails, and texts came through, prompting Emma to look up in surprise.

"I thought I was the only one who had your number?" Her voice was deceptively mild, but Aidan heard the note of jealousy.

"This is my work number," he said, holding up the BlackBerry. "You have my personal, American one. When we land, I'll obtain a mobile for you. With my *personal* Irish number."

She rolled her eyes. "I'm disappearing, remember?"

"To everyone else," he reminded her. "Never to me. I'll get you a secured line."

"Sometimes I forget just how wealthy you are," she murmured, then turned her attention back to the screen.

His defenses rose. "It's just money, Emma. It doesn't define me," he snapped.

"I didn't mean to imply it did," she replied. "I'm sorry."

"Don't apologize to him, lass," Reilly said, walking toward them from the front of the plane, a Guinness in his hand. "It'll just go to his head."

"Les still won't let you in the cockpit?" Aidan guessed.

Reilly's face darkened. "He threatened to call the bobbies when we land if I didn't return to my seat," he growled. "As if they could ever stop me."

Emma watched Reilly silently.

"What?" he asked, shifting under her gaze.

"What kind of things couldn't they stop you from doing, exactly?"

He settled into his seat. "Nothing for you to worry about."

She stared at him so silently for so long, even Aidan felt the need to squirm.

"Emma, ignore him. He's put out about not piloting, is all." Aidan folded his arms.

"Where are we staying?"

"Reilly's, to start. Then I plan to head home."

"Where will I go?"

"With me."

She had the grace to flush. "I've been thinking about it, and I think it's best if we keep things…professional between us."

"Smart," Reilly agreed.

"No one asked for your opinion," Aidan said, resisting the urge to open the emergency exit and toss Reilly into the water below. He concentrated on Emma. "I had an alternate impression earlier today."

She threw him a glare that would freeze the depths of hell. "I'm aware. And I've had plenty of time to think about it. I won't make that mistake again."

Reilly whistled. "Ouch."

Aidan's eyes narrowed to slits. "O'Malley, tell Les that if he doesn't let you in that cockpit, this will be his last flight on my jet."

"Woohoo!" Reilly exclaimed, all five-year-old boy as he leaped out of his seat and charged back to the cockpit door.

"Cian, remove yourself to the washroom," Aidan commanded. Cian, who had been sitting near the bathroom, looking miserable with a bag clutched tightly in his hand, immediately unfastened his seatbelt and closed the small door behind him. Amanda discreetly closed the door to the back cabin.

"Care to explain what mistake you're referring to?" Aidan asked, his voice deadly calm.

She crossed her legs. "You don't scare me, MacWilliam. Everyone else might jump as high as you demand, but I won't."

He didn't move. "That's a poor explanation."

She clasped her hands in front of her. "I made a stupid, rash decision earlier. The universe stepped in and stopped us from making a colossal mistake. I accept that truth. You're not even my type," she finished firmly, apparently not noticing his expression progressively darken.

"Excuse me?" he barked. "What did you just say?"

She blushed, but refused to give any ground. "You're not my type."

He sat back and crossed his arms. "What, exactly, is your type, Emma? From where I sit, your *type* isn't exactly working for you."

"You don't know anything about me!"

He closed his mouth, instantly regretting his words and temper. She sniffed, and his gut twisted at the anguish on her face.

"Did you so truly love him?" he asked softly.

"You don't have the right to ask that question. And you certainly don't have the privilege to know the answer."

He saw it then. Fear, uncertainty, vulnerability. It was written all over her lovely face, tied into her anger. With sudden clarity, he realized he'd need to do more than seduce her in order to gain her heart.

He let out a sigh. He didn't care to argue with her. His phone rang, and he didn't take his eyes off Emma as he answered.

"Colin."

"I have a bad feeling. The same one I had about eight years ago, which preceded a phone call from Reilly detailing your arrival."

Aidan's stomach clenched. "Damn."

Colin—like Reilly—had instincts that were not to be ignored. Both men could bend time to their will when they had to.

"Reilly's not picking up his phone."

"I sent him to the cockpit," Aidan admitted.

"Nah, it's been off longer than your flight. You must've been desperate to get Emma alone if you sent him to fly your plane."

"Did you need me to pass along a message, perhaps?" Aidan asked, annoyed.

"Yes. Let him know that I know what's up, and that I'll take care of things on this end, but he has to get himself back to Brianagh soon."

Aidan didn't envy Colin and Reilly's duties as O'Rourke Protectors, but he did envy their unique travel plans. Colin mostly traveled with Reilly, though Aidan suspected him of doing a fair bit on his own. Reilly, however, could bend time to whenever the need arose, although he claimed he could only do so with the permission of the Fates.

Despite years of asking, Reilly had thus far refused to take Aidan with them on any journey, claiming that he hadn't been given explicit permission to do so.

It was their biggest sore spot to date.

Aidan had been desperate to return to his brother and sister-in-law. From a very young age, Aidan's sole purpose in life was to guard his brother's back. And just when he needed him the most, Aidan ended up in a ditch somewhere, close to death…only to be rescued by Reilly O'Malley and Colin O'Rourke.

For that, he would do anything for either of them. But when it came to Reilly, he didn't have to like it.

Aidan checked his watch. "I'll let him know." He glanced at Emma, who was staring defiantly out the window, her arms crossed. "Any news on our friend?"

"Posted bail from the hospital about an hour ago. He hasn't shown up here, so I'm not sure if he's off the scent or not. It would make life a lot easier if you could just kill the man and be done with it," Colin added with a sigh.

"Modern times are..." Aidan searched for the word.

"Wimpy?"

Aidan snickered. "I was thinking 'refined.' But yours applies too." He hung up and leaned into Emma's seat, trapping her with his arms. "This is not over, Emmaline. I'll be damned if I'm just your *client*."

"Technically, you're my boss," she muttered.

He gave her a scathing look, then went to talk with Reilly. He rapped on the cockpit door. Les swore from inside.

"MacWilliam, I swear, if you don't get him out of my copilot's seat, I will quit before you can fire me," Les threatened.

"O'Malley, I need you in the main cabin. Message from Colin."

Reilly's face changed instantly. His body seemed to grow larger, and he nodded once to the copilot, who stood in the small space between the wall and copilot's seat.

"First time flying with us?" Aidan asked. The man nodded, trying to appear relaxed. Aidan slapped him on the shoulder. "Rule number one: you don't see or hear anything. Right, Les?"

"Get out, MacWilliam. First Officer Davidson, lock that door behind them."

Aidan followed Reilly to the main cabin. The cockpit door clicked closed behind them.

He relayed the message and Reilly sighed heavily. "I have to go back."

Aidan nodded solemnly. "The renovations at my keep are

loud and bothersome. I'll keep an eye on your cottage whilst you're away, then."

Reilly scrutinized him for a full minute. "You're not going to ask me to come along?"

Every time Aidan thought Reilly might be headed back in time, he asked to go. Every time, Reilly turned him down, and every time, Aidan grew a bit more resentful.

But not this time.

Aidan shook his head. "I'm needed here."

* * *

It was really dark.

That was Emma's first thought as she opened her eyes and the jet taxied into the hangar. She glanced at the large clock hanging on the silver hangar wall, illuminated with fluorescent lights outside her tiny window.

Eight thirty.

The jet slowed to a stop, and Les cut the engine. Amanda opened the door as two men wheeled a staircase across the floor to meet it, and a moment later, Reilly went out to greet them.

Emma sighed softly and closed her eyes again. After years of wishing, hoping, and dreaming, she was finally in Ireland.

"Wake up, Emma. We're here," Aidan called.

She scowled. The man couldn't give her a moment's peace. He'd scoffed when she flipped on the latest *Thor* film and made derogatory comments about the superhero. She'd merely turned the volume up and tuned him out.

"Coffee for the road, miss?" Amanda asked, holding a steaming to-go cup. Emma accepted it, then closed her eyes again, mentally exhausted. The aroma of the brew reminded her of her last almost-cup of coffee, when she stood in Colin's kitchen and tried to work his machine. It seemed like a lifetime ago.

"Emma, I'm going to bring your bags to the car. Cian's not fully recovered from the trip." Aidan towered above her, resting his forearm on her seatback. "We'll clear customs before leaving the hangar, then get going. Maybe grab some food. Are you hungry?"

"Is it always like this?" she asked. He frowned, so she clarified, "No time for second thoughts. Go, go, go."

A ghost of a smile played at his lips. "Nay, Emma. It's rarely like this. I hope it will slow down considerably once we get to our final destination."

"Where is that, exactly?" she asked. For the last couple of hours, Aidan and Reilly had huddled together, talking in low voices and mapping out all sorts of plans. After straining to hear them, then realizing they were speaking in Gaelic again, she gave up and put her headphones on, deciding Thor was much better company than either of them. Of course, once Aidan realized she was watching a very beautiful man, he'd become downright belligerent, almost to the point of preventing her from enjoying the movie.

Lucky for her, she was an expert at tuning out white noise. She'd fallen asleep to the surly look on Aidan's face.

"The west coast," Aidan answered.

"Why didn't we fly into Shannon?"

"We were only cleared for Dublin. Tonight, we'll stay at Reilly's cottage outside the city."

"They're ready," Reilly interrupted them, sticking his head inside the door. He caught sight of Cian, who was still green from the trip. "Cian, you head out first. Careful."

Cian managed a nod, then slowly exited the plane.

Emma watched him go. "I feel awful for him. Is he like that every time you fly?"

"Aye," Aidan said. "You'd think he'd get used to it, but he still claims it's unnatural to ride about in the air. He'd much rather a beast under him than nothing at all."

"You mean, like a horse?"

"Aye. Have you ever ridden before?"

Emma grimaced. "Yes."

Amused, he asked, "Did you enjoy it?"

"Absolutely not. It was a nasty thing, kept trying to bite me. I don't like horses."

"How big was it?" he asked.

"Well, I was thirteen at the time, and it came up to my shoulder. So, pretty huge," she replied seriously.

He laughed. "Oh, Emma. That was a pony. Not a horse."

She glared at him. "It was big, and it wasn't worth the five bucks. I didn't trust it."

"Perhaps I can take you for a ride. Show you how trustworthy a true steed can be," Aidan replied.

His eyes told her he was talking about a lot more than horses, but she still hesitated. Yes, she had gone to his room with the hopes of seeing where her feelings led her. But once she came to her senses, her old fears reared their ugly heads.

Aidan was a wealthy, beautiful man. Power and strength oozed from his pores, and he had a killer accent to top it all off. He was sure to have women fall all over him—even if they didn't know the contents of his bank account, his looks alone made him a marked man. And she had firsthand knowledge that he looked even better with his clothes off.

She wasn't immune. Aidan was the most masculine man she'd ever met, and her hormones were all over that like white on rice. But she knew where this kind of thing led. She'd seen it countless times—man and woman meet. Man gets woman into bed. Woman finds out man is married. Someone finds out and threatens to tell, and Emma Perkins is there, ready with the pen, to spin it around.

She'd had enough spinning in her personal life to last two lifetimes. She knew, deep in her bones, if she let Aidan in, she'd never be able to let him go.

She knew she wouldn't be able to handle it when he left, which he certainly would do. Her only relationship was proof enough of her shortcomings. She had thought things with Ben were perfect, and though the pictures of him with another woman had blindsided her, so had the realization that she was more invested in the relationship than he ever was. How would she know when Aidan would tire of her? He was worldly, from a different class than she. He'd get bored with her plain-Janeness, her desire to stay in and read a book rather than go out on the town. She was a homebody, and he was a jet-setter. He was Adonis, and she did not want to end up like Aphrodite in that sad tale. No, it was better if she admired from afar.

She had the perfect excuse. Her temporary insanity this morning aside, she really did work for Aidan. She was contracted not only by him but also by Celtic Connections—of which he was a stakeholder. Therefore, he was totally, completely off-limits to her.

She would not be like Heidi and sleep with her boss.

A voice at the back of her mind whispered that it wasn't the same, but she crushed it.

"I think I'm safest if I stick with what I know," she finally said.

"What would that be?" he asked, leaning forward slightly.

She refused to shrink back. "My own two feet."

"MacWilliam, let's go. They're waiting," Reilly said, popping his head back into the cabin.

Aidan gave Emma a searching look, then apparently let it go. She breathed a silent sigh of relief, and walked out of the jet when he waved her in front of him.

"Thank you for flying with us, Ms. Perkins," Amanda said.

Aidan kissed the back of Amanda's hand, although Emma noticed it was much different from the kisses he gave her on her own hand.

She tried not to examine that too closely.

"Amanda, give your husband my regards."

"Of course," she replied brightly. "Take care, Mr. MacWilliam."

They walked down the stairs, two customs officials waiting to greet them and check passports. Emma pinched herself when a tiny shiver of excitement ran up her spine.

She really was in Ireland. She couldn't wait to explore.

CHAPTER 10

Jet lag was going to be the death of her.

Unable to sleep, Emma rolled out of the exceedingly comfortable bed in Reilly's guest room and padded across the floor, pulling the curtain back. The moon bathed the landscape in a bright blue. She caught her breath at the beauty surrounding the cottage.

Reilly was blessed, indeed. He lived down a private drive, surrounded by trees. The drive opened up to the cottage, like something out of a fairy tale. Inside was just as perfect—the slanted walls, uneven floors, bright paint, and, most of all, the thatched roof.

How she adored thatched-roof cottages.

The back yard (*garden*, she reminded herself) was marked with a low stone wall that extended from either side of the building and straight back, squaring off to create a neat rectangle of perfectly manicured lawn. Beyond the far wall was green, as far as she could see, sweeping gracefully over hills, up to the tree line in the distance, perhaps half a mile or more away. Directly outside the back door was a neatly tilled vegetable garden; empty pots, tools, and baskets lay on the ground, ready for use.

Aidan had, thankfully, backed off her a little. Instead of kissing her senseless in the doorway when he showed her the guest room, he kissed her knuckles and gave a small bow.

She loved and hated how that left her even more breathless than a passionate embrace.

And there was the crux of her problem. She stared out the window, more confused than ever. Never had she been involved in such a complicated nonrelationship.

Drawing the blanket around her shoulders, Emma carefully

unlatched the window and pushed it open. The air whooshed in, and the strands of her hair danced on the wind. She closed her eyes and drew in a strengthening breath.

She had no idea what to do next. She had foolishly opened an emotional door, and while Aidan wasn't forcing it to remain open, he certainly refused to let it slam shut.

Her life was a mess.

A quiet voice caught her attention, and she craned her neck to find its source. Directly below her window, the back door opened, a shaft of yellow light spilling onto the vegetable garden. A shadow appeared, growing smaller as Aidan walked out, ending a call on his phone. He tossed it onto the tiny bistro table on the patio, then drew the sword he'd bought at the auction from its scabbard at his side.

Emma held her breath as he examined it, the steel flashing in the moonlight. He inspected every inch of it, from the hilt to the tip, and then he sat down in the grass, the sword across his lap, a box next to him.

Emma cocked her head, wondering what he was doing. When he pulled out a long metal file from the box, she was intrigued. He slowly dragged the file over first one, then the other edge of the blade, carefully and methodically wiping the metal after each stroke of the file.

He's restoring it, she realized. She'd figured he'd get a professional to do that; after all, he had paid a hefty sum to possess it. Why take a chance and ruin it?

He pulled a small glass bottle and a large, rectangular stone from the box. He tipped the bottle and a shiny liquid poured into his hand. He smoothed it over the stone, then wiped his hand on the grass and picked up his sword again. He dragged the blade against the stone, wiped it, then repeated the motion.

Her eyes almost popped out of her head when she finally understood how he was restoring the blade, and it sent shivers up her spine.

He was sharpening his sword—using a file, oil, and a whetstone. The same way they did in the Middle Ages.

She watched, fascinated, as he rhythmically rubbed the edge of the blade down the stone. He paid particular attention to the tip, honing it to a fine point, then carefully flipped the sword over and repeated the sharpening on the opposite edge. After long minutes, he inspected his work, packed up his supplies, and headed back inside.

Emma stepped back from the window, more confused than ever. Aidan had spent more than a half hour performing a medieval task like he'd been doing it the whole of his life. He could also expertly dress himself in an authentic léine, and he fluently spoke an almost unknown form of Gaelic.

The man had so many mysterious layers wrapped around him, Emma wondered if she'd ever know the real Aidan MacWilliam.

Don't get involved. She closed the window and climbed back into bed, even more confused than when she'd rolled out of it. *Your life is too complicated. Adding a relationship—especially with Aidan—would make it even worse.*

She knew she was right. But she didn't understand why she felt so compelled to ignore herself.

* * *

It had been a full, blissful month of sightseeing.

Aidan had driven her, without complaint, around the beautiful island. Emma had kissed the Blarney Stone, danced after hours in Irish pubs, and roamed the ancient streets of Dublin. She wandered through Bunratty Castle, listening to the tour guide spout interesting facts in one ear while trying to shush Aidan's constant commentary in the other.

Aidan didn't agree with the man on most things about medieval life; apparently his love of the time period extended further than antiquities. Emma was impressed by the number of times Aidan quietly corrected the "facts"—and she wondered what his sources were.

She stood in slack-jawed wonder at the Book of Kells, she

wandered the grounds of Trinity College, and she meandered across the beautiful, many-hued green fields of Tipperary.

And with each day, she fell a little bit more in love with Aidan MacWilliam.

He made it easy, of course. His words were always followed by action. *Are you chilled, Emmaline?* He handed her a stunning Aran sweater from the Blarney Mills. *Who knows when you'll return to this castle, lass. Go ahead and have another run up those stairs. I'll be right behind you.* He caught her as she tripped—again—on the uneven stairs at Dunguaire Castle. *I've arranged a private viewing of the Book of Kells. I thought you might fancy a few hours with it.* He sat quietly at one of the tables in the famous Long Room, surrounded by thousands of manuscripts, patiently waiting for her to go through a selection of pages with one of the staff members.

The man was chivalry personified.

But he made no move to kiss her. He held her hand as they walked from place to place. He even held her hand as they drove across the country and back again. He rubbed distracting circles with his thumb, tracing the sensitive parts of her hand, making her hum with pleasure.

But still, he didn't kiss her.

Maybe, she thought more than once, and more than a bit ruefully, she had been a little *too* successful in her speech, back when they first arrived.

As spring slowly turned toward summer, Emma had seen more of Ireland than she had ever hoped to in her lifetime. Every new place was more beautiful than the last, and she was hard-pressed to think of going back to the States.

Ever.

. . .

"I vow to you, he insisted," Aidan said, resisting the childish urge to roll his eyes.

"I still feel strange living in Reilly's house while he's not here,"

Emma replied. "We've been here for five weeks, and he's been gone almost all of them."

Aidan glanced out the back window of Ry's kitchen, his eyes again scanning the tree line for any sight of his cousin. Reilly had departed a few days after they'd arrived in Dublin, headed back to take care of an issue with Brianagh's eldest daughter, Claire. Before he left, Reilly warned Aidan that he might be a long time in returning. Aidan understood; sometimes Reilly would be gone for a few hours, and other times, weeks.

This time, though, Aidan didn't begrudge the man and his abilities. He hadn't any pressing desire to return to the Middle Ages, not when he finally had a reason to stay in the present.

That reason was currently listing all the reasons why she felt guilty about her current situation.

"Emma," he finally said, holding a hand up. "Relax. You have no deadlines, no bosses demanding your energy. Just you, and me, and wherever you want to go." *As long as we keep a low profile*, he silently added, *and draw no attention to us, you're safe.*

She blew out a breath, puffing strands of her hair outward. "You keep saying that."

"And you keep ignoring it."

She smiled then, and Aidan felt his heart constrict. Had any other woman of his acquaintance ever moved him in such ways? Her laugh, which was frequent now that she had managed to distance herself from her New York life, was the sweetest sound his ears had ever heard. And her face had softened as the worry lines and tension left her.

If he'd thought her beautiful before, now, as she settled into Ireland, she was absolutely radiant.

"We've discussed this to death. You are on a much-deserved holiday. A sabbatical, if you will. Colin's in agreement; he wants you fresh-faced and excited, not drawn and dispassionate."

She pursed her lips. "You're wrong."

"And you're stunning. Finish your breakfast, love, as we're headed to a special place today."

Her eyes brightened, and his chest grew even tighter. The wonder in those violet depths stirred something in his soul, and though he'd been holding himself back for weeks, his heart was very nearly lost to Emma.

If only she felt the same way.

But she had made her intentions clear. They worked together—or would, once Aidan determined she was safe enough from MacDermott to do so—and that was enough for her to put the brakes on their relationship.

He promised himself he wouldn't touch her again until she asked for it. Begging would be ideal, but he wasn't a fool. He didn't think Emma begged for anything.

And though he tried, he couldn't help but hold her hand. It was a simple pleasure, one he refused to deny himself. She didn't pull away, nor did she seem averse to it, so he continued to hold it, embracing the little bolt of electricity each time they made contact.

Never before had a lass so undone him with a look, or a laugh, or—the saints preserve him—a happy sigh.

"So where are we going? And are we taking the Mercedes?"

He chuckled. Her love of that automobile had been obvious from the moment she slid into it. "Aye, we can take that beast. I'd like to show you my home."

"You mean the place you're renovating?"

He nodded, clearing their dishes from the table.

"Reilly told me it has a thatched roof, like this one."

"That it does."

"And that it's bigger than this house, although I think this is charming." She looked around her and smiled. "Though it be small, 'tis mighty."

He laughed. "You're sounding more Irish every day."

She flushed. "I can't take credit for that one. I read it somewhere."

Aidan glanced out the window, and his gazed locked on the lone figure loping across the garden, a sword resting against his shoulder and his boots strapped with knives. A movement further out caught his eye, and he squinted at the second person in the distance, who melted back into the trees almost as suddenly as he had appeared.

"Change in plans," he murmured. Louder, he said to Emma, "Would you mind checking the car for my jacket while I finish up in here?"

"Sure." She headed out the front door, swiping the keys off the table in the living room. The moment the door clicked shut behind her, Aidan stepped out the back door and gave Reilly the signal that all wasn't yet clear for him to return.

Aidan scanned the tree line once more, but he saw nothing. He headed back inside as Reilly made himself scarce, and rubbed his jaw.

Reilly was back. But who the hell had followed him home?

* * *

Aidan pushed back from the table, his belly pleasantly full. Flagging the server, he ordered another glass of wine for Emma and whiskeys for him and Reilly.

"Are you trying to liquor me up?" Emma asked, placing her napkin on the table next to her dish.

Which, he noted smugly, was nearly licked clean.

He had a lot of pride in this restaurant. It had been his first foray into the unknown world of food and food service; Colin and Colin's brother, James, had pushed him to take a risk with it. At the time, he needed to do something more than land ownership (which in modern times had a completely different meaning than it did in his own). After he sold most of his belongings for coin (people paid a lot of money for things he used in everyday life), he figured the next step was to become a landowner. He thought he'd be managing a clan, or at the very least allowing people to live a comfortable life under his lairdship when he purchased a large parcel of land on the coastline of the North Atlantic.

He didn't realize that, in modern-day Ireland, a landowner

was not a laird. It merely meant unpopulated acreage and an overpriced tax bill.

James understood Aidan's need to do something important. Growing up, Aidan's own brother had regularly placed him in charge of obtaining food for their clan. Aidan would ride out, see what he could do to rope a beast or steal cattle, and help feed his people. James thought it might be a good idea for him to invest in a failing restaurant, as it would save jobs, giving employees financial stability. It would also feed others, giving them nourishment.

James was right. It was perfect for him. He managed people well, and was careful with coin. In a strange way, his upbringing gave him what Colin called "people skills" to make this modern business work, and work well.

The restaurant they currently sat in was the original Colcannon. It too was decorated in medieval Irish style, but the decor was not as upscale as his New York location. It had a cozier feel; tables and chairs were mismatched, a fire roared in the much smaller hearth, and the bar stools weren't rooted to the floor. People stood, sat, and milled about, comfortably interacting with each other.

"The food here is delicious," Emma said, interrupting his thoughts.

"Aye. Liam knows his way about a kitchen," Aidan agreed, referring to his head chef.

"He certainly does," Emma agreed. "Welcome back, Reilly. Thanks for letting me crash at your house."

"I'm happy it was of use to you. I hear you're headed to Aidan's home tomorrow?"

"Yes! I can't wait to see it."

"Sorry I derailed those plans today. But his house—you'll enjoy it, to be sure. He secured himself a prime bit of land on the coast. It's his ancestral holding."

"A real estate deal gone well," Aidan corrected.

"Whatever you want to call it," Reilly said mildly, "his family's owned that spot for hundreds of years."

"Family history is fascinating," Emma responded, her eyes

shining. "I traced mine back to England in the 1600s, but that's as far as I went with it."

"There must be *some* Irish in your blood," Reilly mused.

She raised an eyebrow. "Why do you say that?"

He shrugged. "No reason."

Aidan drained what was left in his glass. "Ry, no politics. Especially old news politics. Not today."

"Fair enough," Reilly agreed easily. "It's not really politics, though. Merely a bit of discussion."

"Here we go," Aidan muttered.

Emma laughed. "While you two start squabbling again, I'm going to head to the ladies' room."

After pointing her in the general direction, Aidan watched her until she was out of sight.

Reilly let out a low whistle. "Try not to be quite so obvious in your affections, MacWilliam. I've heard it turns the lassies off."

Aidan raised an eyebrow. "You would know best about turning lassies off, O'Malley." He rubbed a hand over his jaw. "I suggest you leave it alone."

Reilly ignored him. "She's seen your suave side, your business side. She thinks she's seen the worst you have to offer. But she hasn't seen your true side. The uncivilized side. Am I right?"

"Enough," Aidan growled. There was no way in hell she would ever need to know about his uncivilized side. She'd think him daft at best, deranged at worst.

A medieval man, living in the twenty-first century? Oh, aye. She'd laugh herself all the way to the airport.

"It's a hard tale to believe," Reilly continued, ignoring him.

Aidan counted to ten, concentrating on his breathing. Sitting in the same room as Reilly O'Malley and not blowing up every time the man opened his mouth was one of his proudest accomplishments. It had taken him almost five years to master the urge to throttle him.

"I honestly thought," Aidan managed to bite out, "that you and I had come to some sort of peace agreement. Pity. I hate being wrong."

"Takes a man to admit it," Reilly offered. "That will serve you well once you marry."

"I don't plan to marry," Aidan grumbled. "Laird's younger brother. No need."

"Need. A strong term," Reilly mused. "If you've found your mate, then why fight destiny?"

"Why, indeed?" Switching subjects, he asked, "Care to tell me about your latest escapade into the past?"

Reilly's face shuttered. "Believe me when I say you'd best not ask."

For the first time since Aidan had laid eyes on Reilly eight years earlier, he could feel the man's weariness, as though his soul were tired of its destiny.

"Will you suffer greatly for it?"

Reilly ran a hand over his face. "I do not know. I'm hoping they'll not care overmuch."

"Who?"

"The Fates," Reilly replied.

"Do you mean the Tuatha Dé Danann? They're mythical—"

"You do not know," Reilly snapped, then dropped his shoulders. "I answer to a higher power than the Tuatha Dé Danann. You cannot possibly understand, and I hope that you never have to."

Aidan looked at him speculatively. "How old are you?"

Reilly laughed. "Age is irrelevant where time's concerned, lad."

"Are you immortal?"

Reilly shook his head. "No. But I won't die until they decide it, and they've use of me yet."

"The Fates?" Aidan asked, a tremor passing through him at the thought. Growing up, he'd heard the stories of the Tuatha Dé Danann—powerful druid deities. His clan loved a good story, so Aidan had always taken them for tales of morality and warning. But a higher power?

"I won't tell you," Reilly replied firmly.

"Why not?"

Reilly leveled him with a stare. "That's enough. I'll wait for you and your lady in the car." He pushed back from the table and left without another word. Aidan watched him go, his curiosity more than piqued, but Reilly was nothing if not stubborn.

* * *

The next morning, Emma couldn't sleep. Though it was at least a couple of hours before dawn, she was fully awake, excited to see Aidan's home. He'd promised her it wasn't anything spectacular, but she desperately wanted to see him in his own surroundings. She donned a long skirt and long-sleeved shirt, as the mornings tended to be chilly, and quietly headed downstairs to start breakfast.

Walking into the kitchen, she noticed Reilly's cell phone sitting on the counter. She made a mental note to tell him that it was downstairs, then grabbed a glass from the cabinet and headed to the sink. Her eyes drifted out the back window, and in the predawn mist, she saw Reilly walking toward the woods.

Without giving it a second thought, she grabbed his phone off the counter and ran out the door. He was almost to the trees, and she knew he wouldn't hear her if she called out, so she picked up her pace. When she got to the forest, she saw him disappear into a thickly wooded area. She called out then, but he didn't respond.

"Emma!" Aidan bellowed from behind her. She turned. He was headed toward her at a fast clip.

She barely glanced at him, and held up the phone to indicate she was going to give it to Reilly before heading into the forest.

A couple minutes in, though, the entire place seemed to change. There was a thick mist that covered the ground. Every step she took displaced some of the fog, showing her bits of forest floor underneath by the light of the moon. She carefully made her way deeper, looking for any signs of Reilly, before the mist fully descended upon her.

"Uh oh," she said aloud, turning in a circle.

She could make out large tree trunks, clusters of low-lying

ferns, and some tree roots nearby. But everything else remained shrouded in the dense fog, lit by an eerie bluish light.

"Hello, Emmaline."

Emma shrieked and stumbled backward, tripping on a tree root. She looked up, her jaw slack, as Ben materialized from the haze.

"You are so hard to track down, with your rich new boyfriend covering your tracks. A private jet, Emma? Really?" He slowly walked toward her, his eyes glued to hers. His disheveled clothes matched his rumpled hair, and there was at least a week's growth of beard on his normally shaved face.

Haggard, Emma thought dimly. *He looks haggard.*

"We've been over this before. *You. Are. Mine.*"

"We broke up," Emma said, her voice shaking a little. She clenched her fists. "I'm not yours anymore."

Ben laughed, a high-pitched, maniacal sound that frightened Emma more than his threats ever had. "No, Emma. You're mine forever."

She scuttled backward, her hands slipping on the wet forest floor. "What do you want, Ben? You took all my money. I've got nothing left!"

His smile was gone in an instant. "You're not listening, Emmaline. I hate it when you don't listen to me." He reached around himself and drew a gun from the back of his belt. He stroked it lovingly. "I want you, Emma. You're mine. But you left to be with *him*. That's not all right, Emmaline. No, not at all. I told you. I was nothing but honest, you see."

She froze, her eyes locked on the weapon held loosely in his hand. "How did you get out of the States, Ben?"

He laughed again, but this time it sounded desperate. "Oh, I owe some big drug lords a lot of money. They can do so much with the power they have. Getting me to you was easy! But you don't want me anymore. I told you that no one else would ever have you. But you didn't listen. You never listen, Emmaline."

Her throat was dry and her body was shaking, but she slowly stood up.

He watched her dispassionately. "You gave yourself to MacWilliam. Now you're used goods, and I can't have you again. So that means no one can." He raised the gun at her, and she opened her mouth to scream—

She was knocked to the ground at the same time the gun fired. Then someone hauled her to her feet and grabbed her around the waist, swinging her away from Ben.

"Run," Aidan urged, and she didn't have to think twice. She ran...almost smack into a huge chest.

"Me," Reilly said quickly, righting her before grabbing her hand. He pulled her deeper into the forest, running as fast as she could go.

"What about Aidan?" she wheezed.

"He's coming. Keep running, Emmaline."

She didn't have to be told that again. She ran with everything she had.

CHAPTER 11

Aidan knew he wouldn't make it to MacDermott in time to stop another shot, but he did know that he could melt into the unnaturally thick mist around him in an instant. Decision made, he took a swift step backward and listened for which way Emma had run.

"You think to have her?" MacDermott sneered through the fog, his voice clear. "You know she's mine, MacWilliam. I'll find her, or die trying. And if I die, so will she! Your money can't protect her forever."

Perhaps not, Aidan thought grimly. *But my sword will.*

He sent a prayer flying, and headed in the same direction Emma had. MacDermott's insults were loud, and his threats were pathetic, but Aidan wasn't stupid. The man had a gun, and a gun won out over a sword every time.

When he'd seen Emma heading into the forest his heart had nearly stopped. Reilly's woods were notoriously finicky; the time gates located deep in its thickets produced people from all different time periods.

"It's safe for me," Reilly had explained, "for I'm a Protector. I can make the time gate work as I need it. If you try to travel through my forest, there's no telling where you'd end up, MacWilliam. And I'm not going to track you down through the ages, so you'll have to just live where you lie."

MacDermott's slurs and threats faded behind him, leaving him with only the sound of his own breathing.

Where is she? he thought wildly. She wasn't any safer alone in the forest than she was with MacDermott, though the sight of him pointing a gun at her would haunt him forever. He reached for the sword on his back, comforted by the feel of steel in his hand, and strained to hear anything.

When nothing reached his ears, he carried on, hoping he would be able to find her before she landed in someone's dungeon.

* * *

Emma gripped Reilly's hand so tightly she worried she might cut off his circulation. But he didn't seem at all bothered by the fact that she was squeezing it as though it were her lifeline.

Which it was, but that was beside the point.

She noticed his clothing again. The léine wrapped around a really nice tunic, made of what looked like linen. And it had to be handmade, too, for his shoulders were larger than a linebacker's, and his arms…huge wasn't a big enough word.

She was glad he was on her side.

He pulled her alongside a tree and glanced around. His shoulders relaxed and he gently pried her fingers from his own.

"He's gone, lass. All's well."

"Aidan's still with him," she replied, her voice as shaky as her hands. "He had a gun."

"I saw. And there were no other gunshots, so we can assume your Aidan is well on his way to us."

"How does he know where we are, though?" she asked, her teeth chattering from nerves.

Ben had pointed a *gun* in her face. He had fired it at her.

She began to shake in earnest.

"Hold it together, Emma. Aidan will find us, then all will be well."

"Ben found me. He found me in a remote part of Ireland, where I've been for over a month, without any online presence or cell phone or general contact with the outside world." She drew a shuddering breath. "How can you say all will be well?"

He patted her hand reassuringly. "Haven't you ever believed in fate?"

"Maybe when I was young and naïve," she muttered. If fate was a real thing, it was cruel, to be sure.

"Trust in it," he advised. He cocked his head as if listening to something, and Emma stiffened, prepared to run again if Ben burst into the small clearing.

However, it was Aidan who appeared, looking for all the world as though he were out for a morning stroll in the forest. She immediately broke away from Reilly and launched herself at Aidan.

"Easy," he murmured, catching her. "Hey, there's no need to panic. We're both fine."

"Is he dead?" Reilly asked gravely.

"Nay. I only had my sword. To fight him was a fool's errand," Aidan replied just as seriously. "We'll have to think about how he found us later. For now, we have to get Emma to safety."

"We can't go back to the house," Reilly pointed out.

Emma extracted herself from Aidan's arms as the reality fully sank in.

"He'll always find me," she whispered. "He won't stop until I'm dead. I have nowhere to go."

"Nay," Aidan said slowly. He looked at Reilly meaningfully. "There is *one* place he can't reach you."

Reilly groaned. "I'll be knee-deep in manure if I bring you both with me."

"Her life is in the balance," Aidan pointed out.

"Where do you want to go?" she asked. "Because if it saves my life, I'm in."

Reilly's gaze sharpened. "Are you absolutely certain about that?"

She nodded vigorously. She didn't want to die. She wanted a safe place where she could regroup and think through her options for getting away from Ben.

Reilly and Aidan shared a look, then some sort of silent man-communication passed between them. Emma didn't bother trying to read into it; man-speak was beyond her under the best of circumstances. Trying to decipher it while on the run from a man with a gun who wanted to use it on her? She had bigger things to worry about.

"All right," Reilly finally muttered. Aidan grinned, and Emma just tugged on both their hands.

"Well then, let's get going! Come on!"

. . .

Aidan slid his final dirk inside his boot, steeling himself for what lay ahead. Aside from the dangers of the travel itself, he was concerned about ambush attacks, finding food, and getting to safety.

But most of all, he was concerned he wouldn't be able to get Emma back to the twenty-first century.

After sneaking back toward the house, Reilly met Aidan and Emma about a mile from his side of the forest. Reilly drove them the half hour to the site of Dowth, and as each minute dragged out Aidan became more withdrawn, but his mind stayed alert and sharpened its focus, reminding him of his battle days.

Cian sat in the front seat, his own posture vigilant. Aidan knew that beneath his léine, all sorts of weaponry lay strapped against him. Despite being a quiet man, Cian had remained faithful to him and the MacWilliam clan. Aidan prayed for a hero's welcome for him when they returned. After swearing loyalty to first Nick, then Aidan, the man stuck by his word.

Emma sat beside him, her hands clasped in her lap as her eyes devoured the landscape. He watched as she tucked a stray piece of her blonde hair behind her ear, and felt the burden of his decision weigh heavily. He knew he was keeping her alive by anchoring her to his side, but he also knew that came at a price, and she had no idea how much it might cost her. She might wish herself dead after seeing him in his natural environment of cold, war, and hunger.

He glanced down at his satchel on the floor. Emma had declared it a nice accessory when she saw it, but it held much more than just visual value. Food and gold were tucked inside—the former he expected to get them through the first couple nights, and the latter to get them out of a friendly dungeon. The sword in the trunk, he hoped, would be the backup plan.

Backup plans, he was beginning to notice, were used more often than the primary ones.

"Are you sure you're okay with this?" Emma asked him softly, so Reilly and Cian couldn't hear her. "You're very quiet."

Aidan nodded, but didn't answer. After a moment, she patted his knee and turned to look out the window.

He caught her hand before she pulled it away, and held it in place. She looked at his hand, then into his eyes, and a shy smile crept across her face. She gave him a small, reassuring squeeze.

A tiny part of his soul breathed a sigh of relief.

"So, Emma, what's your favorite thing about the Middle Ages?" Reilly asked, glancing at her in the rearview mirror.

"Please don't say courtly love," Cian grumbled from the front seat.

She shrugged. "No, Cian, although I'm sure that was one of the lovelier parts. And it was more England than Ireland, after all. I think the most fascinating thing was how clans worked. It seems like, from everything that's published, clans only banded together in times of war."

"Not all clans," Aidan replied, his voice rough. He cleared his throat. "Some lived and died for each other, in battle or out."

"Fealty?" she asked.

"Family," he corrected.

She glanced at Reilly, then Cian. "Like you three? And Colin?"

Reilly parked the car in a nondescript dirt lot. He turned, noted Emma's hand in Aidan's. "Aye. Like us."

Aidan took a breath. "Are you ready for this?"

Uncertainty clouded her eyes, but she said, "I am if you are. I need some space to think."

Cian's face remained serious. "You didn't tell her where we're going."

Emma pulled her hand away from Aidan's quickly. "As long as

it's away from Ben, I'm fine with that. I just don't want to spend the rest of my life running."

"You'll be safe with us," Reilly replied. "Aidan? Care to elaborate?"

Aidan cleared his throat again, then coughed. "No. " He gave a nod to Reilly and Cian, who exited the vehicle. When Emma made to open her door, Aidan grabbed her hand again.

"You're beginning to freak me out a little," she admitted.

The fear in her voice ate at him; her bravado began to crumble. Without another thought, he leaned forward and kissed her hard. She was shocked enough that she didn't respond before he quickly pulled away.

"I'm taking you to *my* home. If we're separated along the way, know that Cian and O'Malley both would give their lives for yours."

"I hate that it might come to that. They owe me nothing," she whispered, her eyes filling with tears.

"You're one of us now, Emma. You're part of the clan."

"I'm not that important," she said, her voice shaky.

Aidan tipped her chin up, using his thumb to wipe away the tear that escaped. "You are, Emma. Come with me. I'll keep you safe. I promise."

Emma looked out the window at the forest at the edge of the parking lot. "It's a big promise to make, Aidan."

"It's more than a promise, Emmaline. I vow it."

She nodded once. "I trust you."

"And the others," Aidan replied, regretfully letting go of her hand. He grabbed the satchel and opened his door. Reilly opened hers, and Aidan added, "We all vow it."

Reilly helped her out of the SUV and handed her a smaller satchel of her own. "Don't doubt it for a moment."

"Aye, lass, you've my life for yours as well," Cian added, securing his sword to his back.

Emma looked overwhelmed, and Aidan walked around the car. He took her hand and saw fear and trust mingling in her eyes.

"Thanks seem so inadequate," she said with difficulty. She

tightened her fingers around his. "But it's all I have. So thanks. And I'm ready. Let's go."

Reilly slapped him on the back. "Well done, lad. Glad you told her."

Aidan cringed a little, but didn't correct Reilly's assumption.

Trees surrounded them on all sides; while Dowth itself was in the middle of an open clearing, they'd parked far enough away that the police wouldn't ticket Reilly's car for an overnight stay.

Or multiple nights' stay.

"I thought you were about an hour's drive away?"

Reilly groaned. "Damn it, MacWilliam! You *didn't* tell her!"

"She'll see for herself," Aidan answered.

There was a rustle in the trees, and he tensed. He made eye contact with Reilly, and they picked up their pace.

They burst into the clearing, and Aidan didn't pause. He charged toward the rise in the grass before them, stopping short in front of a long, thin crack in the stone. He didn't let go of Emma's hand and moved out of the way for Reilly.

"You'll have to hold tight to her," Reilly said.

Not a problem, Aidan thought. Her eyes were wide, and he knew she could feel the tension around the three men.

"I'm confused," Emma began.

Reilly placed his hands on either side of the crack and said, in a voice not his own, "*Le cumhacht na nDéithe, ordaím duit oscailt chugamsa, An Cosantóir.*"

By the power of the gods, I command you to open for me, the Protector.

The wall silently opened wide, and began to close almost immediately. They all made it inside, Aidan dragging a shell-shocked Emma, and then hurried down a nearly black, suffocating, tight corridor. Suddenly, the narrow passageway opened up, and they strode into the small round chamber, hidden from the rest of the structure. A tiny window, covered by the long grass outside it, was the only source of light. Reilly reached through and pushed down the foliage so they could see the horizon.

Emma looked at Reilly, then Aidan, then Cian. "How did you do that?"

Reilly rolled his eyes and shook his head. "Honestly, lad, just tell her the truth before I do."

"You live in a dirt mound, opened by some voice command control thing?" Emma guessed. "I mean, I've heard the term 'going off the grid,' but I didn't think you were that type…"

"There's more," Aidan said, his voice quiet. "This isn't my home. It's more like a portal to my home."

"Jesus, Aidan, how much money do you have?" she exclaimed, then clapped a hand over her mouth as she turned scarlet. "I'm sorry. That was rude. What I meant to say was: Wow, Aidan, that's really impressive. It seems awfully expensive to build underground portals throughout Ireland, just to get to your home undetected."

Reilly snickered, but Cian remained on alert, glancing out the little window. "The sun's rising," he said solemnly.

"I'll explain soon," Aidan promised.

They stood together silently and a moment later, the rising sun's rays crept into the room. Reilly placed a hand on Cian and Aidan, and Aidan drew Emma to him quickly, sweeping her into his arms. The cave flooded with the full light of the sun. Emma gripped Aidan's neck, and he tightened his hold on her as the world around them exploded into shards of light.

CHAPTER 12

Emma awoke with a screaming headache. She carefully raised her hands and felt her head. No bumps, but just the light touch made her wince.

"Drink this," Aidan said in her ear, wrapping her hands around something rough. "It's white willow bark tea. It should help the pain."

She sipped and made a face. "It's too bitter."

"Drink it," he encouraged her, bringing it to her lips again. "It will help."

She choked down the brew. Darkness surrounded them, but the moon was bright. A cold wind teased the leaves of the trees above her, and she shivered.

Aidan wrapped a piece of heavy wool around her shoulders and fastened it across her collarbone. She glanced down at the cloak, then up at him.

His eyes shone light green in the blue glow of the moon.

"How do you feel, other than your headache?" he asked, smoothing her hair.

"Dizzy," she replied, closing her eyes again. "Weird."

He made her follow his finger with her eyes and performed a few other tests before declaring she probably hadn't suffered a concussion.

"I'll keep an eye on you anyway," he said.

She felt her head beginning to clear, although her brain was still foggy. "What happened? Did you drop me?" The last was an accusation, and she frowned before wincing again.

Her head *really* hurt.

"Nay."

She sat up straighter. "What happened to my clothes?"

He continued to gently rub the back of her neck. "I vow, I changed you swiftly and out of sight of the others."

"Wait, what? Is this…oh my God. Why am I dressed in medieval clothing?"

The dress was dark—she thought it might be a deep blue. The silver braided rope, which circled her ribcage just under her breasts, shone in the moonlight, and the overlay was a sheet of silver gauze.

"Have I been unconscious all day?" she asked suddenly, noting the moon high in the sky above them.

"Nay. Only for about a half hour. We simply came into the night instead of the day."

She paused. "That doesn't make any sense, Aidan. Where are we?"

He paused. "More like when."

Emma blinked. "I'm not following you at all."

"We're in Ireland, but the year is 1465."

"You fell hard," she declared promptly. "It's messed with your brain. What happened in the cave back there? Was it a bomb?"

"Nay, Emmaline. It wasn't a bomb. Reilly brought us back to my home."

Though the man looked all right, Emma had serious doubts. His brain must've been rattled hard by the explosion. Emma gave him a concerned look, but held her tongue. "Where is Reilly?"

"I've found us horses. Can you ride?" Reilly asked, materializing from the trees and making Emma jump.

Horses? "Do pony rides at a county fair count?" she ventured.

"Not in this case. You'll ride with me." Aidan helped her to stand, then walked her over to the largest stallion she'd ever seen.

It eyed her warily.

This adventure was going from strange to downright weird. Why horses? What happened in the cave? And she wanted to get Aidan to a doctor as soon as possible.

But first, she figured they ought to get inside somewhere

quickly. There was no telling if Ben knew where they were, and, as an entire day had passed, he might've caught up to them, wherever they were.

"I can run," she said quickly, taking a step back. She bumped into a hard chest. "Really. I have on my hiking boots. It's fine."

The horse snorted its approval of her plan.

"Don't let the beast know you're afraid of him," Aidan advised, placing his hands on her waist. He effortlessly tossed her up onto the horse's back, and she almost fell off the other side. He hopped up behind her, righted her, then leaned down so his mouth was against her ear.

"Hold onto the horse's mane or my arms, but don't grab these reins. Aye?"

She nodded shakily and adjusted her heavy skirts. She glanced down at the ground and clenched her eyes shut. He kicked the horse, and they galloped off. She heard other hoofbeats, and she managed a small peek through her lids. Reilly rode on one side of them, Cian on the other.

Aidan gave the horse its head, and they flew between the trees in the forest, leaping over small streams and charging through brush. Emma's teeth smacked together in her head, and, after an hour of death-gripping Aidan's arm, she was fairly certain her legs would never work properly again.

Aidan didn't talk, but he certainly kept her warm. He turned her cloak around, and the wind buffeted the wool. His warmth seeped through the dress she wore, spreading throughout most of her body. The pants she wore under her dress kept her legs surprisingly warm as well; although she couldn't claim comfort, she couldn't say she was cold, either.

How did Ben find me? Perhaps Aidan knew. How else would he have known to follow her into the forest? She decided to bring it up with her horse partner, who was currently bent over her, shielding her from the wind and urging the horse to go faster.

She really didn't approve of such an action.

"Aidan," she called.

"No need to yell," he said softly in her ear, making her shiver in an entirely non-cold way. "I'm right here."

"Right," she replied, trying to talk around her clattering teeth. "Um, so…do you know how Ben found me?"

"Nay. But not to worry. He won't find us here."

"If he found us before, and we left absolutely no paper trail or anything, how are you so sure?"

"He can't time travel, Emma."

He was so calm about it, so matter-of-fact. Emma swallowed past a lump in her throat. *Poor Aidan*, she thought. *He's so confused.* She'd heard never to let someone with a brain injury fall asleep, so she kept talking.

"So where are we going?"

"Home," he said simply.

"Right. Of course. And home would be…"

"On the coast."

Emma felt an odd sense of detachment. She should've been freaking out. She was on a horse with a man who needed medical attention, and she had no idea how to steer the creature, much less where to go.

"Stop thinking so hard," Aidan murmured, leaning in again. "You're making our horse nervous."

"I am not," she retorted. With surprise, she added, "You're handling him just fine. Where did you learn how to ride?"

"I believe I've already explained that I grew up here, Emma."

"So, what? Is horseback riding a core requirement of elementary school in Ireland?"

"Never went to elementary school," was the reply.

"Homeschooled, then. Whatever. Don't be obtuse."

"Obtuse? I believe there's only one person on this horse who fulfills that description. And it's not me, love."

She shifted in the saddle and would have fallen had Aidan's arms not tightened when they did. He righted her and she softened her tone. "You weren't born in the Middle Ages, Aidan. I don't know where we are—"

"We came up near the coast," Reilly cut in. "We'll be home before sunrise if we can keep the horses going."

She ignored him. "But," she continued, "it's not possible to travel through time. It just isn't."

"Yet here we are," Aidan said blandly.

She sighed in frustration. "Do you need a doctor?"

"He saw one, once," Cian said. "It didn't go well."

"Bite your tongue," Aidan replied. "It could've gone so much worse."

"Really? How?" Cian asked. "The last time you went, you dove out the front door of the poor man's office, straight into the car, and told me to drive like a 'bat out of hell.' I'm not sure what definition of *worse* you're thinking of, but when that man chased the car almost to the freeway…" He trailed off. "Well, I wasn't happy about it."

Emma tried to smile, but found she couldn't. "Let's just get you to your house; then we'll evaluate you and see if we can't find someone to help."

* * *

At some point, Emma fell asleep in Aidan's arms, while still atop the horse. She woke with a start when the horse stopped, and Aidan slid down the side of the beast with her in his arms.

After Cian scouted a safe location, Aidan gave her privacy to take care of her personal needs and went to confer quietly with Reilly as the horses drank from a stream nearby. Emma stood shakily, her legs screaming in protest, and carefully made her way back to the men, Cian alert and on guard behind her. She patted her hair, which she suspected might never again resemble anything other than a rat's nest, and wished for a brush.

Aidan, much to her dismay, looked effortlessly calm, cool, and collected. His hair was delightfully tousled, and he stood chatting as though he fought off crazy ex-fiancés and rode horses across forests and hills every day of his life.

There was no way they were in 1465.

Right?

The forest around her didn't look medieval, but then again, she didn't really expect a forest to differ much from year to year. The men around her wore medieval clothing, had medieval weaponry, and rode horses, but…that could be part of an elaborate reenactment scheme.

She shook her head hard. She wouldn't be sucked into their delusion.

"Ms. Perkins?" Cian said from behind her.

Emma hadn't realized she'd stopped walking, and she forced her feet to move again. She had never felt more confused in her life.

"We've about six more hours ahead of us," Aidan said as she approached. "If you need to stop, I think this is as safe an area as we're to come across. We're almost to MacWilliam land, and last I knew Nick was friendly with the neighbors."

Reilly held up a hand. "Things can change in eight years, MacWilliam. Don't assume anything."

"Right," Aidan agreed. "Can you continue on, Emma?"

She nodded—really, what else could she do?—and allowed him to help her onto the accursed creature, who snorted and sidestepped away once she was on its back. Aidan didn't release the reins, though, and swung into the saddle behind her.

"I hate this horse," she muttered, her muscles sore and aching. "If I never have to ride one again, it'll be too soon."

"Aw, he's not that bad. He gets us to where we need to be," Aidan replied as they started off again. Moonlight filtered between the trees, casting shadows around them. Emma tucked herself deeper into his embrace. She felt his smile when he pressed his cheek into her tangled mass of hair. "And where we're going, you'll need a story to explain your presence. From this point on, we'll be calling you Lady Emma."

"Because the last thing I want is to appear as a medieval peasant," Emma replied sarcastically.

"Exactly," Aidan replied seriously. "We'll say you're from the

Continent, that I've been traveling and became stranded there. I'm friendly with your father, who charged me with your care."

"Nice story, bro."

He did laugh then. "If you recall, about two-thirds of the way through your thesis, you discussed a woman's role in medieval society."

"I still can't believe you read that."

"Believe it. You wrote that women's hierarchy in the clan depended upon who their sires are or whom they marry. As you're not married, you'll hail from nobility. That makes you untouchable to my clansmen."

She felt a flash of triumph. His story had major holes in it; if the man claimed to have grown up in the 1400s, he should have his facts straight.

"Why would my father ship me off to Ireland?" she asked. "That's not something most fathers would do. More likely he'd sell me to the highest bidder."

"He's avoiding an unpleasant match. He doesn't want to align with a certain family, and they've threatened to take you anyway."

Damn.

"Wouldn't they just take me away?"

"In Ireland they would. But the rest of Europe claims to be a tad more civilized."

"I hate that you have a point."

"What I have is a thorough understanding of the time," he replied with a cheeky grin. "You'll believe me when we reach the castle."

"I thought we were headed to your home?"

"Aye. 'Tis one and the same."

Emma hoped his version of a castle and her version of a castle were the same thing, because their realities didn't seem to be aligning very well lately.

* * *

The sun was just peeking its head over the hills when Emma awoke.

"Good morning."

"How long was I asleep?" She grabbed at the horse's mane when Aidan suddenly slowed the beast.

He chuckled. "About an hour or two. I'm glad you're awake now, though. Look west. Opposite the sunrise."

In the predawn light, hills in varying shades of green cascaded endlessly around them; low stone walls much like the ones in Reilly's garden dotted the landscape. Cattle grazed lazily, swishing their tails, unaffected by the small party making their way to the top of a rolling hill.

"It's lovely," she breathed.

"Keep your eyes trained west," Aidan murmured. "Any minute now..."

They crested a small hill, and suddenly, she saw it. A large castle rose up from the ground, majestic and dark. Behind it, the sea sparkled, catching the first rays of light on its waves. And, situated between the imposing castle and the ocean, a village of whitewashed, thatched-roof cottages sat proudly, small tendrils of smoke curling from their chimneys.

She took it all in, the beauty overwhelming her.

Cian sniffed, and she saw the tears in his eyes.

"I never thought we'd get home," Cian said softly. He looked to Reilly. "My eternal gratitude to you."

Reilly nodded his head, his horse prancing under him as though he, too, was anxious to get to that lovely spot.

"Welcome to the MacWilliam stronghold," Aidan said, pride and relief evident on his face. "Damn, but it's good to be back!"

"There's a moat," Emma exclaimed suddenly, pointing to the castle. "And is that a barbican in front of it?"

"It is," Aidan replied, digging his heels into the horse. "The guards will halt us there before lowering the first drawbridge. Once we're through, we'll proceed straight on to the second, larger drawbridge, into the lower bailey. If my brother is home, I expect he'll meet us there."

Emma stared up at him in amazement. "Wow."

"I take it you no longer believe me a sad head case?"

"How did you know?" she exclaimed. She coughed uncomfortably. "I mean, no, I never thought that. The castle doesn't prove anything. Remember, you took me to Bunratty Castle, where they have the entire place set up as though it was the nineteenth century."

His eyes darkened, and he swiftly pressed an open kiss against her lips. "This isn't a reconstruction. This is the real thing. Medieval Ireland at its best, to be sure. You don't have to believe me. But you will, Emma. You most certainly will."

* * *

"Halt!"

Aidan pulled back the reins of the horse, grateful it was so responsive to the direction. Reilly had a knack for selecting horseflesh—how he'd managed to lead three well-groomed horses out of a stable and into the forest without getting caught was a lesson Aidan would love to learn.

To the guard high atop the barbican wall, Aidan raised both hands in a gesture of peace. The man nodded, his helmet catching the sun, and a few moments later, two riders came over the drawbridge. Aidan sat tall, waiting for them to arrive, and refused to allow even a hint of his nerves to show.

"What's happening now?" Emma whispered.

"They'll determine if we belong in the great hall or the dungeon."

"Dungeon?" she squeaked.

He gave her a reassuring squeeze on the arm, then addressed the men as they slowed their horses to a stop.

"I'm here for Laird MacWilliam." He spoke in Gaelic.

"State your purpose."

Aidan grinned. "Does his only brother ever need a reason to visit?"

The senior-ranking man brought his horse alongside theirs, his eyes widening.

"Hello, Kane. Did you ever manage to marry Keela?"

Kane let out a great whoop and reached over to embrace Aidan in a manly hug. Emma ducked out of the way just in time. She almost lost her balance, but Kane righted her with a "Pardon, my lady."

"I've brought Cian along as well," Aidan said, jerking his head toward the man who was struggling to hold his emotions in check.

"Cian MacWilliam," Kane said with an uninhibited grin. "You wily bastard. We thought the two of you dead and buried! The laird will be very pleased to see you again."

"Do you travel with this man?" the other guard asked Aidan, referring to Reilly.

"Aye. Best to tell Lady Brianagh her cousin has arrived from the mainland," Aidan said. He paused. "The lady is in residence?"

Both guards nodded, and Aidan felt a rush of relief. "Excellent."

"Go ahead and announce their arrival," Kane ordered, and the other guard galloped back to the barbican. "Follow me. We've a new process to follow, what with the attempts on the castle of late."

"What kinds of attempts?" Cian asked.

"An individual trying to breach castle walls," Kane replied. He guided them back toward the drawbridge. "We've caught him twice, and both times he escaped the dungeons, though we don't know how. Nothing to be concerned about."

In Emma's ear, Aidan murmured, "That's medieval Irish Gaelic. In case you were wondering."

She didn't respond, and he tried not to worry. Brianagh would explain everything for her.

They reached the bailey and were subjected to another round of questions, but many of the men were the same guardsmen he'd fought alongside most of his life. They welcomed him back warmly, astonished at his unannounced return after so long an absence.

Kane returned the men to their posts, and the drawbridge to the main castle lowered. Aidan quelled the sudden emotion rising in his breast, and he confidently led Cian and Reilly over the moat, into the dark stone wall of the outer bailey. The echo of the horses' hooves bounced off the mossy walls, and Aidan had never in his life been so overjoyed at the sound.

He rode into the early morning sun, temporarily blinded as they exited the dark tunnel, passing under the portcullis. The courtyard was empty but for the stable master and his charges, who stood waiting.

Aidan dismounted easily, then reached up and slid Emma off. He dragged her down his body, not missing the gasp of breath and the desire clouding her eyes.

He turned his head to the stable master.

"Bernard. Good to see you again."

The man glared at him. "Didn't think I'd ever see you again. What took you so long to return? Horse lose a shoe?"

Aidan threw back his head and laughed. "I missed you too, old man. These horses need a rubdown and some oats as soon as possible. Think your whelps can handle that?"

The young boys waited until Bernard gave them a nod, then they each took one of the horses and led it to a gateway in the stone wall to their right. Bernard took the reins from Aidan and regarded him.

"Well, looks like you survived well enough." He led the horse after the others, leaving Emma staring in consternation at the man's retreating back.

"He doesn't like you very much," she noted, a hint of disapproval in her tone. "You laughed at him. That didn't seem very nice."

"That's about as much emotion as he's ever shown," Aidan replied. He took her hand, then looked at Cian and Reilly. "He missed me. Ready?"

Cian grinned and replied in English. "I've been waiting for this for eight years, my laird." He paused. "I mean, Aidan."

At Emma's confusion, Aidan explained, "When I travel from the clan, I become the acting laird. Now that we're home again, I'm just Aidan."

"Well, Bri will be happy to see me," Reilly said. He wiggled his eyebrows. "Perhaps one or two of the chambermaids, as well."

Before Emma could chastise him, a choked cry drew everyone's attention to the castle steps.

A tall, broad-shouldered man stood at the top of the steps, dressed in a deep blue léine with silver trim. His mouth hung open, his eyes wide, as he took in the foursome standing in his courtyard, and he shook his head.

"'Tis not possible," he stated, staring at Aidan. "You're dead."

"Nah," Aidan replied in Gaelic, his eyes twinkling. "I just wanted to see if absence did indeed make your heart grow fonder. Greetings, my laird."

Nioclas MacWilliam ran down the stairs and slammed into his brother, hugging him tightly and pounding his back. Aidan blinked back his tears, coughing to cover up his displays of emotion, but Nick had no problems pulling back, grasping his brother's face, then pulling him in for a hug again.

"Where the hell have you been?" Nick finally demanded, wiping the moisture from his eyes. "You never came back. I sent men after you, for years. I never stopped searching."

"I traveled a bit." Aidan glanced over his shoulder. Emma stood alone, twisting her hands together nervously as she tried desperately not to stare at them.

"I see you brought back your treasure," Nick replied knowingly.

"Aye. She doesn't speak our language very much, though."

"From whence does she hail?" Nick asked, interested. "Somewhere I know?"

"I believe you know of it," Aidan said carefully. "America?"

Nick gaped at him. "You jest!"

"Not at all." Aidan couldn't help his grin.

Nick pushed past him and grasped Emma's hand in greeting. He said, in perfect modern English, "My lady, I welcome you to my home. I see you've taken good care of my brother, and for that, I thank you. Please, come inside and warm yourself by my fire; I'll have our cook prepare you a meal immediately."

She blinked at him, then looked at Aidan, as if for confirmation, before giving him a small smile. "Thank you. That's very kind."

Nick whooped and laughed. "You really are from America!"

"Um…" She was clearly at a loss, and Aidan took pity on her.

"Emma, Nick is married to Bri. He knows an American accent when he hears one."

"This is so unbelievable," she murmured.

"O'Malley," Nick said, extending his hand. The two men shook firmly. "I suppose I have you to thank for getting him back here?"

"What's he saying?" Emma whispered to Aidan when Nick lapsed into Gaelic with Cian. "I can't understand the accent."

"They're exchanging pleasantries, and Nick is thanking Cian for his service to the clan," Aidan replied. "Don't worry. We'll speak English, mostly. Brianagh will no doubt be ecstatic to hear her mother tongue."

A shriek pierced the air, and a stunningly beautiful brunette flew down the steps, skirts flying, toward Reilly. He easily caught her and swung her around, a huge smile lighting up his face.

"Reilly O'Malley, you didn't even send word!" she exclaimed, laughing over the tears. She buried her head in his neck and hugged him tightly, her next words muffled, and Reilly patted her on the back. When she caught sight of Aidan, her face lit up again, and she launched at him, her arms wide. He caught her easily, careful of the large bump in her belly.

Aidan gave her a hug, then held her at arm's length. "There's something different about you," he mused.

She gasped and replied in Gaelic, "You learned English!"

"I didn't have a choice. I'll tell you about it over a hot meal. Keela still an amazing cook?"

"The best," Bri replied happily. She noticed Emma and smiled warmly, continuing in Gaelic. "Who is your companion?"

"Lady Brianagh, meet Lady Emma. She also speaks your language." He said the last with emphasis, and Brianagh's eyes showed her understanding.

"Pleasure, Lady Emma. I believe I've made enough of a

spectacle of myself this morning, so perhaps we should retire to my solar for some breakfast."

Nioclas wrapped an arm around Bri's shoulders and kissed the top of her head. "Aye. We've much to discuss, and your solar is much more comfortable than mine."

"Come on, then. Lady Emma, Aidan, Reilly? Cian," she added, "we shall send for your sister and nephew. Care you to join us?"

"My thanks, my lady, but I prefer to wait for them in the great hall," Cian replied.

She nodded regally, then walked up the castle steps. Grasping Emma's elbow to steady her—or himself, he wasn't sure which—Aidan was only too happy to follow.

CHAPTER 13

When Emma's vision adjusted to the dim light inside the great hall, she immediately noticed the sheer size of the room. The ceiling stretched up at least two floors, with a large window above the front door. Anchoring one end, an enormous hearth stood empty, save for a small glow of orange in the soot. Guards were stationed all around the room, standing at attention or, in some cases, sleeping on the floor. Brianagh spoke quietly with one of the guards closest to the door, and he headed toward the back of the room, through an open doorway.

"Breakfast," Brianagh said by way of explanation, before heading toward the far corner of the great hall.

"Where are the rushes?" Emma murmured to Aidan, who shrugged.

"Bri hated having hay strewn about. I think you'll find some modern touches to this castle that you won't find anywhere else in Ireland. Brianagh is very adamant that the castle remains clean, for hygiene."

They followed the laird and lady through the great hall, to a staircase tucked in the back. It wound up in a curved fashion, with brackets in the stone that held torches, currently unlit. Twice, Emma nearly slipped on the smooth stone, but Aidan caught her each time.

She became lost as they twisted their way through the hallways of the castle, some seeming to slope higher and others lower. Eventually, Brianagh pulled a key from the large keychain she wore at her waist and unlocked a heavy wooden door. It swung open, and Emma's eyes widened in delight.

Inside, the room was filled with color. Bright tapestries, unlike any Emma had ever seen, lined the walls. Two large couches, made with rough-hewn wood and hand-sewn cushions, flanked the fireplace, in which a fire was already burning brightly. A carved desk was placed against the alcove window, parchment and ink neatly laid out on its surface, ready for use. The desk chair was made of the same wood, but it was cushioned and more ornate than the desk itself.

Books of all sizes lined the built-in shelves on either side of the desk, creating a warm and inviting environment.

Emma loved it.

"It's so wonderful to have another American here!" Brianagh exclaimed. "Oh, you must call me Bri. I'm married to Nioclas, Aidan's brother. But you probably know that already."

Emma smiled at the infectious good cheer in her voice. "Well, yes. I've gotten the distinct impression that you're a big part of this family."

"Pshhh," she replied with a roll of her eyes. "They all feel this need to coddle me, but everyone forgets that I'm quite independent. I even started my own business back in the States, did they tell you that?"

"Yes. I'm actually going to start doing some PR work for Colin," Emma replied. "Well, I was. I don't know how that's going to work out, me being here…and not there."

Bri nearly squealed. "Colin! You know him? How is he? Tell me he's settled down, married. Kids. Something."

Emma bit her lip. "Not married, no. But his house is magnificent. He bought the adjoining neighbor's part and renovated it. The library is phenomenal."

Bri looked at her, interested. "Colin had you in his house?"

"Yes. I stayed there with Aidan and Reilly," Emma explained. Bri's eyebrow raised higher. "And Cian, although I barely saw him."

"He slept outside your room, love," Aidan called over from where he'd settled on the couch.

Bri's expression turned speculative at the endearment.

"Your business is thriving," Emma rushed to inform her. "Colin's taking it international. It's why he hired me."

"So you work for Colin?"

"And me," Aidan said. "It's so good to see you, Bri."

Bri smiled, but it didn't reach her eyes. "We thought you were dead."

"Not dead," he said softly. "Very much alive, some centuries in the future."

Her gaze swung to Reilly. "In all the times you visited, you never said a word. Not once!"

"You know the rules," Reilly said solemnly. He stood against the closed door, arms and ankles crossed. He directed his gaze to Nioclas. "I can't tell you anything that might alter history."

"And another of the rules is that you only travel when there's a threat to the MacWilliam/O'Rourke line. So what's the latest problem?"

Reilly gave a small shake of his head. "We can discuss that later, as it's not a pressing matter. MacWilliam and Emma weren't supposed to come."

"Why did they, then?" Nick asked.

"Emma's run into a spot of trouble with a particularly deranged ex-betrothed."

Aidan quickly explained what happened. "...then I decided it best that we go to Colin's for added protection. Reilly happened to be there, and we all decided to keep Emma under a tight guard."

"That must've been highly annoying," Brianagh replied, leaning over and giving Emma a sympathetic pat on the knee. "Three incredibly overbearing men 'protecting' you? I would've killed them, myself."

"It wasn't so bad. It all came from a good place."

"It always does," Bri agreed. "What did you say you were doing for Celtic Connections?"

"Public relations."

"Ah. Well, Emma, you're amongst friends here. No need to spin this into something positive for the sake of saving face. I've known

Reilly and Colin my whole life. Add in a MacWilliam who's decided you need his protection…let's just say I'm impressed you're not babbling because you've lost your mind."

Emma blinked at her frankness, then burst out laughing. "Wow. You really do have them pinned, don't you?"

"Like you wouldn't believe," Bri concurred.

A knock sounded, and Reilly allowed a line of chambermaids to enter and place trays of food around the room, and Bri added to Emma, "You'll see that food trumps most anything."

"Most?" Aidan asked innocently.

"MacWilliam," Reilly warned, his voice harsh.

To Emma, Bri smirked and patted her pregnant belly. "Reilly can't handle my married status, even when he's the one who dropped me in Nioclas's lap." Bri blew Reilly a kiss and said to him, "Someday you'll see that I'm all grown up, Ry. Since that's not likely to happen today, come eat some food and sit with me. I've missed you greatly."

During breakfast, Emma noted how relaxed Bri made everyone feel. Her warmth radiated from her, stronger even than what Emma experienced at Colin's home. Reilly adored her, although his were brotherly affections. Aidan conversed easily with her, as though they hadn't spent years apart, and Nioclas was quiet, watching his wife with something close to worship in his eyes.

The wistful feeling that crept into Emma's heart was unexpected, and she was stunned to realize it was envy. She'd never seen such a close family before, and she found that, for the first time in a long time, she wanted to feel that kind of connection with others.

Badly.

The three of them brought Bri and Nioclas up to speed as to the events that led them there as they feasted on a breakfast unlike any other Emma had experienced. The fare was delicious—another surprise. From all her research, Emma believed medieval palates were not so sophisticated as to use many flavors. But she tasted a light saffron flavor in her eggs, and wondered at how many other modern marvels Brianagh had incorporated into her medieval life.

When the plates had been cleared, Aidan turned to Nioclas

and got down to business. "I'm not sure how long Emma will need to stay."

Emma froze. *Didn't you mean* we? she wanted to ask, but held her tongue. Maybe that was unintentional.

Unless, of course, Aidan planned to remain in the past.

Sometime between gaping at the great hall, the trek through a very-much-used castle, and sitting across from Nioclas MacWilliam, who definitely had a strong resemblance to his brother, Emma began to accept that perhaps time travel was a possible thing. To start, Nioclas had an air about him that couldn't possibly be acted; the man was leashed power.

He intimidated the hell out of her.

Everything else was too real to be fake—the fire, which was definitely peat, needed to be stoked every so often, and a chambermaid scurried in to do so. The benches, as she'd already noted, were made from stone, and were cold, though the cushions did help with the chill. Even the parchment on the desk in the corner sat in a slightly haphazard pile, as though someone had recently used the quill in the inkpot for jotting down a letter.

A muffled clang sounded, and Nioclas rolled his eyes. "Monaghan. The man is not graceful."

"Monaghan?" Aidan asked in surprise. "But his lands are on the other side of the country! What does he want from you?"

"Not me," Nioclas replied. "My wife."

"He's looking for a wife," Brianagh supplied.

Reilly snorted. "Don't tell me you've made a name for yourself as a matchmaker here as well."

"She certainly has," Nioclas responded proudly. "She's quite sought after. Monaghan is here for his son."

"It's kept me busy," Bri said modestly. "And we haven't seen war since you left, Aidan. It's been very peaceful."

"Even so, Em will need a guard." Aidan swallowed the last of his breakfast. "We're going with the noblewoman story."

Bri nodded. "Good plan."

• • •

When Emma fell asleep on Aidan's shoulder, Brianagh took pity on her. "I'll bring her to her room."

"She stays with me," Aidan said firmly, half rising as the women made their way toward the door.

Brianagh stopped suddenly, her mouth open in surprise. "But… you can't! You're not married!" She glanced at Emma apologetically. "We're not prudes, but truly, your ladyship is at stake. If you sleep in the same room as Aidan, your reputation will be shattered."

"Do I need to worry about a reputation?" Emma asked, raising a brow.

"Oh, very much so," Nioclas said, stroking his chin. "With the current guests we have, added to a large number of guards looking for their next conquest…"

Emma bit her lip. "Oh."

"She stays with me," Aidan repeated forcefully. "No harm comes to Emma."

"My guard wouldn't allow such a thing!" Nioclas replied, bristling.

"I don't think he means to be insulting," Bri said calmly, holding out a hand. "He wants Lady Emma protected at all costs. Which she will be…in the chamber directly next to yours, Aidan."

"Is there an adjoining door?" he asked.

"No," Brianagh replied with a roll of her eyes. "What would be the point of separate chambers, then?"

Emma opened her mouth, but Nioclas opened his at the same time. She snapped hers shut. The man somehow silently commanded deference. She wondered how he obtained such a skill.

"She'll be safe, Aidan. I vow it," Nioclas said, leveling his brother with a stare. "No one will touch her inside of the castle, or on castle grounds. We'll inform the guard together that she's here under your protection, and also mine. They'll honor that."

"I'll have a chambermaid sleep in her room, and post a guard in the hallway," Brianagh added. "Our castle is the most secure it's ever been, and our guards are true."

Aidan looked undecided.

"Aidan, please. I don't want to make any waves while I'm here," Emma broke in. "I'll be fine."

He sighed and nodded, and Brianagh ushered Emma out of the solar before he could change his mind.

* * *

A few twists and turns later, Bri pulled the impressive key ring out again and waved toward the door on the right.

"This is your chamber. I'll have a bath sent up straight away, unless you'd prefer to sleep first?"

"Thank you for being so kind," Emma replied. She grimaced, thinking of their silent walk to the chamber. "I'm normally much more social than this."

Bri leaned forward and spoke so low Emma strained to hear her. "Time traveling will do that to a girl. Trust me. Firsthand experience." She leaned back and said, only slightly louder, "And any amount of time with my family in close quarters couldn't have been good for your mental state. Sleep, bathe, and eat again. I'll fetch you later. For now, I'll send Camille in. She'll be your personal chambermaid. Her entire purpose will be to serve you—if you're anything like I was when I first arrived, and I suspect you might be, you've never asked anyone for help. Enjoy the attention; there's something very special about being important enough to a person that they'd willingly give their life for yours."

"It's an unfamiliar concept," Emma admitted.

"Despite popular opinion, men don't just give the vow of their life for another's lightly. It's only given for a close clansman…or love." Bri waved her into the chamber. "Relax here, Lady Emma. You're safe under Aidan's eye." After she closed the door, Emma heard her give the command to one of the guards who'd been following them to remain outside her door.

Emma surveyed the room. It wasn't large, but it was stunning. Her inner historian was in a state of awe, and after a moment, she decided to ignore her need for sleep for a bit. She ran her hands over the smooth, cold stone wall, marveling at the castle's solid construction. She dragged her fingertips against the wood of the door, awed by its durability. She glanced down and noticed the solid wooden beam propped against the wall, and the metal brackets on the door.

A strong, secure bolt.

She turned her attention to the fire grate before her gaze fell onto the bed and her body took over. She kicked off her boots and climbed into the bed, its softness surprising her as she sank into the coverlets. She fell asleep immediately.

• • •

Brianagh slipped back into her solar, where Aidan and Nioclas were having a heated discussion. She sidled up to Reilly, wrapping both her arms around one of his and laying her head on his shoulder.

"I've missed you," she sighed. "Why did you stay away for so long?"

Reilly's smile was full of tenderness. "Bri, you know the rules."

"Still. I'm your most favorite cousin…" Her sapphire eyes assessed him. "I wonder, then, if you're only allowed to travel when the line is in danger, why you're here now."

"Trust me. We will discuss it later. Instead, why don't you tell me about this matchmaking?" Reilly encouraged her. "Monaghan traveled all the way across the island for your services?"

She nodded. "We're allowing visitors by invitation only. After the first few successes, we had lairds camping outside castle grounds. It became too much, so Nioclas called a council meeting."

Reilly raised an eyebrow. "And he made it out alive?"

She smacked him on the chest. "Yes. Anyway, at this meeting, most of our allies were in attendance, and he laid out the rules for this operation. Inquiries only to start. Once the case is presented, either by parchment or messenger, we would let them know about a date when they were welcome to come to the castle. Or, in rare cases, we would travel to them. Eligible maidens from the clan, as well as their allied clans, are then invited to attend a ball and a skills tournament."

"A ball?"

"Yes. A ball. We have great musicians—"

"Och, aye. I remember those 'great musicians' well," Reilly said with an exaggerated wince. She laughed; the last time he'd heard music in the castle was when she was first married, and she convinced Nioclas to obtain entertainment for her first matching. Everyone's ears had paid the price that night.

"We no longer employ the services of that bard. We have a wonderful trio of musicians and a very pleasant singer. I must warn you, the ball for Monaghan's son is quite soon. Everyone is arriving tomorrow and the next day."

"I thought Nioclas didn't like having anyone know about his prosperous little village?" Reilly replied, looking at the man in question.

"He hates it. But the coin we are given for a successful matching is not insignificant. The success rate has been such that lairds are willing to pay handsomely to see their clansmen happy, and the alliances formed…it's so much better for both clans if the parties involved in the marriage are willing and eager, instead of *forced into it*." She gave him an arch look.

"All I did was return you to your family. I had no part in forcing your marriage…which seemed to work out well," Reilly said.

She grinned. "It really did. And Kathryne and Kiernan visit once per year; it's about as much as Nioclas can tolerate, really. But they adore the grandchildren. I'm happy I have them, but I do miss Colin, James, Evelyn, and Connor."

"All of whom miss you as well."

Brianagh grew pensive. "For how long do you think you'll stay?"

Reilly shrugged. "It's too hard to know."

"What are we waiting for?"

"We're waiting for Aidan to determine when it's safe for Emma to return. But don't worry about the details, my love," Nioclas cut in. He winked, letting her know that he'd been listening to their conversation while holding his own with his brother.

She smiled softly at him, and Reilly groaned. "Have you not worked all that lovey-dovey nonsense out yet? You've been married nigh on eight years!"

She shrugged happily. "It hasn't seemed to fade yet."

"Do you expect Donovan for this event?" Reilly asked, amusement in his voice.

"No, but I think it won't hurt to send for him," Nioclas said thoughtfully. "He'd appreciate seeing Aidan in the flesh."

"No, you can't!" Bri exclaimed, dropping Reilly's arm and stepping forward. "Erin's in her final month of her pregnancy. You know how fast the last child came and you know he'll drop everything to come here at your request. What's worse is she'll support that! Don't put them in that position, Nioclas." She turned to Reilly. "Erin is my dearest friend. She's helped me through so much over these last few years—she's like a sister to me. I don't want her, or her family, in any danger. She's near the end of her third pregnancy, and I cannot ask that of her. Let's not send word."

"Easy, love," Nioclas remarked, pulling her onto his lap and nuzzling her neck with his nose. "There's no need to concern yourself."

Aidan whistled low. "How the mighty have fallen, Nick."

Nioclas didn't even glance up. "I've a feeling you're headed down the same path, brother. Now, if you'll excuse us, we've much to do in preparation for this week. I'll have one of the guards show you to your chambers, and I'll send for you this afternoon."

Brianagh's shy smile and Nioclas's heated glance made both Reilly and Aidan stand quickly.

"I'm to the lists for some light exercise. Join me?" Reilly said.

Aidan nodded. "Aye. Lists. Solid plan."

They heard the bolt slide home a scant second after they closed the solar door, and Aidan let out a laugh. Reilly rolled his eyes in disgust.

Aidan felt lighter than he had in years.

CHAPTER 14

"So what you're saying is that most clans don't allow for an heir succession?" Emma asked.

She and Brianagh strolled the grounds, a bevy of guards behind them, as Bri explained some of what made the MacWilliams different from many other clans in Ireland. The day was almost warm, and people had been arriving for the upcoming tournament, which, Brianagh divulged, would have a grand dinner and dance to start the two-day matchmaking festivities.

Emma's inner historian was cartwheeling around the bailey.

"Not all of them," Brianagh replied. She sidestepped a mud puddle and steered Emma toward one of the inner bailey walls, where the wall opened into another area. "This is where the tournament magic will happen."

"Does anyone ever die at these events?" Emma asked nervously. Through the gate in the wall separating the lists from the courtyard, she spied men hoisting a long beam onto supports in the middle of the training lists. Further down, men were using large metal spikes to outline circles in the dirt.

"Not often," Bri replied, giving her a pat on the arm. "The lists are being set up for jousting, swordplay, and close combat."

"You have it on the castle grounds?" Emma asked.

"Yes. It's safest, and Nioclas hates having his land trampled by overeager participants," she replied.

"I could see that," Emma laughed.

"Don't let his grumbly ways fool you. He's really quite soft on the inside."

"Perhaps he only allows you to see it," Aidan said, stepping from the shadows and grinning when Brianagh jumped.

"You are a menace!" she exclaimed, placing a hand on her heart. "You scared me half to death!"

He gave her a bow. "My lady. Lady Emma."

"What are you doing here?" Brianagh demanded.

"Listening to you lay my very serious brother bare," Aidan replied, his eyes sparkling.

"Don't you dare tell him," Brianagh warned.

"Oh, the price of my silence is high," Aidan replied in mock seriousness. "Perhaps too high."

"Name it," Brianagh challenged him.

"Surely, you can't be so afraid of your husband that you'd be willing to pay someone for silence," Emma protested.

Brianagh shrugged. "I'm not worried about Nioclas. I don't trust what his brother will say, as they have always loved to torment each other."

"My price is the company of your escort," Aidan pressed on.

"Oh, you're good," Brianagh laughed. "I was just giving her the grand tour."

"Then I'm as good as any to take over," Aidan replied with a cheeky grin. He leaned forward and said conspiratorially, "I did, after all, spend the majority of my youth inside—and outside—these walls."

Brianagh relinquished Emma's arm. "I believe she's safe enough with you."

"In public," Aidan murmured so only Emma could hear. She flushed.

"Is four an acceptable number of guards?" Bri asked.

"Yes, within the inner walls," he replied.

"Perfect timing," Brianagh said as a new group of people entered the courtyard. "There are some more of the Monaghans. I'll greet them."

"Would you care to see the inside of the lists?" Aidan asked, winding Emma's hand around his bicep.

Her face lit up. "Yes!"

He grinned in response. "I thought so."

He brought her to where the jousting would take place, and explained in great detail what the men were doing, and how the event would progress. He gave her insight into how the spears were checked for bluntness, chain mail worn, and swords sharpened.

"I saw you sharpening your sword. Back at Reilly's," she admitted. "I wondered at the time why you were restoring it yourself, in the moonlight."

Aidan smiled. "It's something I've always done. Taking care of your weapon is something that's taught from an early age here. Swords aren't cheap. The steel, if it's of good quality, will save your life in a battle. And if it's sharpened correctly, those who attempt to take your life don't get another chance at it." He paused. "That brutality—the *reality*—is part of everyday life here. I took to sharpening my sword in the moonlight because it soothes me. I feel closer to nature, to the earth's cycles and her rhythms."

Emma watched him closely. "Just when I think I've figured you out, you surprise me."

He led her out of the lists, back to the inner bailey. "I'm a man of many talents."

"What else are you good at?" she asked. He gave her a searing look, and she sucked in a breath. "Aidan!"

"What?" he asked, all innocence.

"Can you show me the moat?" she asked, changing the subject.

He pulled a face. "By the saints, why would you ever want to smell such a thing?"

"Because it's a *real moat!*" she replied with glee. "It might be my only chance to ever see one!"

He grudgingly pulled her through the inner bailey, under the portcullis (which she stared at for well over a minute) and through to the outer bailey. He helped her climb the battlements and she glanced over, her eyes going wide.

"This is stunning," she said, awed.

"It's wastewater," Aidan said, disgusted.

"Not that!" she replied. "*That.*" She pointed out to the village and sea beyond.

They stood for a moment, captivated by the view. Before her impromptu trip to Ireland, Emma had never seen such natural beauty before; the closest she ever got to nature was Westchester County.

A cold wind blew her hair around her, and she shivered. Aidan moved to stand behind her, and wrapped his arms around her shoulders.

Before she could voice a complaint, he leaned down, and in a low voice said, "On a full moon, if you were to stand on the battlement and send a wish over its reflection on the sea, legend has it that your wish is carried on the waves until such a time when it can be granted."

Emma let the timbre of his voice rumble through her.

"Others believe that if you cast your wish to the ocean, it holds it safe until your soul mate can retrieve it."

"Have you ever sent a wish out into the sea?" she asked. She felt him nod. "Was it ever granted?"

He tightened his grasp on her as another wind swept across the battlements. "I believe it was."

She twisted in his arms and searched the depths of his eyes, which mirrored the darker green patches in the castle fields.

"You're a complex man," she finally said.

When his lips touched hers, another wind whipped up, and she bridged the distance between their bodies. He slid his tongue into her mouth, tangled it with hers, and she felt herself fall into it. Her heart sped up while everything around her slowed, and he wrapped her in his cloak, creating a cocoon for just the two of them.

Eventually, he pulled back from the kiss, but Emma refused to open her eyes. She didn't want to see the emotion swirling in his, but more importantly, she didn't want to reveal the emotions in hers.

"Coward," he whispered, a smile in his voice.

CHAPTER 15

"All finished, my lady." Camille, one of the chambermaids who spoke a peasant's form of English, smoothed the silvery gauze over the dress and stepped back to admire her work. "You look lovely. Such golden hair!"

Emma self-consciously patted the elegant pile atop her head. "Are you sure it's acceptable to leave it out like this?"

Camille gathered up various things around the chamber. "Aye. Lady Bri dislikes wimples, so Laird MacWilliam's given the womenfolk the option to wear them or not, as is our personal preference. Truly, we are blessed to be part of such a happy clan."

Emma chewed her thumbnail and glanced out the small window again. "All the women out in the courtyard are wearing them," she pointed out nervously.

"Those be the older ones, my lady. If you prefer, I can find you one. It shouldn't take but a moment." She pulled open the door to find Bri, poised to knock. "Oh, Lady MacWilliam! I was just going to find a wimple for Lady Perkins. Excuse me." She bobbed a quick curtsy, but Brianagh stayed her with a hand on her arm,.

"It's quite common to wear a wimple only if you wish to," Bri said, echoing Camille's statement. "We're not alone in this practice. It happens more often than you think…or may have read about."

Emma took the hint, still uncertain. "Well, if you think it best."

"'Tis such a shame to cover such lovely hair," Camille said circling back around Emma, her cornflower-blue eyes shining. "Truly, I've never seen the like of it, all different shades of honey!"

"That will be all, Camille," Bri said gently, and the chambermaid dipped another curtsy before taking her leave.

"Highlights?" Bri noted.

"Yes. And perhaps not the waste of money I originally thought them to be," Emma said. "Camille seems to like them, anyway."

"I think you'll make quite an impression tonight," Bri predicted. "You look lovely." Emma's blue dress was made of a light wool. Much like her original dress, its empire waist was trimmed with a thin silver thread, twisted into a rope that circled her rib cage. This dress, however, wasn't lined; Brianagh had specifically had it made without the extra warmth. Emma would need a cooler fabric, with all the dancing she would be doing after dinner. "I am lucky to have such talented seamstresses here in the castle."

"I'm very grateful," Emma replied, "but, um, I can't find my shoes. I haven't been able to find them since I arrived."

"Oh, right. I have them locked in my trunk. The laces and metal could be construed as fairy-craft," Bri said with a wave. "Don't worry. They're safe until you need them again. The slippers, if they don't fit, can be resized."

Confused, Emma asked, "Fairy-craft?"

"Mmhmm. We're a very supernatural people. When strange things happen, we attribute them to the fairies more than witchcraft or other nonsense. Now come, come. I can't wait to see what you think of the goings-on downstairs. Tonight's a big night—it's the start of the matching!"

"The beginning stage of the matchmaking process?" Emma asked, hurrying to follow Bri.

"Yes, the formal part, anyway. In this case, Monaghan's son, Shane, selected seven ladies from their answers to my questionnaire. I've invited those seven ladies, with their families, as well as a few other choices I'd like him to consider. We have dinner and dancing, and tomorrow, after the tournament, Shane makes his decision. The next day, the lairds—or sires—make up the betrothal agreement, and the wedding takes place soon after."

"Wow. How long is the process from start to finish?" Emma asked, intrigued.

"Five days or less. Life is sometimes short here. People don't hem and haw like they do in our time. They make their decision and stick by it, no matter what."

"What happens if the chosen woman doesn't want to marry Shane?"

"At that point, it's out of my hands. It's up to the woman's father or laird, Monaghan, and Nioclas to come to an amiable solution." Brianagh sighed. "It's only happened a handful of times, when the woman is here against her will. I know history makes us out be property, but we have a lot more power than the books ever gave us. The law states that we are such, but few enforce it. The Irish are a kind people, who love their children and want the best for them. Male *or* female."

"What about what's best for the clan?" Emma was fascinated. She suspected this, but hearing it—seeing it!—firsthand made her almost dizzy with glee.

Bri stopped at the top of the winding stairs. "A laird's daughter holds much the same value as any other daughter in his clan," she explained. "Very few men want a child-bride, so to ally themselves, they'll marry someone else within the other clan."

"What about handfasting?" Emma asked. The process of declaring to marry at a future date seemed like a good way to sidestep the issue.

Brianagh shook her head vehemently. "Oh, no. It's done, but not with any clans we know. That opens doors to all sorts of complications."

"Like what?"

"A rival clan could kidnap the bride-to-be and demand ransom," Bri said, "or the husband-to-be dies in an accident and the bride is left without full clanship rights. It can get messy, so we don't wait."

Emma held her remaining questions. She followed Bri down the stairs, where they waited to be announced. Bri clasped her elbow and they walked arm in arm out of the stairwell, into the great hall, which was about half-filled.

"Tonight, you'll sit with us as a guest of honor," Bri murmured as they made their way to the raised dais. "I'll sit to your right, and Aidan to your left."

A large, slightly overweight man with missing teeth, dressed in a dazzling shade of green, intercepted them before they were halfway across the large room. He said something to Brianagh, giving her a low bow. He continued on, shooting looks of interest to Emma. As he spoke, small drops of spittle flew from his mouth, catching in his silver-and-black beard. They shone in a highly distracting manner; Emma kept sneaking glances at them as he conversed with Bri. She noticed the bits of food clinging to the beard as well. She suppressed a shiver of repulsion as he bowed to her, wafting his own special brand of body fragrance in her direction.

She choked, and Brianagh helpfully clapped her on the back, smiling and saying something that sounded explanatory in Gaelic.

She turned to Emma and, in perfect Middle English, said, "Lady Emma, may I present Laird Monaghan, of the illustrious Monaghan clan in the east of our fair isle."

"A pleasure, my lady. You are the epitome of English beauty. I would be so honored for a dance tonight," Monaghan said in Middle English, the words choppy.

Emma gave a false smile. "Um, that's, um…"

Brianagh spoke in Gaelic again, and the man grinned. He bowed once more—Emma held her breath this time—and stepped back, so they could continue toward the front of the room.

"I told him you would be likewise honored, and explained that you were a lady of few words who spoke a language we're not all that familiar with," Bri said grimly. "Monaghan's interest in you is not going to sit well with Aidan."

"Why not? We're not together," Emma insisted.

"After tonight, I think you might wish to be," Bri warned as another, much older man rounded one of the tables to stop them. Bri made the introductions, the man asked for a dance with the Lady Emma, and Bri granted it.

"Can't you just tell them I don't dance or something?" Emma hissed as yet another man gave a bow.

"Negative," Bri responded through her teeth as she bestowed a smile upon the man before herding Emma onward. "That was a powerful ally. Nioclas would insist upon that even if you were *married* to Aidan. Damn, he is going to be so mad at me."

Emma felt a fleeting sense of panic. "I'm sure it will be fine. They're both older men, old enough to be my father, really."

"Not this one," Bri said under her breath. A man about Emma's age, dressed in the same blazing shade of green Laird Monaghan wore, bent gracefully at the waist. When he stood at full height, he was nearly as tall as Aidan, and he smiled kindly down at Emma, his brown eyes soft. His face, classically beautiful, rivaled any Hollywood movie star, and his manner was relaxed, fully confident. He spoke in fluent Middle English, and Emma had no issues understanding him.

Unfortunately.

"Lady Emma, allow me to introduce you to Shane Monaghan, who resides to the east." Brianagh gave a swift curtsy, and Emma hastily followed.

"My dear Lady Emma, your beauty and rumored wit have captured my attentions. I know you've so promised a dance with my father, but he and I have discussed it at length, and he insisted that I also dance with you, so as to see if we may make a life together."

Emma's jaw dropped in surprise. *At length? He was here maybe three minutes ago!*

He continued, "As the generous lady of the castle has most likely explained, I am here to find a wife, so I can begin fully living as a man ought, with something to live and die for."

Well, at least he was honest about his intentions.

"Sorry, Monaghan, but this lady is unavailable," a familiar voice, undercut with steel, said cheerfully.

The younger Monaghan frowned. "Are we acquainted?"

Aidan said something in Gaelic, and the man's entire countenance changed in an instant. He gave a cordial bow to Brianagh, then kissed Emma's hand.

Shane glanced up at Aidan, gave a smile that Emma could only classify as competitive, and said something back in Gaelic before he headed back to where his father stood and began to talk in earnest.

"Aidan!" Brianagh exclaimed, worried. She glanced nervously at Emma. "You better explain what you just did to her!"

Emma looked at him questioningly, but all he said was, "I saved you from a night of fools."

"I don't know whether to thank you or not," Emma replied. "I mean, I would love to dance, absolutely. But those men looked at me like…"

"A cup of water after a long drought?" Bri supplied helpfully.

Emma kept a placid expression on her face, aware that Shane Monaghan was staring at her again, and wished the floor would open up and swallow her. "Yes. I've never experienced anything like this."

"Well, most people from your land haven't," Aidan pointed out. She rolled her eyes.

"Let's go find Nioclas," Brianagh said, worry in her tone. She glared at Aidan. "I don't know if he can fix what you've done." She dragged Emma away, and Aidan turned to clasp hands with someone, not bothering to say goodbye. He winked at Emma.

"He told Monaghan you're handfasted to him," Bri almost growled. "Unbelievable. That's like dangling a piece of fresh meat in front of a starved dog."

"Did you just call me fresh meat?" Emma wondered aloud.

"Sorry. But the metaphor fits. Shane is a very competitive man. Aidan's just thrown down the gauntlet in the ultimate game of Win the Fair Maiden."

"What did Shane say back?"

Brianagh's mouth settled into a grim line. "The same sentiment as: To the victor go the spoils."

They reached Nioclas, who was chatting with yet another man dressed in different colors, and Emma realized that the different colors must symbolize the different clans. That explained why her dress matched Brianagh's, as well as Nioclas and Aidan's léines.

She was dressed in MacWilliam colors.

Brianagh said something, but Nioclas gave a shake of his

head and turned back to the man. Brianagh's arm tightened around Emma's, and she dragged her off in another direction.

"The kitchens," Brianagh said through clenched teeth. "We need to regroup."

Emma didn't understand what all the fuss was about, but she did understand she needed to move faster to keep her arm attached to her body. They exited the castle and headed into a small outbuilding.

The kitchen was bustling, but all the women stopped to curtsy as they entered. Bri led Emma to a small round table in the corner of the kitchen, and they sat. "This is a disaster. I can't believe he would do this."

"I think he was trying to save me from suitors," Emma interjected, feeling the need to defend Aidan's actions.

"I think you understand the term *pissing contest*," Bri replied, her eyes narrowing to slits. "I won't allow Aidan to ruin this match."

"Should I return to my chamber?" Emma asked, wishing she were anywhere else. She didn't want to mess up a medieval matchmaking soiree, especially as she understood what it felt like to be the second-best woman in a man's life.

She couldn't do that to another person.

"No. If you go there, he'll seek you out."

"Aidan?"

"No. Monaghan."

Emma shook her head. "He just met me. Make him select from his list."

Brianagh slammed her hands on the table in frustration, then sighed heavily. "He will want what isn't his. I seated him with Brigit of the Muskerry clan, his first choice. But you watch. He'll give his attentions to you tonight, offer you his first dance—which you've already accepted by way of his father—and declare a meeting in the lists tomorrow to show his future bride what he has to offer. He'll give his favor to you, and Brigit won't accept him after that. And I, for one, wouldn't blame the poor girl!"

Emma chewed her lip. "There's got to be another way to save this match. Especially as I'm not staying."

Nioclas poked his head in the door. "Ah, there you are. Shane just asked me for use of the lists tomorrow. He said he's excited to announce his choice once he's shown his warrior prowess."

Brianagh dropped her head onto the table in despair.

Emma explained the situation, and Nioclas's face darkened. "My brother is the biggest kind of arse," he growled. "Apologies, Lady Emma. What he's set you up for is either a kidnapping or a marriage."

Emma stood, knocking her stool out from under her knees. "You know that's impossible. I'm not staying here."

Nioclas gave her a steady look. "I wonder how you plan to return, my lady."

She paused. "Reilly?"

"Perhaps," Nioclas said slowly.

Emma tried to ignore the uncertainty in his voice.

* * *

"Lady Brianagh informs me that we're handfasted," Emma said carefully as Aidan placed a piece of bread on their shared trencher.

"Don't worry. We won't *actually* marry."

Her heart twisted at his words. *Why not?* she found herself thinking. *Am I so unlovable, then?* Instead, she took a large gulp of her wine before adding, "Right. Of course not."

His mouth settled into a grim line, and she wondered at his moodiness.

"Your brother informs me that I'm now at risk of kidnapping. From Shane."

He raised an eyebrow as he placed more food on the trencher. "Shane? You're on a first-name basis with the man now?"

"He introduced himself as such, so I suppose we are."

He shrugged. "He won't kidnap you."

"Why not?"

"You're not worth the risk. Besides, guards sleep outside your door. You're safe enough."

Not worth the risk.

As irrational as it was, the words stung. She blinked back an unwelcome prick of tears.

"Aidan," Nioclas admonished him, surprised at his harsh words. "Lady Emma, pay him no heed. I've doubled your guards for the duration of your stay, so you are quite safe."

"Thank you, my laird."

Bri gave Emma a sympathetic glance, and Emma looked away. Aidan was in a fine temper for some reason, and though he'd made her no promises, he had kissed her a time or two as though he meant it. She should've known not to look into it too deeply. He was being kind. They'd been through a lot together, but now that she was out of danger (by a few hundred years), he had lost interest. He was the white knight who rescued maidens in distress, and she wasn't in distress anymore.

She wasn't surprised by his determination to steer clear of a real relationship with her. She wasn't real relationship material.

"Well, handfasted or not, your first dance of the evening is with the young Monaghan," Bri declared.

"Like hell it is," Aidan snapped.

Emma felt her own patience break. "As you *just* stated, we're not really getting married. So it shouldn't matter to you who I dance with."

He refused to make eye contact with her. "Fine. Do as you want. I don't care. I'm just trying to save Bri's party."

"Don't bring me into it," Bri objected. "You're the one who issued the challenge to Monaghan."

Emma straightened. "Right. About that. I refuse to be in the middle of some testosterone-fueled brouhaha."

"Brouhaha?" Reilly asked, interested.

Emma's eyes narrowed. "*Yes*, brouhaha." She turned her attention back to Aidan. "Let's take a moment to remember that I am not your wife, or your handfasted…whatever—"

"Betrothed," Reilly supplied.

"Handfasted betrothed," Emma continued, "or someone to

toy with, so I suggest you cut the BS immediately. I don't want to add *kidnapped* to my stupidly long list of bad things that almost happen to me."

Reilly leaned over his plate so he could see her around Aidan's silent form. "Your appearance here has caused quite a stir, my lady. You're quite beautiful, and many men have made their interest known to Laird MacWilliam. Perhaps you should speak with him about your recourse. Most of the men here would find you more than worth the risk."

"Shut it, O'Malley," Aidan growled.

"It pains you that I speak the truth." Reilly wagged his eyebrows at Emma. "But that cannot be what keeps me silent. If given the choice, Lady Emma, would you stay here with MacWilliam with his boorish self, or return to your homeland, with its challenges?"

Emma froze. *Given the choice? He's really not going back?*

Aidan refused to look at her.

"So you'd stay here?" she questioned.

"I haven't a choice," he replied curtly.

She blinked. "Oh." She looked at Reilly. "He doesn't have a choice?"

Reilly shrugged, then returned his attention to his trencher.

"She's going back," Aidan said abruptly.

"That's up to Lady Emma," Reilly replied without inflection.

A vein in Aidan's neck began to throb. It seemed as though whatever temporary truce the two men had was suddenly null and void.

"We will have private speech later," Aidan replied angrily to Reilly. To Emma, he growled, "You're going back."

"You don't get to make decisions for me," she replied hotly. To Reilly, she added, "I didn't agree to that."

"Maybe not, but you agreed to everything else," Aidan spat, angry now. "Every last decision. You signed the contract, you got in the car, you got on the plane."

Her eyes narrowed further. "If you want to circle back to

the source of all those decisions, perhaps we ought to start at the beginning."

"When the pictures of your client and your ex went viral?" he asked sardonically, tearing a hunk of bread from the loaf in front of them.

Emma stopped cold.

"Low blow," Reilly murmured, then held silent.

"I was referring to your insistence that I work for you. Fool that I am, of *course* it started with the pictures," she replied coldly, past her very dry throat.

"The job offer was Colin's doing, wasn't it?" Reilly interjected. "Weren't you scouting Emma for his PR position?"

"Perhaps we ought to take this to my solar," Nioclas cut in.

"No one can understand us," Reilly pointed out. "We're also too far from any of the other tables to be overheard."

"This seems like something my brother and the lady should discuss in private," Nioclas tried again.

Emma didn't hear him over her spinning mind. "Are you saying that you didn't want me as your publicist?"

"That's exactly what I'm saying," Aidan affirmed. "I was scouting you for him. Your circumstances, unfortunate as they were, aligned perfectly with my goals. I got you to him."

So the protection he offered her…it was to ensure that his cousin would have someone to fill a position?

She was ten times a fool. Of course it wasn't about her. It was about what she could do for someone else. Like always.

"What about Ireland?" she asked, hating the catch in her voice.

Aidan turned cool eyes to her. "What about it?"

Bri's look of miserable sympathy was almost more than Emma could take.

And just like that, Emma decided she'd had enough. No more teasing kisses, or holding hands. No more pretending that maybe she could have a relationship with Aidan MacWilliam. He was out of her league, sure. But he also was a first-rate jerk for allowing her to think there might be something between them. She always knew she wasn't relationship material, but seeing as how she'd fallen right into his plans for her…Apparently, her taste in men hadn't improved since she'd sworn them off after Ben.

In a low voice, she hissed, "I am so very grateful we never finished what was started back at Colin's."

"What, exactly, did you start at Colin's?" Brianagh asked, her curiosity fully piqued.

"I tried to dissuade her," Reilly said matter-of-factly.

"Perhaps you should save your speech for another time," Brianagh said.

"But then you said you didn't really mean it!" Emma exclaimed, ignoring her. "I am so grateful Cian interrupted us. Talk about a sign that sleeping with you is a bad idea!"

Aidan turned a cool gaze on her. "When I finally take you to bed, it will be the best night of your life. I vow it."

Brianagh choked, and Nioclas clapped her on the back as he exclaimed, "Saints above, Aidan, she's a lady!"

"And that seals it," Reilly said with a sigh. "Tomorrow, in the lists. Choose, swords or joust."

Emma glared at Aidan. "You will *never* get me in your bed."

"Challenge accepted," Aidan snarled.

Emma's eyes narrowed.

"Joust," Aidan answered Reilly, his gaze locked on hers. "And when I best him, you'll marry me, here. Because you," he leaned closer to her, "are," their noses almost touched, "mine."

The words felt different, coming from Aidan. The threat wasn't one of violence…it was a sensual warning that made her lose her breath. And that made her even angrier.

"Then I will pray for your failure," she snapped.

"The terms are set, then."

Emma looked up in surprise. She hadn't noticed Laird Monaghan and his son standing at the table in front of them.

Emma risked a glance at Bri, whose face was grim.

Nioclas stood and the hall quieted. He spoke in Gaelic, and the crowd broke out in cheers.

"Nioclas just announced that Aidan would be showing his prowess in the lists tomorrow, using the joust as his combat of choice," Bri translated, squatting down next to Emma's chair. Hands shot up, and Aidan sat back, crossing his arms with a deadly expression on his face, as men made their way to their table to have speech with him and declare their place in line for the morning's activities.

"And those men are going to challenge him for your hand."

"What?!" she nearly shrieked, then remembered herself. After determining no one was paying much attention to her at the moment, she hissed, "No!"

"Look at the bright side," Bri offered. "Now that Aidan's declared he wants you as his wife, Shane won't. He'll be expected to participate, as most of the eligible men will, but if he does it halfheartedly, the match with Brigit can be saved."

Emma blinked. "I don't think I understand your social rules as much as I thought I did."

"They're way more complicated than what is written," Bri agreed. "But trust me. This fixes everything."

"Except the whole me getting married part," Emma replied flatly.

"Oh. Right." Bri chewed her lip. "Well, let's cross that bridge when we get to it. For now, Aidan may have just saved my behind."

"Which, I might point out, he put in jeopardy in the first place," Emma argued.

"Perhaps," Brianagh agreed.

In that moment, Emma hated Aidan MacWilliam. She didn't want to be a prize. She didn't want to be bartered for. She didn't want to owe anyone anything, ever.

Surely the laird of the castle wouldn't force her to wed someone she didn't know. She hoped, anyway. She also hoped that Reilly would be able to return her to the future sooner rather than later.

CHAPTER 16

"You are the biggest kind of fool."

Aidan wanted to ignore his brother, but he knew it would be fruitless. "I won't argue the fact."

"By the time you're done tomorrow, your arms will fall off from exhaustion," Nioclas continued in disgust. "Is she truly worth this?"

Aidan nodded.

"And you want this?"

"Aye."

"Said with such certainty," Nioclas mocked. "You understand that if Monaghan decides he wants her, you'll have to fight him truly?"

"Aye."

"Is that all you're capable of saying?" Frustrated, Nioclas threw his hands in the air. "I vow, Aidan, you would try the patience of a saint!"

"I spoke with O'Malley earlier," Aidan said heavily. "He isn't certain he can get her back to the future."

"You took a calculated risk in coming back," Nioclas replied, "and it didn't work out. So now she's stuck here, as are you, and you think marriage is the only option for her?"

"It's her only solution," Aidan replied grimly.

"Oh, just what every woman wishes to hear from her lover," Nioclas snapped. "Your lack of romance insults our clan."

Aidan sighed. "I've changed, Nick. Romance isn't as important as the facts right now. She thinks she understands our time—but she doesn't, not really. If I don't marry her, she'll end up dragged to the altar against her will and I'll have to go kill someone to rescue her."

"No one will drag her anywhere. She's under my protection."

"Oh? And what if Monaghan decides that you're not that much of a threat after all? Or if he decides to carry her away into the night? Once he forces her to marry him, you'll have to get approval from the clan council to go to war for her. You know they'll never agree to it, not for a lady who was under your protection for less time than it takes to blink." Aidan flexed his hands, wishing he had something to punch. "Do you expect the clan to go to war for someone who has absolutely no impact on their lives, except for a bit of grief the lady of the castle might suffer?"

Nioclas looked as though he wanted to argue the point, but he blew out his breath. "Nay," he admitted.

"Of course not. Do you not realize I've thought all this through?" Aidan asked, angered. "Because I have, in great depth. I've got a man after Emma's head in the future, and quite a few men after her skirt right now. There's no choice *but* to show my hand."

Nioclas rubbed his hand over his face. "Couldn't you have at least given the lass some sort of proposal that would make her more amenable to your suit?"

"I had hoped to, but then I lost my head a bit. O'Malley wouldn't stop with his incessant chatter, Monaghan came rushing to Emma's aid, and I saw how those men were staring at her during dinner. I don't regret the action," Aidan replied wearily. "I'll make it up to her later. I'll have the rest of our lives, after all."

"If she accepts you," Nioclas reminded him. "And if she is, in fact, unable to go back from whence she came."

Aidan spun around. "What?"

"I've never forced anyone to marry another. I don't intend to start now."

"Are you in jest, or did you imbibe too much at supper tonight?"

Nioclas shook his head firmly. "Neither. You must woo her on your own, and she must go to the altar willingly."

"She'll go willingly," Aidan growled.

"Oh, aye, that's convincing," Nioclas retorted. "She seemed so very amenable to you at dinner tonight."

"She wants me," Aidan retorted. "She's just scared."

"If you stopped growling like a wounded beast, perhaps you could show her some of our legendary charm," Nioclas suggested.

"Not that it's any of your concern—" Aidan started.

"Oh, brother mine, your happiness is my utmost concern," Nioclas protested with a smirk.

"—but Emma has seen my more charming self. She's had a rough time lately, and I *had* planned to give her time to work through her concerns."

Nioclas chortled. "It didn't seem as though your Lady Emma was as susceptible to your charms as you might think."

"Oh, she's susceptible," Aidan snapped.

Nioclas finally released his laughter. Aidan crossed his arms, staring at him in exasperation as he wiped his eyes.

"The Aidan of yore had females falling at his feet. By the saints, you had lasses claiming you'd been in their beds just for the chance at the glory of it all! Yet here you are, insulting a woman, thinking it would win her heart. Apologies if I find the situation more than amusing."

"I have never seen you laugh so hard before," Aidan observed dryly. He forced a smile. "'Tis good to see you so happy, after so many years of melancholy."

"A good woman does that to a man," Nioclas admitted. "Truly, I am fortunate. And I'd like nothing better than for your own fortune to be as strong as mine."

"It will be," Aidan replied with a confidence he didn't feel.

"Susceptibility," Nioclas agreed. He clapped him on the back. "Chin up, brother. You're a brilliant strategist. I've no doubt you can overcome this battle to win the war."

* * *

Emma was out of breath by the time Shane returned her to her seat. He signaled for more wine.

"You are a good dancer," she said, gratefully accepting the cup.

He flashed white teeth at her. "For not knowing the dance, you kept up very well yourself."

Emma avoided his eyes, although she couldn't help but smile. His eyes crinkled at the corners endearingly. Her heart should've been thumping with excitement from his attention, but the only thumping she felt was from the dance steps that echoed through the floor. Emma had no idea how to direct his attentions elsewhere, but luckily Brianagh joined them.

"I do believe Brigit of Muskerry would love a dance, while Lady Emma recuperates," Brianagh noted, taking the seat next to Emma. She turned imploring eyes on Shane. "Perhaps you'll oblige her?"

"Of course, my lady." He bowed, then winked at Emma before sauntering off.

"What I don't understand is why he would need your services," Emma said, her eyes following him across the room. "He's handsome, charming, intelligent, and the son of the clan leader. All in all, quite a catch."

"His father wants to secure an alliance," Brianagh replied, also tracking Shane's movements. When he reached Brigit, she relaxed slightly. "He wants to ally with the Muskerry clan, but Laird Muskerry has no daughter and the women of that clan are...um..." She paused, trying to find the right words. "Well, they're not as attractive as other women," she finished. She cringed. "I hate even saying that."

"Brigit is very pretty," Emma said, watching the raven-haired beauty dancing with Shane.

"That she is. She's a Muskerry cousin, who hails from Scotland. She's here on an extended visit, and if we can get them married, it'll be a wonderful match for all parties."

"I don't want to encourage him," Emma sighed. "I don't know what to do to turn his attentions away, though. I don't know what to do to turn *any* of their attentions away."

"You could go along with Aidan's plan," Bri suggested. "Pretend you're excited to be engaged, and pretend you're in love."

Emma raised an eyebrow. "Aidan told me how you and Nioclas fell in love. I smell a matchmaker at work here."

Bri grinned. "Well, it *did* work for us. And it would be so nice to see Aidan settled and happy. But I'm suggesting it out of purely personal reasons. I want Shane and Brigit married."

"To keep your successful reputation?"

"The businesswoman in me says yes, but the romantic in me says it's for a happy life." Bri's eyes misted a little. "I do love a happy ending."

"How can he not get a happy ending?" Emma asked. "Add to the good looks and charm, he's just plain *nice*."

"They're all nice when they're trying to win a lady's heart," Brianagh said with a small laugh. "And I believe Shane to be a good man."

"Any ideas as to how I can aid in the match?" Emma asked.

Brianagh smiled blandly at a laird who passed by their table, then replied, "Well, you gave him the obligatory dance that his father secured. So, the next dance he asks of you, kindly inform him you're waiting for your betrothed. Then ask him how his dance with Brigit went."

Emma nodded her assent, and when he approached her again, she did exactly that. His enthusiasm dimmed, but he remained cordial and pleasant before excusing himself.

"Works like a charm every time," Bri noted with satisfaction. "The language of love is the same no matter the century."

Emma snorted. "At least I'm learning a lot about medieval matchmaking."

"There is that," Bri agreed, and they dissolved into giggles.

"I wonder what you ladies find so humorous," a masculine voice asked from behind them.

Brianagh dropped her head back and gazed adoringly at her husband. "Girl talk. Where did you go for so long? Lairds have been asking for you."

"We went to his solar, to weep over the expense of your little event," Aidan said as he approached them. "Saints, Bri, there must be at least a hundred people here, eating through your larder!"

"I'm not worried," Bri replied. "They're here to see a wedding, Aidan. I plan to give them just that. Speaking of, how was your dance with Monaghan?" Brianagh asked Emma.

Emma shot her a murderous glare, but Bri kept her expression serene.

Aidan's face was stony. "Perhaps I could have the next dance, Lady Emma?"

He waited patiently for her answer, and despite her anger, her heart began to thump in triple overtime. She nodded her head wordlessly. He slowly brought her hand up from her lap, turned it over, and kissed the inside of her wrist. She gasped softly, and felt his smile against her skin.

Carefully, he placed her hand back in her lap. "I'll find you when the musicians strike up another chord, then." He turned to his brother and murmured in Gaelic, "Susceptibility."

Nioclas tipped his head, and Aidan left the three of them staring after him, Bri and Nioclas in amusement, Emma in angry confusion.

Again.

* * *

When the music started up, Nioclas offered Emma his hand before Aidan could make his way across the great hall.

Emma took it, suspicious. Something was up, but she couldn't figure out what. Instead of leading her to the line of people forming for the next dance, he walked with her slowly around the room. He greeted various people as they circled the tables and introduced her to almost everyone. Emma knew better than to question what he was doing in front of others, her language aside. He was the laird, and if he wanted to walk her around the room, he would walk her around the room.

After awhile, Nioclas leaned down and said quietly, "If I might ask you a few questions, Lady Emma?"

"Um, sure," she replied nervously.

"I do not mean to intimidate you," Nioclas informed her. He motioned for her to head toward the enormous hearth.

"Well, you do," she replied boldly. "You're very serious."

"In comparison to my younger brother?" he asked, stopping when they reached the wall.

"Not just him. Everyone. You seem like someone I don't want to cross."

"Intelligent observation. A key trait in a life partner," Nioclas mused. Before she could respond to that, he went on, "Aidan was seven years old when our mother was killed. He witnessed it. He came to me, terrified as any child would be, and unsure who he could trust. You see, it was our sire who killed her. Aidan's faith in people was shaken that day, and I made certain that he could always rely on me to be the one constant in his life. He needed a lot of time to learn how to trust again, but he did it. I never left him behind, never put him in a place where he wasn't safe from the world. When he was old enough to begin training, I ensured he stayed at the castle instead of being sent to a neighboring ally, because—again—he needed reassurance that he had at least one person on his side."

"I had no idea," Emma whispered.

"When he went missing on a mission I had assigned him, I was destroyed. I blamed myself for many years, and just when I'd given up hope of ever seeing my brother in this world again, he comes riding into my bailey as though he just left last week. I must wonder why he came now."

Your guess is as good as mine, she thought with a snort.

"I believe he came because he needed the reassurance that the most important thing in his life would be protected while he dispatched the threat." Nioclas surveyed the crowd, then back at her. "It is a difficult thing in your time to dispatch a threat."

"He plans to dispatch Ben?" Emma asked, her mind whirling. "As in kill him?"

"I'm unsure. Do not think him cruel or evil," Nioclas warned. "Our time has certain rules that govern it. Death is the only thing that will stop the man who wants you dead. You or him, Lady Emma." He took a breath. "I'm asking you to try to place your trust in the man Aidan is."

She pressed her lips together. "With all due respect, Laird MacWilliam, your brother has made it very clear that I'm nothing to him."

He inclined his head. "It seems to be a very large thing to bring you here if you truly mean nothing to him."

"You cannot hide behind my brother," Aidan interrupted as he approached them, smiling. "I've come for my dance, Lady Emma."

Nioclas gave her a swift bow and walked away without further comment.

"Your brother is a little scary," she admitted, watching Nioclas as he rejoined Brianagh.

"He only appears so, to properly intimidate the other clans. He keeps peace through his reputation of war."

"Reputation of war? Yeah. Scary."

"Unfortunately," Aidan said as he led her into the throng of dancers, "that's life here. Peace one moment, war the next. Do you know the steps?"

"Of war?" she asked.

"No, the dance," he said, laughter in his eyes.

"It's hard to keep up with you sometimes," she said on a sigh. "You change topics very quickly."

"I like to keep your mind engaged. So," he responded with a cheeky grin, "do you know the steps?"

"No," she admitted, refusing to be stymied by his sudden, inexplicable good cheer. "But then again, you knew that."

"True, I did. Which is why I told Nick to take you around the hall during the first set. This one is not a structured dance."

"You are making my life difficult," Emma announced as he pulled her in close.

"You realize that if you just gave into my charm, your life would be so much easier."

Charm? For a moment, Emma thought back to the Aidan of

the last few weeks. She thought of how easy it would be to wake up next to him every morning, laugh with him every day, and feel the erratic beat of her heart each time his eyes devoured her, dark with desire. She thought about what his brother said, and oh, how she wanted to give in to him. But she'd given her heart away before, hadn't she? And all she received from that was constant fear and a very real death threat.

Here she was, her heart so entwined with this man, and Aidan had all but admitted he only needed her to fulfill some obligation to his cousin.

She had to untangle herself, and fast.

Aidan spun her suddenly, then drew her even closer to him.

"Stop thinking so hard," he murmured. "Let me help you separate the men from the boys, Emma. Men stand by their vows."

"And boys don't?" she replied, leaning back slightly.

"I think you know the answer to that."

He spun her again, bringing her flush against his chest. "Sometimes, when your soul finds its mate, it lets out a great sigh, and with it, you fall."

"When you fall, you get hurt," Emma replied curtly.

He placed his lips against her ear. "I'll catch you, Emmaline. I vow it. Let yourself fall."

The music stopped, and the people around them clapped for the musicians. Aidan bowed slightly. "When you're ready, I'll be here. Arms open." He winked. "Guaranteed catch."

She watched him take his leave of the floor, nonplussed. Nothing was ever guaranteed.

She'd be a fool to forget that.

CHAPTER 17

Emma strolled along slowly, marveling at the order of the garden outside the kitchen. The rows stretched out neatly, twenty or more plants in full glory in each row. They were all labeled—garlic, onion, leeks, cabbage, celery, spinach, carrots. The rows were extensive, and had a surprising amount of variety.

"Reilly sends seeds back here with various travelers he comes across."

Emma nearly jumped out of her skin. She spun around. "Lady Brianagh! I thought I was alone."

Bri's expression was faraway as she gazed at the bounty. "It's quite amazing what grows in the soil here. I was never much of a gardener growing up, but here, we have to grow or raise everything. And it's not just us we have to feed," she went on, bending down to check one of the plants. "It's an entire clan."

"This doesn't seem like enough to feed a clan," Emma said dubiously. It was a great garden for a family of four, but a family of five hundred or more? She couldn't see it.

"We've cultivated it so these can be grown in the fields adjacent to the castle." She added in a whisper, "Though I chose to live in the Middle Ages, I insert a bit of the twenty-first century whenever I can." She straightened and brushed her hands on her skirt. "Of course, only when it won't impact history. If it's not elsewhere in Ireland, we don't trade it."

The sun broke free of the clouds, and a ray of sunshine lit up the garden. Emma raised her face to the sun, enjoying the warmth. After a moment, she whispered, "Was it worth it?"

Brianagh didn't have to ask what she meant. "Absolutely."

"Even when it's cold, and war comes to your front door," Emma pressed. "And when you can't take a hot shower, or call your cousin, or even pop down to your local supermarket for some ice cream?"

"Aside from the ice cream, which is cruel to bring up in front of me, being as my lifelong hiatus from it is detrimental to my overall well-being, all the other stuff is just filler. It replaces meaningful relationships with fluff. Unnecessary fluff. I'd love to call Colin, or James, or my aunt and uncle, but I can't. It's a fact of life that I've come to terms with." Brianagh leaned down and pulled a couple of leaves from another plant. "Hot showers mean nothing to me anymore. I love a long soak in the tub—it's a time for me, when I can relax and fully unwind. I never took that kind of time for myself when I was working all the time. Celtic Connections is a great accomplishment, but I'm so thankful I'm not part of it anymore. It would've sucked me dry."

Brianagh looked at peace. There were no dark circles under her eyes from working late, no hunched back from too many hours at a computer. Her hands bore some calluses, but the ring on her left hand shone brightly in the sun. She was completely at ease with herself and her home.

And her choices.

Emma felt a prick of tears. She hadn't felt at ease with herself in years—she had worked herself into the ground, only to come up for air and see that there was nothing to show for it. Her home was four walls in the middle of a city—generic art hung on the neutral-colored walls, neutral-toned wood floors did nothing to warm her toes, and her kitchen consisted of a two-burner stove with a half-size oven, a small broken microwave, and an apartment-sized refrigerator.

Well, it used to, anyway.

"When was the last time you had a long soak in a tub, with nothing but happy thoughts in your mind?" Brianagh asked softly, slowly twirling a stem of basil between her fingers.

Emma watched it spin and fought the tears. "Maybe when I was a child. But if it happened, I don't remember it."

"What about your family?" Bri asked. "When you visit them, are you relaxed?"

Emma swallowed with difficulty. "I have no family."

"I'm so sorry," Bri murmured.

Emma dashed a tear from her cheek. "Some people in life get everything. Success, money, family, love. Then there are others who work really hard, but the only thing they get is another day of hard work without reward."

"Hmm," Bri said, her eyes full of compassion. "How would you define those words? Success, money, family, and love?"

"With pretty standard definitions," Emma replied with a shrug, striving for nonchalance.

"Humor me, then. Let's start with success," Bri said, leading her down the rows toward a bench set in the stone wall. "For some, it means becoming the president of a company or the laird of a clan. For others, it's raising happy children or saving an injured animal."

They sat down. Emma refused to look at Bri, afraid her tears would overflow the moment she saw the understanding in the woman's eyes.

"Money," Bri continued thoughtfully. "Well, in another lifetime, I would've said you need money to be successful. And money is important, no doubt. But how much do you need? A lot? A bit? I've come to realize that I only need what it will take for me and my family to stay warm with full bellies."

Emma let out a sigh.

Bri stretched her arms above her head and smiled into the sunshine. "The last two—family and love…well, those are there for the taking."

Emma's head snapped up. "That's where you're wrong. Love isn't something you can find—trust me, I looked. In fact, I thought I had it, and look where that landed me."

Bri frowned. "Not all men are bad, Emma."

"But love doesn't happen to everyone. I don't think I'm cut out for love. There's too much you have to give of yourself to see any reward. And, as my history has demonstrated repeatedly, giving doesn't get me anything but pain." Her voice caught on a sob. "I don't think there's anything left of me to give, anyway."

Brianagh put her arm around Emma and gave her a squeeze. "I think you have a lot to give, Em. More than a lot. I'm not the only one who believes that."

Emma gave a self-deprecating laugh. "Oh, Bri, if you're referring to Aidan, you're so wrong. He's one of the lucky ones— crazy success, ungodly amounts of money, and the love of an amazing family." She shook her head, not bothering to check the tears anymore. "But he doesn't need me. He sees me as a challenge. He's been trying to get back to this life for years, and my life isn't here…I could never make his life any better, and eventually he'd get bored, like they all do. I won't risk feeling that way again."

Bri wrapped her other arm around Emma. "Some risks are worth taking. I say this from experience, Emma." She pulled back and searched her eyes. "Love is a risk worth taking. True love is more than the lust, more than the overwhelming feelings of joy. It's in the mundane. The way he puts food on your plate before serving himself, when he gives his cloak when you're without. The way he puts your life above his own, always. The number of guards he employs to ensure nothing happens to you when he can't be there to protect you himself. The way he holds you, as though you're both the most delicate and strongest creature in the world… That's true love, Emma."

Emma's eyes filled again as memories flooded her mind. Aidan covering her body completely, to protect her body from the shattering glass when they were shot at in New York City. The way he wrapped her in his cloak as they made their way to the MacWilliam castle, the number of guards dedicated specifically to her safety…

Did Aidan love her? Because, damn the man, she certainly loved him. But that wouldn't be enough.

A loud cheer sounded from behind them, and Brianagh stood. "Come on. The tournament's set to begin soon, and we need to get cleaned up."

Emma took a deep breath and let it out shakily. Nodding, she took Brianagh's arm, and they hurried back to the castle. Was she ready to fall?

She thought that maybe she ought to find out.

* * *

"Oh my God."

Brianagh laughed at Emma's expression. "It's amazing, isn't it?"

Emma stared out over the lists, awed. Clan-colored flags hung from a series of long wooden beams, placed end to end on supports, directly through the middle of the enclosure. The same flags hung in the wooden stands, where people were quickly filling up the seats in their respective areas. The largest section was decorated with blue-and-gray flags, and hung from what looked like a president's box above the tallest stand was a large tapestry emblazoned with a shield. On it, a hawk proudly flew, its wings spread wide, a shield on its chest…and that shield displayed the letter M, leaves of ivy snaking their way around each line of the letter, with a sword slicing across the M and its foliage.

Just like the napkin at The Colcannon, Emma remembered. She felt a strange sense of worlds colliding as she studied the tapestry.

"We're heading up there, to the best seats in the house," Brianagh said excitedly, dragging her up the steps.

From the higher vantage point, Emma could see clear across the crowd, down into the jousting area, and the one marked for swordsmanship. The MacWilliam section was filled with a few hundred people, all waving flags or wearing blue. The Monaghans wore their bright green, and though they were small in number, they certainly made up for it in noise. Emma counted eight different clans gathered for the tournament, and she concluded that this was a very big event. She hadn't ever read that eight clans gathered together peacefully. One or two, perhaps, but eight…

"How do you do it?" she asked Brianagh, unable to overcome her amazement. "All these clans, in one place, without fighting?"

"Love conquers all, Emma." She glanced out at the crowd, a happy grin on her face. "It really does."

A horn blew from below, and there was a mad dash to find seats. People were cheering wildly, and women were lining the front row, displaying their ample charms.

"They're hoping for a flag from one of the warriors," Bri explained. "In exchange, they'll give him a favor—in our case, instead of a ribbon, it's a kiss!"

Emma laughed. "I guess that's one way to go about it."

The horn blew again, and this time, a line of horses galloped in, kicking up dust as they circled the arena, the men holding their clan's flag high. Each man was dressed in chain mail, the sounds of it just audible under the beat of hooves. The arena pulsed with energy as the ladies in front started calling and cheering, and the men behind them booed until their own clansman passed by, at which point they went wild.

The warriors galloped around the arena twice, then they broke the line and each headed in a different direction. The noise in the arena shook the wood beneath Emma's feet. She gripped the edge of the box and grinned at Brianagh and Nioclas, who stood next to her.

Aidan rode over, expertly reigning in his horse, and he made a show of walking the beast back and forth, looking at each woman who waved and called out to him. He rubbed his chin thoughtfully, as though he were contemplating which woman to give his flag to when suddenly he vaulted off his horse and hopped over the banister, into the crowd.

Noise unlike any Emma had ever heard ensued. Clansmen were cheering madly, women were jostling each other to get to him, but he charged up the steps and stopped directly in front of Emma.

"A flag, my lady?" he asked, unable to contain his smile.

"How much does that chain mail weigh?" Emma wondered.

"A very savvy publicist once told me that responding to a question with another question just invites more questions." He held the flag out, and she took it, momentarily speechless, as the world narrowed to just the two of them.

"Do you forget nothing?" she asked, emotion welling in her throat.

He wagged his eyebrows playfully, then offered his cheek, waiting for her kiss. She leaned in, and at the last moment, he turned, capturing her lips with his. He didn't linger, but he gave her a quick bite on her lower lip before pulling away and facing the crowd in triumph.

Emma covered her mouth and started laughing.

He shot her a wink over his shoulder and said, "It weighs about fifty pounds," before he charged back down the steps, hopped the banister, and vaulted himself onto his horse.

"Showoff," Emma murmured, a bubble of joy enveloping her. She let out a breath.

Emma watched with amusement as Shane brought his horse to the Muskerry clan and offered a flag of green to Brigit, who curtsied before accepting it. She clasped it to her chest, and he tipped his cheek toward her. She leaned forward and gave him a very chaste kiss, and the Muskerry and Monaghan clans cheered.

Brianagh gave her a smile of relief. Match saved.

* * *

Aidan shifted, ignoring the sweat under his chain mail as he stood next to his horse. He placed a calming hand on the beast's neck, murmuring to it as he watched a rival clansman land in a cloud of dust.

Aidan hadn't jousted in almost ten years. It used to be his favorite sport; unseating a man from atop his horse gave a feeling of triumph like no other. Of course, being the unseated gave a feeling of pain like no other. He remembered nursing a very sore backside for the better part of a se'ennight during his training years.

"Do you remember how the healers here set a broken bone?" Reilly asked from behind him.

Aidan's horse snorted and danced a couple of steps away, and Aidan patted the beast reassuringly. He murmured to the horse, "That's exactly how I feel about him too."

Reilly leaned against the stable wall, watching the now-hobbling warrior make his way off the field. "No one's been able to unseat Monaghan."

"Or perhaps they're allowing him a good show for his soon-to-be bride," Aidan responded.

The recently unseated clansman made his way into the stable, holding his wrist and swearing.

"Is he that good, then?" Reilly asked the defeated warrior.

The man breathed hard and nodded. "Is the healer nearby?"

"I believe she is down there," Reilly replied, pointing. "Back of the stables. Get in line."

He limped off, muttering about fools on horses and hurting his sword arm.

"You're sure?" Reilly asked in his most uninterested voice. "Because—and this is important, so keep those ears open, lad—I wouldn't want you to forget that you've still got to unseat me to get to your lady."

Aidan slammed his helmet down and dug his heels into the horse's side, spraying a satisfactory amount of dirt into Reilly's face.

If Emma was stuck here, Aidan would ensure her happiness. He would make her smile every day, show her how important she was to him, show her how much he loved her.

He definitely loved Emma.

But he knew she might choose the future over him. The thought twisted like hot metal in his gut. Could she love him back? He wasn't sure how to know. Last night, he'd panicked when he'd heard the detachment in her voice about being handfasted. He sought to arm her with the knowledge that she wasn't being forced to do anything, but she'd taken his comment about marriage entirely the wrong way. And as the conversation wore on, Aidan realized that he loved her enough to let her go…and that she didn't love him enough to stay.

Not that he would ask that of her—he knew exactly what she would be giving up.

But a part of him wished she might want to give it up for him.

The crowd, as expected, went crazy when he galloped out, and he waved his MacWilliam flag as he sized up his first competitor. Monaghan had already bested four of the eight, and he showed signs of fatigue; his posture wasn't as straight, and he was rolling his right shoulder to ease the pain.

The horn blew, and Aidan cleared his mind of everything except Monaghan's sore shoulder. The two men brought their horses to their respective ends of the track, and at the second horn, they took their positions. Aidan hefted the long, blunt-tipped lance from the squire. He tucked the handle tightly against his side and raised his shield, and he steadied the horse with his knees.

The third horn blew, and the horses charged, one on either side of the beam. Aidan urged his horse to a breakneck speed and, just before impact, he raised the lance slightly, loosened his grip on the handle, raised his shield to meet Monaghan's lance, and braced himself for the impact.

His lance hit Monaghan squarely in the shoulder, on his bone. Monaghan toppled from his horse, unable to hang on. He rolled when he hit the dirt, showing Aidan he was not seriously injured, and Aidan slowed his own horse.

Aidan dismounted and walked toward Monaghan, who, despite the hard fall, was standing on his own. They reached out and shook hands, more gently than they would normally, and Monaghan grimaced and called him a foul name.

"To the victor, my friend," Aidan said. They both glanced up toward Emma, who was hugging herself and watching them silently. Her golden hair, piled atop her head in a complicated pattern of braids, highlighted her beauty, even as she stood in the shade of the laird's box.

"You are a damn lucky man," Monaghan said to Aidan.

Aidan nodded once, then watched as his competitor took himself from the field to hollers and heckles.

Aidan gave a sweeping bow toward Emma, then returned to his horse amidst the cheers. He prepared himself for the next competitor…then the next, and the next, and the next.

When he stood on the field, victorious as the last jouster standing, he looked up toward Emma, wondering if she understood how truly serious he was about marrying her.

The horn blew again, and Aidan spun around. "What the hell?"

"A late entry, my laird!" one of the squires called out to Nioclas, who nodded regally and took his seat again.

"Bastard," Aidan grumbled, knowing that Nick was only allowing a late entry to show the MacWilliams' prowess. He had barely managed to keep his seat with Muskerry, his final competitor. His legs ached, his back was stiff, and his arm cramped in places he didn't realize were even part of the extremity.

"The O'Malley clan!" the squire called out.

The crowd hushed for a moment, unsure as to what an O'Malley was doing there, but they apparently decided they didn't care. Cheers, hoots, and boos intermingled as Reilly took his place at the end of the beam, waiting for Aidan to mount his steed and fight one more time.

Aidan cursed him. Reilly gave him a salute.

Aidan mounted, then brought his horse around and took his position once more. He snapped his helmet down, slowed his breathing, and waited, poised, for the sound of the horn. When it came, he encouraged the horse to faster speeds, hoping to knock Reilly off-balance with a quick joust to the shoulder.

Reilly slammed into him with a force Aidan hadn't felt from any other, and he tottered on his seat as Reilly's lance snapped in half, wood shards spraying around him. His horse, bless him, took that moment to turn, which was all that saved Aidan from making his own cloud of dust.

Aidan swore and saw Reilly watching him closely. He very subtly rotated his right shoulder—where Reilly had almost, but not quite hit—and held back his grin when Reilly's eyes narrowed. He spun his own horse around to take the position again.

Aidan raised his shield slightly, as though to protect his shoulder, which left his left shoulder all but exposed. He traded his damaged lance for a new one, pleased that he'd made at least some contact with Reilly's shield, which, even from where he sat, looked roughed up.

The horn sounded, and Aidan kept his shield over his right shoulder. At the last moment, he moved it to the left, deftly blocking Reilly's blow, and caught Reilly full on in the stomach, where he hadn't been expecting Aidan to be able to hit. Reilly fell spectacularly, and when the dust cleared, he remained seated, knees bent, with his forearms resting on his knees.

Aidan didn't bother to get off his horse. Instead, he walked the beast over to Reilly and shook his head.

"Why did you let me win?"

Reilly squinted up. "Who says I let you?"

Aidan gave him a suspicious glance. "I get the feeling you don't fail at anything."

"Strange," Reilly mused, "I get that same feeling about you."

Aidan reached a hand down, and Reilly took it, popping onto his feet as though he hadn't just fallen from a tall horse. The crowd cheered, and Reilly looked at him once more.

"You must realize that I'm not your biggest challenge. That is up in the stands, with very little idea as to what happens next."

Aidan dismounted. "Do I have a choice, O'Malley?"

Reilly looked at him silently for a moment. Then, softly, he said, "I don't know, Aidan."

He walked off the field as the MacWilliams jumped the barrier, heading for Aidan. Reilly tipped his head toward Nick, Bri and Emma, leaving Aidan standing, victorious yet disheartened, in the middle of a horde of happy, boisterous clansmen.

He'd never felt more alone.

CHAPTER 18

When Emma finally tore her eyes away from Aidan, who was accepting help from clansmen to remove the chain mail, she grinned widely at Brianagh.

"I can't believe he won!" she cried, excited. "I can't believe I just saw a real tournament!"

Brianagh's smile was tentative. She wrung her hands nervously. "Um, Emma, there's something you should know."

"He has to do swords next?" Emma guessed, craning her neck toward the swordplay area.

Brianagh exchanged a glance with Nioclas. "No, that's not it."

Laird Monaghan was jostling his way through the MacWilliam crowd, headed toward them. Bri was saying something, but Emma was again distracted by the sheer amount of food stuck in the laird's beard. She wondered if she'd missed a food hawker during the event. She would have loved to try the medieval equivalent of popcorn, or a snow cone, or even a hot dog.

She wrinkled her nose. On second thought...no on the hot dog.

"Emma, pay attention! You need to know—" Brianagh stopped short as Monaghan reached their box.

Laird Monaghan said, in very broken English, to Emma, "Well, that settles that, I suppose. In case you were wondering, I thought you'd make a lovely Monaghan. But the Muskerry lass will do nicely, too."

"Um, thank you?" Emma replied uncertainly.

"As you're his ward, it should be easy enough to settle the papers," Laird Monaghan said. He directed his gaze at Nioclas. "My son is disappointed, you see."

Nioclas inclined his head. "I see."

Laird Monaghan nodded his head slowly. "I do not want to become involved in any…conflict…with the Muskerrys. They outnumber us here, aye?"

Nioclas agreed.

"Then I suggest, for all clans involved, that the ceremony happen immediately." He turned his attention back to Emma. "Before my headstrong offspring gets any ideas in his thick skull."

Emma thought Shane seemed intelligent, but she wasn't going to contradict his father, so she agreed enthusiastically without any idea as to what the man was talking about.

Laird Monaghan gave a brisk nod, then made his way back down the steps.

Brianagh groaned loudly. "This is a disaster."

"Perhaps you ought to take Lady Emma to her room for immediate preparations, and explain to her what's happened," Nioclas said grimly. "I'll find that arse and tell him he needs to be in my solar to sign papers."

"Wh-what?" Emma said, looking back and forth between them. "I'm not getting the warm fuzzies here."

Brianagh signaled to Kane, who immediately brought forth her personal guard, before saying, "I'll explain it once we get to your chamber. Kane—send for Sinead immediately."

"Who's Sinead?" Emma asked, allowing Brianagh to steer her out of the box.

"My best dressmaker."

Emma licked her dry lips nervously. "Why would you need your best dressmaker?"

Brianagh set her jaw. "Because Aidan never breaks a vow. Let's leave it at that until we reach your chamber."

Silently, Emma hurried toward the castle, her stomach sinking. Brianagh called out instructions to various people as they made their way to her chamber. Emma didn't know what she was saying, but she understood the urgent tone.

Brianagh flung open the door, and an older woman was standing in the center of the chamber, surrounded by bolts of fabric, a small stool, and six teenage girls. Right behind them, four men lugged a large tub into the room and placed it off to the side.

"Right," Brianagh said briskly, rubbing her hands together. To Emma, she said, "We have four hours." To Sinead, she said something in Gaelic, and the woman blinked, then began barking orders like a general.

Two of the girls came forward and grabbed Emma's arms, hauling her to the stool, where they encouraged her to step up onto it. Sinead placed her arms in a T, and Emma looked at Brianagh in concern.

"Okay. First things first. Don't pass out," Brianagh warned. "Sinead will poke you with a needle to revive you. I'm not kidding."

As if to demonstrate the point, Sinead stuck a long, thick needle into her mouth, then began to measure Emma.

"Next. Last night, Aidan announced that you were handfasted. Shane took that as a challenge. When Aidan charged out today, he cut Shane off to reach the MacWilliam side, and, in going back and forth in front of the clan, didn't allow him the opportunity to come anywhere near you. Shane was not happy, but thankfully, he went with his second choice."

"Brigit," Emma supplied.

"Yes. And when Aidan unseated Shane, he was telling him, in stupid man-code, that you were his, and to back off." Bri chewed her lip. "Laird Monaghan was, in no uncertain terms, demanding that you become unavailable to his son immediately."

"I'm not available to him, though," Emma pointed out. "Aidan already announced we're engaged."

"Which, if you remember, is a perfect excuse to snatch you away," Brianagh reminded her.

"Why would he do that? He seems completely logical and level-headed. Ow!"

Sinead barked something at her.

"She said to stop fidgeting," Bri translated.

"I barely moved!" Emma complained.

"Breathing constitutes fidgeting," Bri replied apologetically. "So, there's more. No—don't respond. Just try to be completely still. Last night, at dinner, Aidan made you a vow, did he not?"

"He didn't say the *word* vow…"

Bri snorted. "I like how you're trying to twist this one, Em, really. But you know, and I know, he made a vow that when he bested Reilly, he was going to marry you. Here." She glanced at Emma nervously. "Now."

"Now," Emma echoed, realization dawning. "Wait, now, as in, *now*, now?"

"Yes. *Now*, now."

"No!"

"Yes."

"I'm being measured for a wedding dress?" Emma asked incredulously as the girls each held up a bolt of fabric for her.

"Pick a color?" Bri responded hesitantly.

"I have to sit down," Emma said, stepping down from the stool.

"Not until you pick a color," Brianagh said, again apologetically, as Sinead chased Emma back onto the stool with the needle. "She's all business, all the time. For what it's worth, I think the gold would look stunning with your hair and eyes."

"Fine. Gold," Emma said, exasperated. "This is ridiculous. I can't marry him. I can't!" She paled. "Does this mean I'm stuck here, in the past?"

Bri said something in Gaelic to Sinead, who immediately began barking orders to the girls.

"I don't know," Bri admitted, then added softly, "but if you are, believe me, there are worse fates than being Aidan's wife."

Emma put her head in her hands. "My choices aren't that great," she said, her voice muffled. "Marry a man who doesn't love me, or face one who wants to kill me."

Sinead patted her shoulder. Emma smiled at her gratefully, then realized the woman was trying to get her off the stool.

All business. Right.

She got down, and a thought occurred to her. "Bri, if I marry Aidan here, but then can go back, am I still married to him?"

"That's dicey," Bri replied slowly. "If you are sent back without him...well, who would know, right? And the vows do say 'until death do you part.' And, technically, he'd be long dead."

Emma's heart constricted at that reality. "Oh, God."

"But if you were to both stay, then you'd be married for life. If you both leave, well...I suppose that's up to you, how to handle it. You'd have no proof that anything happened here." Brianagh clasped Emma's hands. "I'm so sorry this is being thrust upon you. But, if I were in your shoes—and trust me, I've been almost exactly where you are now—I would believe in Aidan. He wouldn't play with your heart. He knows what I just told you, and my guess is that he's protecting you in all possible ways."

"How can you be so sure?" Emma asked. "Because I've been pretty confused since the moment I met him. One side seems so confident, and trustworthy. But there's this other side. A darker side, one that he doesn't let me see, but I can feel it's there. It's almost uncivilized."

Bri squeezed her hands. "I can't say for sure, but I suspect that's his medieval warrior self sparring with his modern self—I would think they'd tend to be at odds more often than not."

Sinead inserted herself between the two women, placed a tape around Emma's chest, then grunted and gave a nod.

Emma raised an eyebrow. "This has to be the most insane day of my life." She looked at the girls, who were furiously cutting long swaths of gold fabric, and Sinead, who was using a knife to outline a pattern in a large sheet of parchment.

Bri laughed. "I bet it is."

"Do I have a choice?" Emma asked in a small voice.

"You'll always have a choice. But there are consequences to each choice, and the one that's most likely to ensure your safety is to marry Aidan."

"Damn it."

"Come on. Let's get you ready for a wedding."

* * *

Aidan stood next to the desk in Nioclas's solar, his arms folded. "When you leave, will you have the ability to take Emma back with you?"

"Are you giving up on her?" Reilly asked in surprise. He tossed a dirk into the air and caught it, then repeated the action. "That's unlike you."

"She needs to understand her options."

Reilly caught the dirk again and scratched his cheek with it thoughtfully. "I wonder why you care so much."

Aidan wanted to smack Reilly's forehead into the nearest hard surface. "I care because she will be my wife. But if she's not willing to stay here, I need to tell her that she can return."

Reilly shook his head in pity. "You poor sap. Of course she can come back with me. In fact, I believe she has to return with me."

"What?" Nioclas broke in.

Aidan felt his chest constrict. "I thought you said you weren't sure?"

"Once I take care of my business here, I've been given orders to return to the future."

Aidan saw the seriousness in Reilly's eyes, and he felt as though he'd been punched in the gut.

"So what you're saying is that Aidan has to choose between Emma and his family?" Nioclas demanded.

"I'm not saying that at all. In fact, I don't think the choice will be up to Aidan," Reilly conceded.

"You think I'm supposed to be here," Aidan concluded, a hollow feeling spreading through his chest.

"Isn't that what you've been working toward for the better part of the last decade?" Reilly asked, seemingly indifferent.

Aidan didn't respond, the enormity of it slamming into him. He blindly groped for the edge of the table.

"Fate isn't always what we think it is," Reilly said, sheathing the dirk in his boot. "I'll leave the two of you to settle the marriage contract."

Aidan sat down heavily, his mind reeling. Fate had handed him his soul mate, only to rip her away?

He didn't want to believe it.

Nioclas gave him a concerned look. "I'll return momentarily."

Aidan nodded, still too shocked to speak. Was his place truly here, at his brother's side? He had always believed that. His brother risked everything for him, everything for their clan. He avenged their mother—if not his own mother by blood, certainly of heart— and saved Aidan from following in the footsteps of an evil sire.

Aidan owed Nioclas everything. He'd sworn his loyalty, and he couldn't break it. He'd already been gone too long. If he left again… he couldn't put his brother through that. But could he let Emma go? Could he convince Reilly to keep her here? Would she *want* to stay here, with him?

His eyes fell on the tapestries that lined the wall behind Nick's desk. Great battle scenes, in which a tall figure with long dark hair fearlessly rode a stallion into a battle. The men on foot, fierce expressions on their faces, were engaged in swordplay, arrows high above their heads in midflight.

On the opposite wall, the tapestry showed a different scene altogether. A woman sat in a chair by a blazing hearth, cradling a small child in her arms. Behind her, in an open doorway, stood the man with the long hair, home from battle. His attention was focused on his wife and child, and his bloodied sword hung above the door. Woven into the blood on the sword were the Latin words, *Pro domo focoque pugnamus.*

We fight for hearth and home.

The MacWilliam clan did not want to expand across Ireland; they were happy with their lot. They had everything they needed— fish from the sea, fertile fields bearing food, peat for their fires, and a strong clan pride. Expansion would mean some would have to give that up and settle in other parts of the land to keep a stronghold. It meant constant war, constant demand, constant giving without receiving.

That was not the legacy Nioclas wanted to leave for his children, nor his children's children. He wanted—and had achieved—peace in a time of greed and war.

No, there was no way Aidan could leave his brother. He glanced at the tapestry behind the desk. If another clan declared war against them, it was Aidan who would protect Nioclas's back during battle.

He knew marrying Emma was the best protection he could give her, for however long she was here. If Monaghan decided he wanted her, he could steal her away in the night and pay any number of priests to perform the marriage, fully against her will. She'd be locked up, too far from O'Malley to ever return to her time.

If she were married to him, the MacWilliams would fight to bring her home, if it came to that.

His gaze traveled back to the tapestry of the woman, his heart torn. Home.

He needed to be here to fight for his brother's hearth and home. After all his brother had done for him, his own happiness was a small price to pay. He knew the truth of it in his mind…now, he needed only to convince his heart.

Nioclas reentered the room. "Are you sure you want this, Aidan?"

He nodded briskly, resolved. "I am. She needs the protection of the clan if she's here for any length of time."

"Is that all it is?" Nioclas questioned.

Aidan rubbed his hands over his face again. "Aye. It's all it can be."

"Then let's draw up the marriage papers."

* * *

What a difference four hours, a bath, an exceedingly determined head seamstress, six seamstresses, and Brianagh's personal chambermaid could make.

Emma smoothed her hands down the fine gossamer silk, unable to stop touching the soft fabric. The square neckline of her long-sleeved, lightweight woolen gown was lined with a deep blue ribbon. Sinead used the blue ribbon around each upper arm, and she encircled Emma's natural waist, separating the top and bottom of the dress. The gold gossamer silk overlaid the gold wool of the skirt, which had a slit up the front to allow a panel of dark blue silk to peek through. From the ribbon bands on her arms fell a swath of the same blue fabric in the skirt.

"This is stunning," she murmured, humbled by the amount of speed and work Sinead put forth. "*Go raibh maith agat,*" she said to Sinead.

Sinead curtsied at the thanks, then hustled her girls out.

"So you do know some Gaelic," Bri said, impressed.

"Not as much as I thought I did," she admitted, "but I think I got 'thank you' right."

"You did," Bri assured her. She walked around Emma, a dreamy look on her face. "You look stunning."

"*Go raibh maith agat,*" Emma said again with a quick curtsy. Her smile faded. "I feel sick when I think too much about what my life has become."

Bri took her hand and patted it. "I wanted to go home when I got here, too."

"What changed?" Emma asked.

"Love. My home is where Nioclas is. And his home, for better or worse, is here."

"I don't know if I love Aidan," Emma blurted out. *Liar. You've loved him for weeks.*

"Do you think that, given time, you could love him?" Bri asked softly.

Someone knocked on the door and called out. Brianagh answered, and looked at Emma.

"Showtime."

"I really think I might be sick," Emma answered.

"No, you won't," Bri said firmly "You'll be fine. Just trust that Aidan knows what he's doing."

Emma took a few deep breaths. *Trust Aidan. Trust him. He knows what he's doing.*

She opened her eyes to find Bri watching her curiously. "You know, Emma, you don't have to go through with this. But, I think you know that if you don't, and something happens here…you won't have a clan to call your own."

"I get it. Where are we headed?"

"The chapel." Bri opened the door. "Aidan!"

He stepped into the room, and Emma's breath caught. He looked resplendent, fresh from his own bath, in a clean léine.

"I need a moment alone with Lady Emma," he said in a low voice. "We will meet you at the chapel."

Bri waited for Emma to nod her assent before exiting the chamber.

Aidan smiled at Emma. "You look beautiful."

She flushed. "Thanks. You look pretty amazing yourself."

"Em, I know you think you're being forced into this. I get that you're between a rock and a hard place. By marrying me, you will have the protection of the clan, no matter what happens to me."

"Are you planning to go somewhere without me?" she joked.

Serious green eyes regarded her steadily. "Nay. But you'll be able to go somewhere—or rather, some*when*—without me." He took a step away from her, closer to the door. "Reilly says he can take you home. To the future."

"You wouldn't come with me?" Emma asked, her heart dropping.

Aidan shook his head. "My life is here. I'm not sure when you could return, but if we marry, you'll have protection for as long as you're here."

Emma felt the icy tendrils of dread spiral in her stomach. "So this will be a marriage of convenience only?"

He nodded briskly, all business. "Aye. There's no need to worry that I'll force anything upon you."

Emma felt the blow to her heart, and could almost hear it as it fully shattered.

She felt the prick of tears, but somehow pushed them back. "Of course. Thanks for reassuring me, Aidan. I feel much better now. If I were to disappear, would that leave you free to marry for love later?"

"Aye, I suppose. But I'm not the loving type, so it's a moot point."

"Okay, then," she said, waving toward the door. "Maybe we should, uh, get this thing done?"

"After you," he said, once again all charm and affability, as he opened the door and gave a swift nod to the guardsmen standing at the ready. He extended his arm, and she took it, her insides hollow and her heart in pieces.

CHAPTER 19

As the priest droned in Latin, Aidan stood at the head of the chapel, wondering if he had made a strategic error.

He thought he could make her fall in love with him.

Her face, though she tried to shield it, showed otherwise. She would choose the future; he knew it.

He tried to catch her eye, but she was having none of it. She steadfastly watched the priest and kept her hands folded tightly in front of her.

Damn. He was in serious trouble.

The priest cleared his throat, then gave Aidan a pointed look.

"Oh. Aye," Aidan said quickly.

The priest turned to Emma, who gave a soft "Aye," then he blessed them. A moment later they were announced as man and wife, and Aidan gave Emma a chaste kiss on her lips.

Which were ice cold.

Afterward, they faced the people in the chapel, and Laird Monaghan appeared pleased. Shane and Brigit were giving each other heated looks.

At least one thing was going according to plan, Aidan thought wryly.

Aidan and Emma led them out of the chapel toward the great hall, where the wedding feast waited.

"Are you all right, Emma?" he heard Bri whisper as they strolled across the courtyard. The chapel began to empty, and clansmen began cheering.

"Later," Emma whispered back, then pasted on a false smile.

Reilly joined them at the raised dais and clapped a hand on

Aidan's back. He said, in Gaelic so that Emma would not understand, "Why does she look so miserable?"

Aidan glanced at Emma, who was in deep discussion with Brianagh. "I informed her before the ceremony that this marriage is in name only, and that she was free of it once she returned to the future."

Nick smacked him on the head. Clansmen cheered, but Aidan glared at him.

"You are a horse's arse," Nioclas said succinctly.

"My exact sentiments," Reilly agreed.

"Why?" Aidan demanded. "I ensured the lass has a life when she leaves here. One without a long-dead husband."

Reilly grabbed a fresh roll from a tray as a kitchen maid passed by. "Och, you are the biggest kind of dolt."

"There is truth in his words," Nioclas agreed.

"Look at her," Reilly demanded. "Does she look like a lass who's relieved? Or one who's had her heart broken?"

Aidan rolled his eyes, but he felt his stomach churn. "Lay off, O'Malley."

"Did you ask her if she would be willing to stay here with you?" Nioclas asked.

"I didn't have to," Aidan admitted grimly. "It was written all over her face."

"I see naught but confusion and perhaps a goodly amount of sadness," Nioclas replied in a low voice. "Perhaps you should ask her directly."

"There's no need. I know what she's thinking, brother. She wants to return to her time."

Nioclas sighed heavily. "Good luck to you, brother. Though it seems you have more work to do than time available in which to fix it."

Aidan met Emma's sad eyes and realized that his brother had it right. He didn't know how much longer Emma had in his time, but he needed to fix things between them, starting immediately.

. . .

As Brianagh reassuringly patted her hand and Aidan served her the best bits from the trencher in front of them, Emma thought she might be sick.

She was a fool, and it hurt.

She must've misunderstood Aidan's intentions. He probably just wanted her to know that he liked her enough to give her the protection of his name. He never declared love, or any sort of feeling, really. Sure, his kisses left her breathless and dizzy, full of wonderful feelings, but who knew if he felt the same? Maybe when he kissed her, it was the same for him as when he kissed a different woman. Maybe he kissed different women all the time.

Maybe she really and truly couldn't read men.

She was so weak. Emma had allowed Bri's words to open her heart, and now she was paying the price. She mentally kicked herself. She should've walked away from Aidan back in New York. She could've paid off Ben, given enough time. She would've figured out how to escape him, somehow.

Should've, could've, would've. The three words she had vowed, the day Ben went to jail, to never say again.

"Perhaps we might have speech after we dine?" Aidan murmured. He refilled her wine cup. "I fear I may have misled you."

Emma ground her jaw to avoid replying in haste. She managed a nod. Misled her? That was an understatement. But he had clarified his intentions mere hours earlier. She had no idea why he wanted to rehash that conversation, but if she could survive a marriage ceremony, she could survive another round of business talk with her husband.

Emma needed a quick distraction to avoid tears, so she focused on Brianagh. "I was thinking about the publicity plan for Celtic Connections. I love what you've done here with the ball and tournament…maybe we can incorporate a modern version of those in the company, and tie it back to these roots?"

"Oh, that's brilliant! A ball would be easy enough. But the tournament…let's see."

As Bri excitedly brainstormed, Emma tried to focus on her

future. Maybe Reilly could bring her back immediately, so that she could do business with the man currently sitting next to her, holding the broken pieces of her heart in his rough, strong hands.

* * *

Aidan closed the chamber door and slid the bolt home. He paused a moment, hoping that he could right his wrongs, then walked toward Emma.

She stood by the window, her arms wrapped around herself as the breeze teased the golden tendrils of hair that escaped her pins. She gazed to the ocean, the moonlight reflecting clearly on the deep waters. The sounds of their boisterous, happy clan drifted through the window as the main castle door opened, then closed.

He started to speak, but she beat him to it.

"It's a beautiful land, isn't it?" Her voice was wistful, far away. "These people...they celebrate life unlike anything I've ever seen. With all of the wars and famines, it's easy to see why they live openly and joyously." She rubbed her arms, the silk that covered them rustling. "There's a simple beauty in it, but there's such hardness as well. I'm grateful I'm not experiencing the terrible side of the Middle Ages."

He remained silent, unsure as to how to respond.

Emma returned her eyes to the sea. "You once told me that if I were to cast my wish into the ocean, it would remain safe until my soul mate could return it. Do you still believe that to be true?"

He took another step, captivated by the longing in her words. He was next to her now. "Aye."

Emma pressed a kiss into her palm, then gently blew her wish into the night.

Aidan pulled her into his arms. "I've been a fool, Emma."

Her eyes swam with unshed tears. "No, Aidan. I've been a fool. I understand how you feel now. You were trying to show the Monaghans that I was an unsuitable choice, to save Brianagh's reputation. And I allowed myself to believe you cared about me, even though I'm certain I knew deep down that it wasn't real. You're right—we can't have a relationship. Who knows when Reilly will return me to the future? We can't—"

Aidan couldn't help it. Emma's sweet smell, her voice, her beauty and wit and everything in between called out to him, and he needed to kiss her. More than he needed to eat, or sleep, or breathe.

He grasped her face with both his hands and threaded his fingers into her soft hair. He lowered his lips to hers, his entire being centered on their mouths. He traced her lips with his tongue, silently asking her to open for him, and when she finally sighed and granted him access, his body celebrated.

Home.

He deepened the kiss, tasting every inch of her mouth. Emma's arms wrapped around his waist, and she melted into him, her body fitting against his. He removed her hair pins, his mouth never leaving hers, and their tongues tangled in a sweet, lilting melody only they knew.

Because she's the one, his soul whispered.

Aidan pulled back momentarily, searching the depths of her eyes. Her face, softened with wonder, rested in his hands, and he knew he could never let her go.

She staggered back, her face pinched with grief, and she shook her head vehemently. "No, Aidan. I'm—you're—this is business only."

He stood frozen, unable to move in the face of her declaration.

"Protection. Name only. I can't do more than that." Her voice broke on the last word, and a sob escaped her.

"What did you wish for when you sent your kiss to the sea?" Aidan asked, his voice hoarse.

She looked at him with wet eyes. "To go home."

CHAPTER 20

"Something's wrong."

Late in the evening, Aidan stared down into his still-full cup, disgusted at himself. He couldn't even drink himself into a proper stupor to forget his colossal mistakes. "Aye," he muttered. "I'm a bigger fool than even you thought."

Nioclas slammed his hands down, causing the table to shake and Aidan to look up, startled.

"Nay, brother. Your wife has gone missing."

"She must have left with O'Malley."

"Nay, she hasn't," Nioclas shot back, his patience wearing thin. "O'Malley sits with my own sweet wife in my solar. Cian is with them, distraught, and her *entire guard* is searching the grounds."

Aidan shoved back his chair and pushed Nioclas out of his way. "To your solar, then, and tell me what happened!"

Together, they hurried to the solar, as Nioclas told him that Emma hadn't left their chamber after Aidan. When a chambermaid entered to bring her dinner, the room was empty, and her entire guard swore up and down that she hadn't left the room.

"The passageways?" Aidan surmised.

The castle had winding tunnels that connected the rooms, but they all eventually led outside, deep into the forest. Many times it proved a wise way to hide people and precious items when the castle was under attack.

Nioclas pushed open the door to the solar. "Aye, it's the only logical way. The window is too high, and she's angry, not suicidal."

"How do you know she's angry?" Aidan asked. "Eavesdropping, Nick?"

He glared at Aidan. "You left your bedchamber not more than fifteen minutes after entering it. You either shirked your duties to consummate the marriage, or you don't love the lass. Either way, the entire clan is less than pleased with you."

"That's enough," he snapped. "Are the guards on their way to the forest?"

"Nay. They're searching the passageways, but she could have left hours ago," Cian reported.

Aidan opened the door. "I'm headed for the forest."

"We all are," Reilly agreed. "I'll have Bernard saddle the horses."

"No time," Aidan called over his shoulder, halfway down the hallway. "We'll do it ourselves."

"I'll join you," Nioclas called. He gave swift instructions to the guards, then kissed Brianagh. "Stay, in case she returns."

She nodded. "I'll stay. Come back safely." She looked at Reilly. "The same to you. Bring her back. To whenever she wants to go."

In minutes, the four men thundered out of the castle walls, toward the forest line in the distance. The closer they got, the tighter Aidan's throat became.

* * *

Emma shivered, the chill of the night seeping in through her woolen bodice. She sat on a tree root, looking anywhere but at the silver glint of the revolver in Ben's hand.

His dark hair was almost blue in the moonlight, his skin a wrinkled mess. He looked even worse than the last time they'd come face to face.

Which she had thought might truly be the last she ever saw of him.

When the wall behind the hearth in her chamber had swung open, Emma was too surprised to scream for help. And when Ben pointed the gun at her and calmly commanded her to place her hands in front of her so he could bind them, she did. Then, when he demanded she walk, Emma's legs did as they were told, despite their wobbly shaking the entire mile out to the forest.

After emerging from a well-concealed exit deep within the forest, they walked down a small hill, then deeper into the trees until they approached a small clearing. At first glance, Emma swore it looked like the fairy rings she'd read about in her traveler's guide to Ireland. A circle of trees, ringed inside with large mushrooms, stood before them, the air seeming to shimmer in the moonlight.

Emma got the shivers just thinking about stepping inside its circumference.

Ben had no interest in entering the circle; he had Emma sit on the exposed tree root and wait.

"How are you here?" Emma whispered, afraid if she spoke too quickly, he might pull the trigger.

His eyes were wild. "I told you I'd find you, Emmaline. I watched a man come in and out of the forest by your lover's house. I followed him. I thought at first I was crazy, that I was seeing things. But no, no. It was real. He kept disappearing."

He stepped forward and traced a hand down her face.

She shuddered, and his expression grew angry.

"I followed him the other night. He did something with his voice, and he disappeared again. But this time I ran into the same spot he was and then I was falling…and there you were, walking along the beach with *him*. You looked so happy, like you used to with me. But that doesn't matter. You'll get us back. Then we can fix us."

Emma's heart jumped into her throat.

Ben looked up to the sky. He continued calmly, "I know you think you married him today, Emmaline. See, I found that little entrance into the castle all on my own. It was overgrown, but I was so hungry. Sometimes my medicine makes me hungry."

"Medicine?"

"Why do you think I need the money, Em? I need my medicine!"

Drugs.

"But I'm here now, and I'll take you back home, and we'll live together forever."

"You wanted to kill me, Ben!"

"Oh, I was just a little upset that you took another man to your bed. But I'll move past it because you're mine, and I don't want you dead yet. I need your new bank password first."

Emma's mouth dropped open. The man was certifiably insane; she was certain of it.

"There was a large deposit placed into your account a few weeks ago. But the account has a lot of security on it now, which is unfortunate. It doesn't matter, though, because I have you now and you're going to give me your money so I can pay off the people I owe."

"Who do you owe, Ben?"

His red, watery eyes flashed. "I just need to get a little more, okay?"

"More what?"

He glared at her. "I just need a small hit, then I'll be okay. Then we can get married and get the house with the fence you always wanted. Don't you want that anymore, Emmaline? Or did your new boyfriend convince you an old pile of stones was better?"

She glanced at the gun in his hand, but didn't answer him. Instead, she asked, "How do you think we're going to go back?"

"We're waiting for your boyfriend to find you. I saw him carry you to that cave. I'll give him the choice of sending us back through this grass ring here, or killing you both."

Emma felt ill.

The barrel of the gun slammed into the base of Emma's neck, making her gasp.

"You're not paying attention to me, Emmaline. You know how I hate it when you don't pay attention."

"Step away from her, MacDermott," Aidan commanded, emerging from behind a tree. Cian, Nioclas, and Reilly followed suit, each holding their swords.

They all froze when they saw the gun. Ben leveled it at Aidan's chest.

"Glad you could join us. Emma and I need to go somewhere a bit more futuristic, if you know what I mean. You're going to help us get there."

. . .

"What is that he holds?" Nioclas asked in a hushed tone.

"The deadliest, fastest weapon you were never meant to see," Aidan muttered. He raised his voice. "What do you want?"

"Emma," Ben replied steadily. "But you've always known that, haven't you?"

Aidan stepped forward and Ben tightened his grip on the gun. "One more step and I'll shoot you. Then her."

"I can take you back," Aidan bluffed. "I'll give you all the money you want. Just let her go." Aidan's eyes met Emma's, and hers filled with tears with his next words. "I love her, too, MacDermott. I'll do whatever you want to keep her safe."

Ben's hand started to shake with anger. "She's mine!" He turned to Emma, keeping the gun on Aidan. "Tell him you're mine, Emmaline. Or I swear to God I'll kill him for trying to steal you."

"I'm yo—"

"No, Emma. It will never end if you tell him that," Aidan said solemnly. "You're not his. You belong only to you."

Ben looked at her. "Are you choosing him over me?"

"I love Aidan," she said, her voice strong. "I'll never love you, Ben. After loving Aidan, I don't think I ever did love you."

Calmly, Ben swung the gun at her and pulled the trigger.

"No!" Aidan shouted, rushing forward as Emma crumpled to the ground.

Another shot sounded, but Aidan couldn't look away from Emma, soaked in her own blood. "Emmaline!"

She didn't respond, and Aidan felt for her heart. "No healer here can help this wound," he said, his voice raw. He looked over at Ben, lifeless on the ground, then searched out Reilly. "You've got to take her, O'Malley. Save her." His voice broke on a sob. "Please."

Reilly didn't hesitate. He knelt and slid his left arm under Emma, then held out his right hand, fingers splayed, and murmured something in a language Aidan couldn't understand. He quickly twisted his outstretched fingers into a tight ball, curling in from his smallest finger to his thumb, and an almost feral sound burst from his lips. The air shimmered, and Reilly swept Emma's lifeless body from Aidan's arms before rushing into the fairy ring. It swallowed them both.

Aidan looked first at MacDermott's lifeless body, then at the spot where his love had disappeared. All that was left was a puddle of blood, and his own broken heart.

CHAPTER 21

Beep. Beep. Beep.

Her left shoulder blade burned. She tried to move, but the pain was too intense. She let out a moan.

"God, Emma. Emma, can you hear me?"

"Reilly?" she tried to say, but her throat was too dry. A straw was placed at her lips, and she greedily drank the cool, crisp water. She couldn't remember anything tasting so good.

"Emma, you're in the hospital. Just rest. There will be plenty of time later for talking," Reilly's voice said from somewhere near her.

Another voice—a woman's. Irish accent, English language. "I'll give her some more pain medication. She's due for her next dose, anyway."

"Where's Aidan?" she tried again, but her tongue felt thick and foreign. Why couldn't she open her eyes?

"You're safe here. Sleep, Emmaline."

She couldn't do anything but comply with Reilly's softly spoken command.

* * *

Beep. Beep. Beep.

Emma's eyes felt as though they were made of sandpaper. She blinked, working through the grit, until she could focus on something.

A fluorescent light, switched off, on a drop ceiling.

Her fuzzy brain couldn't grasp that, so she carefully turned her head to the left and found the source of the incessant beeping. A blue machine displaying green digital numbers stared at her. Every few beeps, a piece of paper dropped from it, landing in a wire basket.

She moved her eyes from the machine, and realized she was in a bed. The white blanket was tucked around her tightly, and she noticed the safety bar alongside her leg.

Colin sat nearby in a black plastic chair, with his elbows resting on his knees. His folded hands propped his head.

She swallowed, and before she could even attempt speech, he placed a straw against her lips. She drank, savoring the water, and when she finished she gave him a smile of gratitude.

"Where's Aidan?"

Her voice was scratchy from disuse, her throat raw.

Colin placed the pink plastic cup on the side table. "How are you feeling?"

She tried to sit up, but her back screamed in protest. She gasped, and Colin helped her to readjust.

"Emma, don't try to move. You were shot, and they had to do some serious digging to get all of the bullet pieces out of your shoulder."

"Shot?"

"Yes. Relax. Reilly's talking to the nurse now; he'll be back in a moment. You had us worried for a while there."

"Colin, where's Aidan?" Emma asked again.

Colin's eyes were so deep, as though they held secrets a normal human couldn't possibly understand. And so sad, as though his heart were breaking right alongside hers.

"You made it home, Emma…but Aidan didn't."

Her world stopped. Tears spilled down her cheeks, and she tried to form words, but nothing came out. Her monitor started beeping rapidly, and she let out a sob, ignoring the pain ripping through her at the movement.

She had one coherent thought slamming through her brain: She didn't care if he didn't love her. She didn't want to live, if it wasn't with Aidan.

. . .

Six weeks later, Emma sat in a very stuffy office. The lettering on the door read FINN O'ROURKE, ESQ., SOLICITOR.

She still didn't know why she'd been asked to come.

She didn't care, either.

She knew Colin was worried about her. Reilly, too. According to the hospital, about a month ago she was released into the custody of her cousins, who were her next of kin. She had a passport that said she was Emmaline Perkins MacWilliam. A marriage certificate verified that, too.

Aidan had certainly ensured she had full clan protection on this side of the time continuum, too.

Her heart hurt too much when she thought about anything having to do with a certain green-eyed warrior, so she focused on where she was at present. Diplomas lined the wall. A mahogany desk stood about two armlengths away. A black leather chair, probably placed on the tallest setting so the lawyer would look larger and more commanding, sat behind it.

The door opened, and a stocky man entered. He shook her limp hand, apologized for his tardiness, and set a folder on the desk.

"Mrs. MacWilliam, I'm very sorry about your loss. As you may or may not be aware, Mr. MacWilliam set up some provisions for you, in the case that he went missing or passed away." Mr. O'Rourke forewent the leather chair and perched on the edge of the desk. He picked up the folder, and Emma noticed it was more of a binder.

A white binder.

Tears threatened, but she held them at bay. The man was still talking, and she tried to pay attention, more to stop the emotion than anything else.

Emotion was very, very bad.

"He left you everything he had," Mr. O'Rourke said. "That is standard procedure for most married couples, and you can rest assured that he had this all fully legalized and witnessed. There won't be any problems as far as your joint account, and Mr. MacWilliam's other accounts overseas are in your name also. He didn't have life insurance, but he did leave you this." Mr. O'Rourke pulled a sealed envelope from the binder and handed it to her.

She glanced at the wax seal, and her eyes filled with tears.

A silver M, ivy twisted about it, with a sword straight through. His letter. His symbol.

The tears came fast and furious, and with a murmured "I'm so sorry for your loss," Mr. O'Rourke placed a box of tissues on his desk and quietly left, allowing her privacy.

After a few moments, Emma wiped the tears, and studied the envelope. She even sniffed it, hoping to catch his scent, but all she smelled was the paper.

The stab of disappointment cut through her like a knife.

Carefully, so as to not disturb the wax, she used a letter opener on the desk to slit the envelope. She pulled out a piece of parchment, and she stifled a sob. She smoothed the paper onto the desk. The parchment was something he'd touched—it was as close as she would ever get to him again.

She began to read.

> *Dear Emmaline,*
>
> *If you're reading this, that must mean that I didn't make it back to you. You're either crying or laughing while reading this, and I find myself curious to know which—did I succeed in convincing you that we're meant to be? Or did I screw it up? If it's the latter, let me assure you that, when we next meet, be it heaven, hell, or in between, that means I've an eternity to convince you. If it's the former, please don't grieve for me. Our souls are forever intertwined, my love, and you must continue on in this life, realizing that we will be together again someday. I love you, Emmaline Perkins. You are my soul mate, and I recognized that immediately, although I fought it. I think you did as well, but you were understandably scared. I hope I was able to ease your fears. I*

will always be there to protect you—listen to your heart. I'll forever speak to you through it.

Right now, you're asleep on my plane. I'm watching you as we fly together over the Atlantic, and you look so peaceful. I need to keep you safe. Family is important, Emma. Don't shut out the one you've been given; Colin and his brother, James, will always be there for you if I am not. O'Malley, too, although I'd caution against staying near his cottage (too many strange visitors). On second thought, O'Malley's an arse. Look to Colin.

I believe that even before I met you, I knew we were fated. My job, from this moment on, is to protect you, love you, and provide you with everything you could ever need.

Again—if I've somehow mucked this up, I'll spend eternity fixing it, when we're together again.

I bequeath you everything. All my money, properties, and restaurants. And, perhaps most importantly, my family. Take care of them, Emma. James needs to visit more. Colin needs to be bossed a bit, and O'Malley...well, hit him over the head a few times for me. He'll understand.

I love you more than you could ever know. Be at peace, love, and take solace in the fact that I am yours, eternally.

All my love,

Aidan

Emma carefully refolded the letter, smoothing the edges as she went, and placed it back in its envelope. Mr. O'Rourke poked his head in the door.

"Can I get you anything, Mrs. MacWilliam?"

She nodded and took a shaky breath. "My family, please."

"I'll bring them in," he said. A moment later, Reilly and Colin entered, and she felt her chin quiver.

Reilly opened his arms, and she flew into them. He held her, avoiding her recovering shoulder, and let her cry for as long as she wanted.

• • •

Colin stared out the window of the small cottage, watching Emma as she sat motionless on the cliff. The wind whipped her hair around her, but she was as still as stone as she stared across the sea.

"A storm's coming," Reilly noted, glancing at the dark clouds rolling toward them. "I hope this shack can hold up."

"Aidan custom-built this house," Colin said. "I'm sure it will withstand a storm. He did like to be prepared for anything."

"That he did," Reilly agreed. He watched Emma for a moment. "Except, perhaps, this."

"Yes," Colin agreed quietly, "except this."

Emma's grief was almost palpable. She ate, but only enough to survive, and only at the prodding of Colin or Reilly. She functioned—she did some work for Colin, agreeing that she needed to occupy her mind, but every assignment he gave her she completed in record time. When finished, she would spend the rest of her day outside, staring at the sea, lost.

"If only there was some way to bring him back," Colin said for the umpteenth time. "What good is our power if we can't use it to heal people?"

Reilly placed a hand on his shoulder. "Col, have I taught you nothing over the years? It can't be used for personal gain. O'Rourkes can only travel when the line is in danger."

"I know," Colin replied. "But look at her. She's devastated. And I can only imagine what Aidan's going through; he has no idea what happened to her." He paused. "Why is it that you never told Aidan that he could just hop the open time gate near your house?"

Reilly didn't take his eyes off Emma's profile. "If I closed the gate, he never would have met Emma. He had to meet Emma."

"Are you a time bender to the future?" Colin asked. "Tell me, Reilly. Because I need to know if this works out."

"I can't go to the future, Colin. I'm just a man."

"I don't understand you."

"I suggest not trying."

Colin dragged a hand through his hair, his attention back on Emma. "I don't know how to help her. Nothing we've done has worked. Is she doomed to live this way until she dies? Is that what the Fates want for her?"

"I don't pretend to know what they want," Reilly said, bitterness in his tone. "They change their minds so often, I can't keep up."

"It's always just a matter of time until they change them again."

"Everything is a matter of time with us," Reilly replied wryly.

"Hopefully what I have next will help distract her."

"Another Celtic Connections assignment?"

Colin nodded. "We're ready to start in the UK and Ireland. But I need some positive press from the natives, so to speak."

"You're turning to the paparazzi?"

"I'll let Emma determine that. But we need some locals on our side."

"What happens if they're not on your side?"

"Then I'll do whatever it takes to lead them to the light," Colin quipped with a smile. It faded as he looked back at Emma. "I wish I could do more."

"I understand the sentiment," Reilly murmured. "Good luck. Let me know if she needs anything."

Colin gave a wave and headed out the front door.

Reilly left through a time gate.

CHAPTER 22

Swords clashed, and Aidan threw himself into the fray, not caring if he was marked or killed. Steel met steel in a clash so intense his hand ached.

He recognized that he needed to feel something—anything. A piece of him had died the day Reilly carried Emma away. He doubted he would ever fully recover.

Nioclas swore. "Aidan, get yourself out of there and let my guards train! I don't want them worrying about killing you, with your mind in places it ought not to be!"

Aidan shrugged. "If they kill me, it's just practice, Nick. Accidents happen. I wouldn't hold it against them."

"Don't let my wife hear you speak as such," Nioclas warned. "She'll string you up by your toes until you take the words back. Come, let's walk."

"I've no need of exercise." Aidan sheathed his sword.

"Let me rephrase. I order you to walk with me."

Aidan rolled his eyes. "Aye, I'll go. But only if you drop the laird act."

"We're going back into the forest."

Aidan braced himself. "For what purpose?"

"Your heart is broken," Nioclas announced.

"You want to talk about this now? Six weeks after the fact?"

"I didn't think you were ready before," Nioclas explained. "But now…"

Aidan swore, then followed his laird out of the castle walls.

"This reminds me of how you acted when you were ten-and-three, and didn't want to clean out the stables," Nioclas chortled as they walked. "You were so angry at me. Thought you knew everything."

Aidan smiled at the memory. "You never lost your patience with me."

"I never did," he agreed.

"I owe you everything, Nick. I don't think I ever thanked you for saving me. From Burke, or from myself."

Nioclas's eyes looked wet. He started coughing and muttering about the inordinate amount of dust in the air. "If you had the chance to go back, would you?" Nioclas asked, wiping his eye under the guise of scratching it.

"Moot point."

"It's more than your heart that's broken, Aidan. It's your soul. I have tried to put myself in your shoes, and I must admit, the pain I imagined was too much for me to handle. I cannot fathom how you're managing."

"I don't have a choice," Aidan said hollowly, "so I make do."

"When you disappeared all those years ago, it nearly destroyed me. And when you returned, I thought that, were I to lose you again, I wouldn't be able to survive it. But I was wrong, Aidan. Seeing you like this, so broken, is killing me." He stopped walking and grasped Aidan's shoulders. "If given the chance, I need to know that you would take it. That you would return to your other world, live a long and happy life together. That you would make a family, create a clan, live in peace…I need to know, Aidan."

"Aye," Aidan choked out, "I'd take it, you bastard. But I don't have that choice!"

"Then, brother mine, I wish you well. Godspeed, and may we see each other in the next life."

Aidan looked at him, confused, then he heard something behind him. Reilly leaned against a tree, ankles and arms crossed.

"I will pay dearly for this, MacWilliam, so for you to make up for that, you will vow to your brother, here and now, that you will spend the rest of eternity making that woman feel loved. Every.

Single. Day." Reilly held out his hand, fingers splayed open. "Vow it, and I'll bring you back to her."

Aidan locked eyes with Reilly and slowly nodded his head. "I vow it."

Reilly looked at Nioclas. "I want it noted that I'm doing this for Emmaline, not this arse."

Nioclas managed a smile. "Aye. Duly noted."

They were gone immediately.

• • •

Aidan saw Emma first, and his heart pumped faster, harder. His breath came in short gasps, and he tried, in vain, to steady his breathing.

She was here.

Emma sat on a flat outcropping. The winds of the North Atlantic whipped the loose strands of her hair. Her arms were wrapped protectively around herself, and all Aidan could sense was her loneliness.

As he approached, the wind carrying his footsteps away from her ears, his concern skyrocketed. He saw her closed eyes were swollen from tears, and her nose and cheeks were red. Her frame was smaller; whether that was from the injury Reilly told him she had sustained or the fact that she was barely eating, he didn't know, and with a start, he realized it was more than loneliness that enveloped her.

It was grief.

Even over the roar of the wind and the crash of the waves below, Aidan could hear his heart shatter. He had done this to her. If he had left her alone from the start, she wouldn't be sitting here, outside his house, overcome by emotions she should never have to feel.

He vowed, then and there, that if she let him, he would spend every day of the rest of his life making it up to her. He swallowed past the sharp lump in his throat, and sent a prayer flying that she would find it in her heart to forgive him for his transgressions. He knew he didn't deserve her, and she certainly deserved better than him, but he couldn't imagine living without her in his arms, or his bed, or his life.

He needed her more than he needed to breathe.

She drew a shuddering breath, tearing him from his thoughts, and her eyes fluttered open. She blinked and slowly turned her head.

He saw her take a breath, and he held his own in response.

• • •

Emma caught sight of a man standing to her left. She turned slightly, and her breathing stopped.

The wind tore at his black hair, his eyes a stormy, tormented green. His jaw had at least a week's worth of scruff; his hands were fists at his side against a blue and silver léine, and as the wind whipped into a frenzy, her heart stuttered.

His name came out of her mouth, and she felt her world start to spin dangerously out of control. Her breath returned in short gasps, and she clutched herself even tighter, unsure if he was a figment of her imagination.

If he was, she never wanted to see reality again.

Then he was next to her, his arms open, and she launched herself into him with a guttural cry, her sobs muffled against the soft tunic. He was stroking her hair, whispering Gaelic in her ear, and she couldn't formulate any thought beyond—

He came back.

His lips found hers, and she was crying, kissing him, practically climbing him. He leaned back, let out a loud laugh, and then gazed down at her, love shining from his eyes.

"Are you really here?" she choked, furiously wiping her tears away so that she could be sure.

"I am," he confirmed.

"How?"

"Turns out O'Malley isn't as big of an arse as I thought he was."

Emma grinned, then wrapped her arms around Aidan and pressed her lips to his. He kissed her hard, then led her back toward his—their—cottage.

"There's a storm coming," he noted, looking over his shoulder at the dark clouds gathering in the distance.

"I know just what we could do until it passes," Emma shouted over the wind.

"I thought you would want to talk?" Aidan replied, a grin spreading over his face.

She threw her head back and laughed. "You're really here!" She choked on a sob. "I thought I'd lost you forever."

"You will never lose me, love." He kissed her nose as the first fat raindrop landed on her shirt. "I'm yours forever."

"About that…it seems we're married in this time, too," Emma managed to get out. She drew a deep breath, trying to control her emotions.

His eyes twinkled. "Ah. You received my letter."

She nodded, and when he opened his mouth to speak, she placed her fingers over his lips, silencing him.

"It's all in the past, Aidan. You showed me that I'm finally ready for a future." Emma gazed at him. "I let myself fall, Aidan. You're ready to catch me, right?"

He swept her into his arms and rested his forehead against hers. His green eyes blazed as he stared into hers. "I've been ready since I met you, Emmaline. Don't you see? I'd wait an eternity for you."

"You don't have to," Emma whispered against his lips. "I'm yours. Then, now, and forever, Aidan. I love you."

His lips captured hers, and he carried her home.

CPSIA information can be obtained at www.ICGtesting.com
Printed in the USA
LVOW08s0630160416

483833LV00005B/5/P